MARILLA
before ANNE

MARILLA
before ANNE

Louise Michalos

Vagrant
PRESS

Vagrant Press is an imprint of
Nimbus Publishing Limited
3660 Strawberry Hill St, Halifax, NS, B3K 5A9
(902) 455-4286 nimbus.ca

Printed and bound in Canada

NB1512

This story is a work of fiction. Names, characters, incidents, and places, including organizations and institutions, are used fictitiously.

The character of Anne of Green Gables is owned by the Anne of Green Gables Licensing Authority.

Design: Jenn Embree
Editor: Whitney Moran

Library and Archives Canada Cataloguing in Publication

Title: Marilla before Anne / Louise Michalos.
Names: Michalos, Louise, author.
Identifiers: Canadiana (print) 20200388509 | Canadiana (ebook) 20200388568 | ISBN 9781771089289 (softcover) | ISBN 9781771089661 (EPUB)
Subjects: LCGFT: Novels.
Classification: LCC PS8626.I24 M37 2021 | DDC C813/.6—dc23

Nimbus Publishing acknowledges the financial support for its publishing activities from the Government of Canada, the Canada Council for the Arts, and from the Province of Nova Scotia. We are pleased to work in partnership with the Province of Nova Scotia to develop and promote our creative industries for the benefit of all Nova Scotians.

This book is dedicated to my grandson, Jack Scallion,
of Baker Creek, BC, whose heritage, like Anne's,
is deeply rooted in the soil of East Coast Canada

*"It may be the ludicrous escapades of Anne that render
the book so attractive to children, but it is the struggle of
Marilla that gives it resonance for adults."*

—

MARGARET ATWOOD, *MOVING TARGETS:*
WRITING WITH INTENT

CONTENTS

PART I

INTO *the* ABYSS

CHAPTER 1

Saturday, August 7, 1841

Avonlea, PEI

THE WARM AUGUST BREEZE RUFFLED MARILLA'S HAIR AS she climbed onto the roof of the back porch. Her crinoline rustled beneath her dress, breaking the stillness of the night as she dropped to the ground to make her escape. Imagine, having to escape your own home! She'd tried it once when she was seven years old, and even now, ten years later, the sting of her mother's slap was sharp in her memory. But Marilla knew if she didn't brave this one act of defiance against her parents, she would simply die.

The full moon lit her way as she tiptoed across the yard, praying her parents wouldn't hear her. She lifted her petticoat and started to run. A giggle, long buried, broke free and filled her with what she'd always known was missing from her life. That which she was now running toward, and the one thing that didn't exist in the house behind her: joy. Pure, life-sustaining joy.

As far as Marilla was concerned, it had been choked to death a long time ago by her mother's piousness, superiority, and self-righteousness. Tonight, Marilla would risk her punishment and the wrath of God almighty himself, just to have William hold her. She hoped and prayed this one night would change all the others to come.

She ran toward Rachel and the flickering lantern that waited for her at the end of the lane and together they raced toward town, where the dance hall was already aglow with lights. Where the sound of laughter filled the air. Where the face of the man she'd fallen more in love with every day since they met would smile just for her.

☙

William leaned against the doorjamb. His jacket, the only one he owned, felt tight across his shoulders. He'd laboured long these past months and his muscles had broadened across his back. And though he was more comfortable in work clothes, he wanted Marilla to see that he could present himself as well as any other man. Or at least as well as John Blythe. He stood taller than John ever would, but he'd learned that privilege and status in a community as small as Avonlea brought its own form of stature to a man.

The last of the sun had slipped below the trees and the peepers had begun their rhythmic symphony. William sighed, his impatience at last getting the best of him.

"She'll get here, don't worry."

"Who? What are you talking about?"

The snort of laughter from behind and the clap of Duncan's hand on his shoulder made him turn.

"Willy, my man, there's no hiding it. A blind man could see what you so stubbornly won't. And you can mark my words, that little filly who caught your eye when we landed here back in June is at this moment braving life, limb, and most likely mortal soul to get here."

William swatted the hand from his shoulder and smirked. He jumped, leaving the steps behind, and landed in the dooryard, releasing the excitement that exploded at the mention of Marilla's limbs.

Duncan headed back inside, leaving William to stare down the darkened road, his words drifting behind him as he retreated.

"I'd be careful, William. John Blythe won't take kindly to a mainlander stealing his girl."

∾

The lantern held between the two young women shook as Rachel's words hissed into the darkness. "You can't possibly love him, Marilla. Get hold of yourself. You've only known him a few months. What in the name of God will your mother say? She'll not have it."

Marilla looked into Rachel's eyes, made all the more fiery by the glow of flame between them, and spat words she'd had little practice using: "I don't care." With that she grabbed the lantern and started walking away.

"You don't care? Why, Marilla Cuthbert," Rachel said, racing to catch up, "in all my life I have never heard words like that coming from you. You, who has cared for everything and for everyone for—well, forever!"

"Precisely."

"But what about John? Are you saying you don't have feelings for him? Everyone knows you're his girl, Marilla. Always have been, always will be."

Marilla's rigid stance stopped Rachel in her tracks. "I am not his girl. Just because everyone thinks it, doesn't make it so. John, with skin that's never seen a hard day's work in the sun and hair the colour of straw! He pales next to my William. I'm certainly fond of him, we've known each other for years...and I guess I thought maybe that's what love was. But Rachel, I didn't even know what love was until I met William. Now I do."

Rachel's voice softened. "William is quite handsome, anyone can see that."

Marilla placed a hand over her forehead and feigned a swoon which made Rachel giggle. "But you haven't looked into his eyes... they are the deepest brown with bits of amber that sparkle when he smiles. And his teeth. They're perfect."

"Oh for heaven's sake, Marilla, he's not a horse."

"And he's sweet and thoughtful and so strong." Marilla,

anxious now and breathless at the thought of seeing him, looped her arm through Rachel's. "And best of all, he loves me too!"

The sound of fiddles reached them and the glow of lights shining in the distance made them squeal with excitement as they ran together toward the dance hall.

~

William stopped pacing and listened. The sound of her laughter reached him, and he started down the road. He could see the light from the lantern bouncing through the pines and he began to run.

She saw him, shouted his name, and, leaving Rachel behind to hold the lantern, ran headlong into his arms.

The next moment was a swirl of crinoline and the familiar sweetness of her skin as he buried his face in the tender curve of her neck. She squealed with laughter as he whirled her off her feet. His arms tightened around her tiny waist, pressing her breasts against him while his lips sought her mouth.

"You made it," he whispered. "Thank God." He lowered Marilla but held her tight. "You look beautiful."

"Thank you, William, so do you. From down the road I wasn't sure who it was, standing there looking so handsome," she teased, then stood atop her toes to reach his lips.

Something in the way she spoke, her lightheartedness, raised suspicion and he leaned back and eyed her. "Marilla, your parents were well aware I'd be here tonight, so now tell me, how did you get them to agree to let you leave?"

"I didn't. I just left."

William released her and stepped back. "You just left?"

"She just left." They turned toward Rachel, who'd by now caught up to where they stood. Rachel had carried what they kindly called baby fat for most of her life, and walking at a pace that was more than a stroll often left her winded. She took a deep breath and wagged a finger in their direction. "And you'd better be worth it, William Baker. 'Cause there's gonna be you-know-what to pay."

"Marilla, this is not going to help with my petition for your hand. If your parents find out you disobeyed them, they will not give their permission, let alone their blessing."

"They refuse to listen," Marilla said, folding her arms across her chest. "And besides, I don't need their blessing,"

"Maybe not, but you do need their permission. You're not eighteen till October, and if we want to get married before I leave at the end of the month, then they need to sign the certificate."

"I don't care. What difference will a couple of weeks make anyway? We'll go to the courthouse in Charlottetown. We'll lie. We'll run away," Marilla shouted, shocking them both with her anger. "But one way or the other, William Baker, I will be on that ferry boat when you return to Nova Scotia. Do you hear me?"

They'd reached the steps of the community hall and people turned to stare.

"I think everyone can hear you," Rachel said, taking Marilla's arm and steering her toward the entrance. William followed discreetly behind. He had no desire to add fuel to the heated gossip that was undoubtedly spreading throughout the hall at their arrival.

Those dancing paid no heed, and within minutes had reached for their hands as they were caught up in the high steps and heated calls of the Virginia reel. By the end of the dance, their worries and anger were forgotten amid the fun and laughter. Marilla clung to William as he danced her into the shadows at the far end of the hall and out of view. When they emerged, sweaty and breathless, their lips were tender from kisses their hungry mouths had desperately sought.

While they were catching their breath, Rachel made her way across the floor carrying two full glasses of punch while a tall young man trailed behind, carrying two more. "Marilla, you remember Thomas?"

"Of course," Marilla said, hoping Rachel wouldn't notice how dishevelled she felt, having quickly settled her clothes and hair back in place. "Hello, Thomas. I almost didn't recognize you. What with the beard and all." She reached out and accepted the glass he offered. "Nice to see you back. How was college?"

"I must say, I enjoyed my time in Charlottetown," he said "There was so much to do. But I'm relieved my studies are finished."

"He just got back last week," Rachel said, eyes gleaming as she stared shamelessly up at Thomas, whose previous crop of unruly hair was now quite tame, with only a few curls falling carelessly over his forehead. "Isn't he—I mean, isn't that wonderful?"

Marilla, who had been worried their absence would be questioned, realized it had never been noticed, and waited for Rachel to come to her senses. And when the two continued to stare, oblivious to anyone else, she coughed into her hand to break the spell.

"Oh, and this is William," Rachel said, snapping out of her trance. "Thomas Lynde, meet William Baker." The two men shook hands. "William has spent the summer in Avonlea with a shipbuilding crew from Halifax."

"From the big city of Halifax. Well, I bet you can't wait to get back there and away from all these farmers," Thomas teased, passing a glass to William while dodging Rachel's playful swat. She handed Thomas a glass and as their four drinks sloshed together, they toasted congratulations to Thomas on graduating from veterinary college and a wish for safe passage back to Nova Scotia for William.

∾

At four in the morning, with the mist of early dawn dimming the moon's glow, the two couples made their way, giggling, whispering, and shushing, along the road to Avonlea. Thomas had driven the wagon as far as he could without being seen or heard, and they now crept barefoot over the rise leading down to the small sleeping village.

Thomas, once the boy next door, was now all man; he held tightly to Rachel's hand and turned right, following the lane that would take them toward their homes. William and Marilla turned left, tiptoed down the long path toward Green Gables, and quietly slipped into the barn that sat back from the main road, hidden from view.

The rum that had spilled into the punch throughout the night took the edge off Marilla's fear, leaving her warm and glowing with desire. Her heart beat wildly as William lowered her onto his jacket, thrown hastily over a bed of hay, and reached for her buttons.

The sensation of bare flesh when they finally touched made her gasp. His mouth roamed over her body, taking her breath away until she pleaded for him to make love to her. William waited, poised above, and looked into her eyes. When he saw the answer he needed, he softly whispered her name.

She inhaled sharply, then sighed as he slowly, gently claimed her. She clasped him tight against her body and softly spoke his name. The rhythm of movement—primal, instinctive—delivered them to a time and place that would forever belong to them, and left them quaking and breathless when they returned.

They fell asleep in each other's arms and only stirred when the rooster's crow welcomed the day. Marilla's eyes flew open and she shook William awake. "You have to go. Quick! Before my brother comes to the barn."

Clothing rustled and hay scattered as they hurried to dress. William opened the barn door, stuck his head out slowly, and breathed a sigh of relief.

"He's no where in sight. Thank God."

"Hurry, William, you must leave."

They smiled as lovers, kissed each other gently, and crept through the door. William raced along the lane and onto the main road, keeping to the trees and hedgerows. Marilla stepped onto the lid of the water barrel at the back of the house and hoisted herself onto the back porch. She shimmied through her bedroom window and buried herself under the quilts on her bed.

Her lips, once so prim and proper from a lifetime of obeying her mother, now held a smirk. And for the first time in seventeen years, Marilla was filled with the kind of joy her heart had always longed for.

CHAPTER 2

"**M**ARILLA, WAKE UP."

The voice, distant and muffled, reached her through the deep fog of sleep. She was buried beneath the quilts, and the darkness confused her. Why was her mother up so early? What time was it? Marilla poked her head out to look at the clock on her bureau and was startled awake by the brightness of the room.

"Marilla, church starts in forty minutes and you haven't even had your breakfast yet. It's been sitting on the table for half an hour. Get up this minute and get yourself ready."

"Yes, Mother," Marilla croaked. She placed both feet on the floor and sat up. Her stomach lurched forward and she waited for the dizziness to pass. Memories of the night before swirled inside her head and the sickly sweet taste of punch made her gag. She felt a tenderness deep within her and reached down to cradle her belly. William's face swam before her and the knowledge of what they'd done felt all the more real in the light of day.

Her mother's footsteps retreating down the back staircase that led to the kitchen propelled Marilla forward. She stripped, dropped her clothes to the floor, and reached for the pitcher of water sitting on the commode. As she bathed, the water's hue turned red and the memory of giving herself to William made her tremble.

Twenty minutes later, with her thoughts gathered and emotions in check, Marilla stepped into the kitchen. Her father and brother stood at the wash basin in the corner, scrubbing the morning's chores from their hands, while her mother stood at the stove, placing firewood in the grate. A roasting pan sat on the sideboard, waiting to be placed in the oven.

"I could have sworn I heard someone outside last night," Mrs. Cuthbert said just as Marilla sat down. "Your father didn't hear a thing, was dead to the world...as usual."

Her father bristled at the tone she most often reserved for him. "I'd been up since five, Nora. And I was exhausted. What would you expect?"

Her mother sighed with impatience and turned away. "Your window faces the back, Marilla. Did you hear anything?"

The spoon Marilla held stopped midway to her mouth and she looked up in terror.

"That was just me," Matthew said, wiping the last of the soap from his arms. "I went to check on one of the cows. She'll be calving in the next day or so, I suspect." He winked at Marilla as he passed and dropped something in the folds of her skirt. When she looked down, her face flushed with heat. One of the pink ribbons that decorated her corset was now sitting on her lap.

Her dear, sweet brother. A man of few words. Knew which ones not to say more than he knew how to say them. She slid the ribbon into her pocket, finished her cold oatmeal, and waited while her father and brother headed to their rooms to change.

Twenty minutes later, Marilla stood in the hallway struggling to pin her bonnet in place when Mrs. Cuthbert rushed past. "We'll wait for you in the wagon," she shouted, letting the front door bang shut behind her.

Her father, normally rushing to keep up with her mother, was slow this morning heading down the hall. He stopped and smiled at Marilla in the mirror. When his eyes suddenly glistened with tears Marilla spun around. "Father, what is it?"

"You've grown so much this summer, Marilla. I hardly recognize my little girl."

Marilla smiled. He hadn't called her that in a long time.

"But I guess maybe you're not, now that William Baker has caught your eye."

Marilla blushed with thoughts of William's body lying next to hers and turned from her father's knowing stare.

"I won't always be here, Marilla, and it's a comfort to know—"

"Oh for heaven's sake, will you stop that? You're starting to sound like old Mr. Webber now."

Her father laughed and settled his hat in place. "You're right, my girl, I am. Come along now. Let's not keep Her Majesty waiting."

Marilla laughed at their private joke and took one last look in the mirror, at the woman, no longer a young girl, looking back. Her thick brown hair, normally braided and hanging the length of her back, was now twisted into a bun at the base of her head and held in place with hairpins her aunt had sent from Halifax. Marilla peered closer. Her eyes were the same blue, though rimmed with red from lack of sleep. Her brows looked the same, though the frown that normally creased them had softened. When she leaned closer to inspect her lips, still tender from last night, she gasped at the sprig of hay stuck on the brim of her hat and was still laughing as she joined her family for the ride to church.

~

As she entered, Marilla breathed in the familiar smell of polished pine and the lingering scent of a wood fire, lit to chase the chill. She stopped for a moment and stared. On a morning when she would have preferred fewer faces, the church was packed.

Children from Avonlea and the surrounding communities had formed a choir, and under the direction of the Sunday school teacher, were performing for the first time. Mrs. Cuthbert, who hadn't missed a church service her entire life, was indignant that her pew at the small Presbyterian church was now occupied by another family. "A family not even from Avonlea," she muttered as they squeezed into a back row.

John Blythe, the pride and joy of his mother and the only son and future successor to his father's mercantile, sat with his family in the pew across the aisle, and Marilla couldn't even look at him when he waved and called out her name. The organ music pumped louder and people rose to begin the service. John tilted forward and stared past his parents to catch her eye. She briefly caught a glimpse of his expression and knew Rachel's prediction that there would be hell to pay had already come to pass.

The minister, leading both the senior and junior choirs, blocked John from view as the procession made its way up the aisle. When the final note of the opening hymn strained toward completion, the congregation settled noisily in the pews. Marilla stared straight ahead, avoiding the glances of those who may have seen her the night before.

The altar, illuminated by the yellow hue of stained-glass windows, was draped in green as it always was in August, a time of green crops and lush growth. She recognized the vases and knew it was her mother who had filled them. White lupines, Marilla's favourite, though her mother would not have known, were displayed on either end. She tried her best to settle and worried others would guess the reason for her angst.

Halfway through the service, from the corner of her eye, Marilla caught the outline of a man making his way down the aisle and startled her mother when she yelped.

William, in his full Sunday best, squeezed into the pew directly in front and smiled boldly in her direction. Her mother's intake of breath startled the whole pew and Marilla thought for sure she'd die right on the spot. This couldn't be happening. John glaring from across the aisle, William sitting directly in front, and her mother pressed beside her.

"Excuse me, Mrs. Cuthbert, but Marilla is needed to help prepare tea for the reception." Rachel, that most loyal of friends, reached over and pulled her from the pew before Marilla's mother could respond and the two made their way toward the hallway that led to the church hall.

"What is he doing here?" Rachel whispered when they were finally out of earshot.

"I didn't think he'd really do it," Marilla said, grabbing Rachel's hands.

"Do what? What is he going to do?"

"He told me last night—well actually, it was this morning—" she corrected, blushing, "that if my mother wouldn't let him come to the house, which she won't because you know she doesn't approve, then he would come straight to the church." A note of pride crept into her voice for anyone bold enough to face down her mother. "And he did." A smile began to form but quickly vanished when Rachel's hands squeezed hers too tight. "Ouch."

"And now what?" Rachel asked, forcing Marilla to focus.

"Well, I think he's going to ask for my hand in marriage."

"In the middle of the church?" Rachel's whisper rose in panic.

"No. For God's sake, Rachel, he's not without some sense. He's going to wait until the service is over and approach my father when he goes outside. Or at least that's what he told me last night, I mean this morning…."

The voices of the children's choir faded behind them and applause for their efforts, hesitant at first, became loud and enthusiastic.

"Marilla?"

They turned toward the voice and stopped to stare at John Blythe, who was approaching them with an expression on his face that made Marilla back up.

"What in hell is he doing here?" The voice that never whispered boomed into the hallway, and if not for the applause, would have been heard by everyone in the church.

"John, we've talked about this," Marilla pleaded. "You know my feelings. Please leave." ·

"I'm not leaving until you tell me what he's doing here. If you think for one minute that I'll just hand you over to that uneducated, lowlife excuse for a man—"

"Hand me over?" Marilla thrust her face forward, forcing John, a man who thought volume could compensate for height, to take a step back. "Who do you think you are? I am not yours to hand over. Do you hear me?" Her voice found strength as she stared him down. "I do not belong to you!"

The doors to the sanctuary opened and Marilla hurried past the people who'd stopped to stare. She could hear Rachel behind her, running to catch up, and prayed John wasn't following. She ran through the crowded vestibule and out the front entrance, past the minister, past the choir, past the surge of people making their way to the hall. Only when the warmth from the midday sun touched her face did the tears begin to flow. Marilla sobbed as the reality of all that she had done and said set in.

When the footsteps behind her caught up, she spun around, but instead of Rachel, it was William, and without heed to who was watching or the consequences of such a display, she threw herself into his arms, where he held her until her trembling and tears subsided.

"What is the meaning of this? Marilla Anne Cuthbert, come away from that man this instant." They turned to see her mother glaring at them, with her father and brother hurrying behind. When Marilla stepped back from William's arms, the shock from her mother's slap threw her off balance and she fell to the ground.

Her father caught his wife's arm midair and moved her aside. "Enough!" he shouted. "Enough!"

He reached down and, together with William, helped Marilla to her feet while Matthew, furious at what he'd witnessed, grabbed his mother and led her away. "You stay with Marilla," he said to his father. "I'll deal with her."

"Mr. Cuthbert," William said, head lowered while Marilla clung to his hand, "this is all my fault. I came here today to tell you that I'm in love with Marilla and want to marry her. I'm so sorry. I didn't mean for any of this to happen."

The words "marry her" reached Mrs. Cuthbert just as she stepped up into the wagon. "Over my dead body" was all they heard; the snap of Matthew's whip as he pushed the horses on and the crunch of pebbles beneath the wheels drowned out the rest.

Her father took a deep breath and steadied himself before speaking. "This is not your fault, young man. But neither is this the right place for such a discussion." He turned and watched the wagon leave. "I'll tell you what…Marilla's mother will be gone tomorrow after lunch to clean the church. Drop by and we'll talk this over then." He raised a hand as William began to speak. "I'm not saying I'll agree. Marilla's been spoken for by the Blythe family for a long time." He looked up and held William's gaze. "But I can see plain as day how much you care for my girl." He winked at Marilla and shook William's hand, then hurried to catch up with the wagon.

Marilla looked across the churchyard, seeing the people who'd gathered to watch begin to disperse, their heads tilted together in hushed conversations. Rachel rushed to where they stood, and while they embraced she explained how Thomas, her hero, had come to the rescue just in time to take a raging John Blythe out the back door and away from the church.

"I will never forgive him for this!" Marilla said.

"Where is he now?" William asked, taking a step away from Marilla and toward the church.

"He's gone. His parents got him away as fast as they could. To say they were embarrassed would not quite tell the tale. Mortified, more like it. He's always been strong-willed, but to be the cause of such a scene in the middle of a church service—well, you can imagine." Rachel stopped talking suddenly and looked at Marilla's face. Her eyes opened wide and she peered closer. "Marilla, what happened? Who…?"

"Who else? You should have seen her. She…" Marilla choked back tears and couldn't finish.

"Come on," William said, taking Marilla's arm. "Let me walk you home. It's done. You heard your father, he'll listen to reason. You don't need her approval. We'll be together soon and you can leave all this behind."

As comforting as the words sounded, Marilla couldn't let go of the feeling that the events that had taken place over the past few hours, from clinging to William in the barn to the confrontation at the church, had upended the world she once knew and hell was still waiting to be paid.

CHAPTER 3

❧❀❧

Monday, August 9, 1841

MONDAY IN AVONLEA WAS LAUNDRY DAY. ALWAYS HAD been, always would be. And the measure of a good house-wife was based on what time her sheets and towels were pegged on the line. Heaven forbid if the time crept toward nine and the line was bare, because every woman in the small community would know and the chatter would begin.

By noon, the clothesline at Green Gables was still bare on this particular Monday. The pile of wet sheets and wooden pegs, spilled when the basket was dropped, lay scattered on the grass. The cows, not yet milked, were bawling loudly in the field, and the chickens fluttered and clucked in the yard, their nests too full of uncollected eggs to nestle and roost.

Marilla walked slowly down the lane toward the house and took in the scene before her. With all that had happened since early morning, it was the emptiness of the clothesline that brought her to her knees. She bent forward, buried her face in the folds of her apron, and wailed. Her father, the one who provided sanctuary against a life hardened by her mother's bitterness, was gone.

One minute she could see him at the far end of the pasture, urging the cows toward the barn; the next she couldn't see him at all. Before she had a chance to wonder why, she could see Matthew running from the lower pasture. He stopped suddenly and fell to his knees. She strained to see but the sway of tall grasses kept him hidden. It was only when Matthew shouted her name that she felt the first prickle of fear. She dropped the basket and ran. Halfway across the field, the image of Matthew rising, holding the limp body of her father, pulled a scream from her body so fierce it left her with little breath to run. She watched as Matthew staggered and swayed under the weight. She remembered reaching for her father, pale and lifeless, just as Matthew's knees gave way and together they lowered him to the ground. She could hear the words "Stay with him, I'll get the doctor" fade behind her as Matthew ran. She clutched her father's hand and watched helplessly as he tried to speak. When his eyes, pleading and terrified, looked into hers, she knew he was dying. She laid her head across his chest as he heaved his last breaths and felt the shudder of his heart when it stopped.

As she kneeled remembering that moment, she heard the scuffle of feet behind her and lifted her head. Matthew laid his arm over her shoulders as he knelt beside her. His voice cracked when he spoke.

"Marilla, I tried so hard. I tried to carry him, to get him back from the field. But I couldn't…I just couldn't."

"It's not your fault, Matthew," Marilla whispered, reaching for her brother's hand. "There's nothing more you could have done."

With great effort they stood, and Marilla held Matthew while he cried. When he straightened and wiped his face with the back of his hand, Marilla was startled to see how angry his expression had become.

"She made his life miserable," he spat, "and it finally broke him."

"Don't, Matthew. Don't say that. He had a stroke. That's what Doctor Timmins said. You heard him. You can't blame this on—"

Matthew started walking away, cutting Marilla off, his voice growing louder with every step. "I heard him. But you and I know the truth. He cowered…for Christ's sake, we've all cowered."

Marilla watched him storm off, kicking dust and scattering hens as he made his way to the barn. She walked slowly to the clothes basket to complete the task that would let the neighbours know they were home. Word of what happened had by now reached them, and a procession of the shocked and mournful would soon begin.

Marilla carried the basket into the house and placed it in the porch. She looked into the emptiness of the kitchen and then headed upstairs. She hugged her shawl and settled at the window, rocking and waiting. What would happen now? William was supposed to drop by after lunch to meet with her father and discuss their future. He'd no doubt heard the news. And knew, like her, that all of that changed with the last beat of her father's heart. William could appeal to her mother under normal circumstances, but not now. Not to a widow. A woman struggling to hide her indignation at the trouble her husband's death was causing. With a funeral to plan. With the pain of loss embittering an already hardened soul.

From a distance, Marilla caught a glimpse of William at the end of the lane, and, with heart pounding, rose to watch him walk the path to the house. He stepped around to the back and stopped beneath her window. Through a blur of tears, Marilla stared into eyes that held all the words he would never have a chance to say. He sent a kiss on fingers that looked desperate to reach her and she placed her hand against the pane and cried out to him: "William, I love you!" And though bereft and overwhelmed as he walked away, she felt a small measure of comfort in knowing William never had to ask. Denying her mother the pleasure she would have gained in refusing his plea afforded Marilla a small measure of satisfaction amidst the pain of losing her chance to be free.

∾

Aunt Martha, Marilla's favourite aunt in the whole world, arrived three days later. She always visited in August and had arrived in Charlottetown the week before to visit with friends before heading to Avonlea. She'd boarded the train as soon as she received word and arrived just in time for the wake. The wagon that brought her from the train station dropped her off at the end of the lane, and Marilla ran to meet her. She clung to her aunt now, breathing in the familiar fragrance of lemon-scented soap and rosewater. At forty-two, her aunt, so like her brother, was still wiry, though her love of sweets, Marilla suspected, had rounded her curves and softened her embrace.

"I'm so relieved to see you," Marilla said, linking her arm through Martha's and walking together toward the house. "And I know how happy it would have made father…knowing you were here with us." Tears slid down her face and Aunt Martha gently reached up and brushed them away. "Marilla, dear, of course I'm here. I came as soon as I could. Well, as soon as I could find a decent dress. You know how few I own."

Aunt Martha, her father's only sister, was never one for frills and lace, preferring overalls over aprons, and though she was eight years his junior and lived in Halifax, their closeness had never diminished.

"How is Matthew taking this? He was so close to his father. And how"—her aunt hesitated before continuing—"how is your mother? It must have been—"

"You can ask her yourself," came the reply.

Martha's sister-in-law, a woman she'd disliked from the first day they'd met, stood on the front porch. Her back was ramrod straight. Refusing to show any human tenderness, it had never slumped. Her hands, strangers to comfort and consolation, were tightly clasped in front of her.

"I'm so sorry for your loss, Nora," Martha said, walking toward her. Just at that moment, the door behind Nora opened and a neighbour stepped out. Her sudden appearance forced a politeness from Marilla's mother that otherwise would have been absent.

"Thank you for coming, Martha. You must be very tired after your journey. Marilla, don't just stand there; bring her bags inside."

The neighbour glanced back and forth between the women and hesitated before speaking. "Mrs. Cuthbert, the minister would like to begin."

They stepped through the door and Martha stood for just a moment inside the kitchen while Nora hurried behind the neighbour. The delight she'd always felt at seeing her brother sitting by the window was gone, and though the kitchen was warm, she suddenly felt chilled, realizing, as if for the first time, where he lay. She clung to Marilla's arm and walked slowly down the hall. The parlour had begun to fill early that morning and now spilled out into the narrow hallway, with some standing on steps leading upstairs. As they passed, friends who'd known them all their life murmured their sympathy and removed their hats. Nora had not even thought to lower the blinds, and the room was bright with sunshine. Martha bristled; the frill of white lace against the glare of glass felt gaudy and frivolous amidst the pall of grief.

Martha wept for her brother as the minister said the final prayers and the casket was closed. She stayed close to her niece while Matthew and Thomas Lynde, along with two of her brother's oldest friends, carried the pine box from the parlour to the front door where a wagon sat waiting in the yard. Neighbours lined the roadway and joined the procession of mourners as they made their way to the cemetery, and Marilla felt a wave of gratitude and comfort for the kindness shown to her father.

When they reached the entrance to the graveyard, William, whom she hadn't seen since the day of her father's death, the day that was meant to be the beginning of the rest of her life, stepped forward and reached for her hand. She moved into his arms, returning to his solid presence, the only place that felt safe, and tears she'd held in check began to flow.

"I'm so sorry," he whispered. "For your loss…for your father… oh God, Marilla…for everything." Something in his tone alarmed her, and she looked up and searched his face. His eyes were shrouded in sadness, but was it grief she saw, or regret?

A gentle hand on her back reminded her where she was and she pulled away.

"I assume this is William?" Aunt Martha said.

Marilla nodded. The procession of mourners had reached the open grave ahead of them.

"I need to talk to her," William said.

"I'm sorry. As much as I appreciate you being here for my niece, you know you can't stay."

"But I just want to—"

"There will be plenty of time later, when all this is over, to talk." She took hold of Marilla's arm. "Marilla dear, your place is beside your family right now."

William reached out to her as she passed and their fingers briefly touched.

"Come along now, Marilla, they're waiting."

Marilla took her place beside the grave and watched as the pine box was lowered. The earthy smell of red clay, recently dug and piled high, stung her nose. The shovels stuck in place on top, waiting to throw it all back, looked crude and offensive. She watched the mourners, heads bowed, dutifully murmuring prayers that would commit her father to his final resting place.

She raised her head and saw William, shoulders slumped, slowly walking away. She tossed a flower, handed to her by Matthew, on top of their father's casket, and even while the sun warmed her back she felt herself grow cold. Her beloved father was gone, and when she looked back toward the empty road, something inside told her William was gone too.

CHAPTER 4

Friday, August 13, 1841

"MARILLA, WOULD YOU LIKE ANOTHER CUP OF TEA?"
"No thank you, Aunt Martha. I've had enough tea in the past few days to last me the rest of my life."

"How about you, Rachel? Would you like a cup? How about another biscuit?"

"I'm fine, thank you," Rachel said, leaning back in her chair.

Marilla's mother, rocking quietly in the corner of the kitchen, lost her patience and spoke sharply: "For God's sake, Martha, we've had enough. We've all had enough. Sit down and stop fussing."

The four women had been gathered in the kitchen all morning. With the routine of their lives thrown into turmoil by the rituals of grief, they sat not knowing what to do. A reading of the will was scheduled for Sunday afternoon. The family solicitor along with a representative from the Agricultural Society had requested the meeting and were arriving together. Mrs. Cuthbert's supply of geniality and social decorum being nearly depleted, this last remaining duty and the unexpected request from the representative to attend had left her nerves completely frayed.

A knock on the front door interrupted the heated response her aunt was no doubt preparing and gave Marilla a chance to dispel her own pent-up emotions by running to answer it.

Mrs. Webber, who operated the Avonlea post office from the front parlour of her home, stood on the front porch. Her presence alarmed Marilla; mail was only delivered on Mondays, and this was Friday. And the mail was only ever delivered by Mr. Webber, not his wife, a woman given to anxiousness, which she now clearly displayed.

"Mrs. Webber," Marilla said, opening the door.

"I feel terrible disturbing your family at such an awful time, but…."

"Oh not at all, Mrs. Webber. Please do come in."

"No, Marilla, could you come out here? I need to talk to you in private."

Mrs. Webber peered past Marilla into the front hall, no doubt checking to see if her mother was close by, and Marilla quickly stepped out and closed the door. Mrs. Webber had always shown kindness to her, and without ever saying so, Marilla knew she disapproved of her mother, long before she'd witnessed the scene at the church six days ago.

"After the funeral yesterday, when we got back home, a young man was waiting in the front porch. He gave me this." She reached into her handbag and handed Marilla a letter addressed to her.

Marilla instantly recognized William's handwriting. And with her fear that he had left the Island finally confirmed, her heart began to beat wildly. She gulped back the tears forming in her throat and whispered his name.

"He didn't want to post it because he wasn't sure you would actually get it, with your mother so obviously set against him. He pleaded with me to bring it to you myself."

"Thank you, Mrs. Webber." Marilla's voice trembled. "You've always been so kind."

Mrs. Webber placed her hand over Marilla's and leaned in close. "If there is anything you need, my dear girl, anything I can do, I want you to know I'm here."

Marilla could no longer speak but found comfort in Mrs. Webber's unexpected embrace. She watched the postmistress walk away, then tucked the letter deep into her apron pocket, wiped her eyes, and headed back inside.

"Was that Mrs. Webber I saw walking across the yard?" her mother asked as soon as she stepped into the kitchen. "What did she want?"

"She only wanted to pass along her sympathies, that's all."

Before her mother could ask the questions that Marilla knew she would, she whispered in Rachel's ear, "Would you mind walking with me down to the spring?"

Marilla reached for the water pails sitting in the pantry. "I need to refill these and you can help me carry them back."

"Of course, Marilla," Rachel said, leaping to her feet. Matthew's arrival at that moment, back from the barn and looking for lunch, provided the distraction they needed to slip out the back door and head to the spring.

Rachel knew her well enough to have understood the hidden message behind the request. She grabbed Marilla's arm and practically dragged her down the lane. With pails swinging and skirts flying, they made their way to the privacy of the spring, to the large cluster of granite boulders at the end of a winding path through the woods, where a pool of trickling water lay at its base. Marilla's heated face and pounding heart welcomed the air, always fresh and cool in the shadow of the branches that spread like a canopy above.

Freed from the stifling boredom of the kitchen, Rachel plopped herself down on the moss, tucked her legs beneath her skirt, and waited. Marilla settled beside her and reached into her pocket. She passed the envelope to Rachel, whose eyes lit up with surprise.

"Is this from William?"

Marilla nodded.

"It can't be. He can't be gone. What happened? Why would he do this?"

"I don't know. I assume the explanation is in there," Marilla said, pointing to the letter. "I need you to read it. I don't think I can."

"Are you sure? What if it's very personal and he says things, you know, that you might not want me to hear?"

"Open it, Rachel. Please. Whatever it is, you would eventually wrench it from me anyway."

Rachel tore at the envelope and unfolded the small, one-page letter tucked inside and began to read.

August 12, 1841

Dearest Marilla,

I can't begin to tell you how sorry I am for leaving you the way I have and for not being able to talk to you the day of your father's funeral. I wanted so much to see you before I left, to explain, but the circumstances would not allow.

That I'm leaving you so soon after your father's death is cruel enough, but to leave so soon after discovering how deep our love for each other has grown over the summer is nearly killing me. I ache to hold you as before and the memory of our time together is all that keeps me going.

Marilla, sitting with her hand held to her lips, began to cry, and Rachel, stifling a gasp, placed a tremulous hand on Marilla's arm as she continued reading.

I was told on Monday morning, before receiving news of your father, that our ship, scheduled to leave in two weeks, was leaving in four days. And instead of going to Nova Scotia, as was planned, it is heading to Boston. As a fourth-year apprentice, I must accompany the ship to its final destination.

I will be back, Marilla. That I promise. The journey as well as the sea trials are expected to last two months at the most. I love you, and by the time I return you will be free to marry me.

Until then, you will remain in my heart. And my hope is that you'll forgive me, so that I may remain in yours.

With love and affection,
William

Marilla bent forward and collapsed onto Rachel's lap. "I can't bear it," she cried. "I can't. My father, and now this. I feel as if my heart will break."

"Shh, Marilla, don't cry, he's coming back. He promised," Rachel consoled. "Try to feel the happiness in his words. He loves you, Marilla, and he's going to marry you. This is wonderful news. And look," Rachel continued, trying her best to rouse her friend, "there's an address where you can write to him."

Her curiosity piqued, Marilla sat up, wiped her face, reclaimed William's letter, and read the address at the bottom.

Always the optimist, Rachel stood and reached for Marilla. "You can write him every day. And two months will pass in no time. You'll see."

With that hopeful thought in mind, Marilla felt her strength begin to return. She took Rachel's hand and stood. They filled their water pails and headed back to the house.

"Are you going to tell your mother? You know she'll never approve."

"Oh, I'll tell her, but not without Aunt Martha present. She'll support me, I know she will." Marilla stopped walking and looked at Rachel. "I know this sounds terribly disrespectful, maybe even cruel, but after what happened…." Marilla reached up and touched the tender spot on her cheek. "I can't wait to see the look on her face when she realizes there's nothing she can do to stop me. William will be back and…." The thought of her next words made her back straighten in defiance. "We will be married."

"Well then," Rachel said, a bold smile spreading across her face. "Let's get going. We have a wedding to plan."

CHAPTER 5

THE HOUSE WAS QUIET WHEN THEY RETURNED. AFTER placing the pails of water in the pantry, Rachel left for home, promising to come back later that evening. From the window, Marilla could see Matthew walking through the potato field. The plants swayed in the breeze and her brother's hand brushed over them lovingly. Where the field ended, the blue sky began, and off in the distance the Gulf of Saint Lawrence sparkled under a brilliant sun.

Marilla tiptoed past what had always been her parents' bedroom, just off the kitchen. The room was now her mother's. The closed door looked strange in the middle of the day. She made her way up the staircase, and when she found her own bedroom door closed she opened it quietly, not wanting to disturb her aunt, who always slept in her bed whenever she visited.

The lace curtains were drawn, dimming the room, and the scent of lavender filled the air. A small cot was set up under the slope of the ceiling. Marilla gathered her shawl around herself and sank comfortably into its folds. The slats strained under her weight, a reminder that the cot no longer belonged to a little girl.

Her aunt stirred, rolled over on her side, and faced Marilla.

"I'm sorry I woke you," Marilla said, lying still to quiet the squeaks.

"I wasn't really asleep, just resting."

"You look tired, Aunt Martha. Are you all right?"

She hesitated as if unsure. "Your mother can be so difficult. I could always cope with my brother here. He always seemed to know what to say to keep her in check and to keep me from.... I'm sorry, Marilla. This is so unkind of me. She is your mother, I shouldn't let her bother me so, but now that he's gone..." Her words caught, then released in a sob. "I miss him so much."

Marilla had little experience with adults crying. And certainly not her aunt, who always wore a smile. So when she buried her face in her pillow and cried as if broken, Marilla rose quickly and crawled in beside her. The sound of her aunt's grief filled the room. She clung to Marilla and wept, reversing for the first time the roles they'd always held.

Moments later, her aunt sat up, reached for a handkerchief to wipe her face, then straightened her hair. Her moment of self-indulgence had passed and her attention was now fully on her niece.

She took a deep breath. "So now, tell me, what caused the great rush to the spring with Rachel? The pails were still half full and it was quite clear nobody wanted another cup of tea."

"This," Marilla said, pulling the letter from her pocket. "It's from William. That's what Mrs. Webber wanted at the door. And he really is gone, just as I thought...and he wants to marry me and...." She took a deep breath. "I don't know how to tell my mother. I need your help."

"Marilla, dear, what do you mean he's gone? Where is he?"

"Read this," Marilla said, handing the letter to Martha. She stood and paced the floor while her aunt read in silence.

"Dear God. I feel terrible. This is what he wanted to tell you and I forced him away. Well, truthfully, it was your mother. She made it very clear he was not to come anywhere near the house or the cemetery, and most certainly not you. I'm so sorry. I just didn't realize." Martha placed her hands gently around Marilla's shoulders as her niece plunked next to her on the bed. "Marilla dear, how can I help?"

The look of determination in Martha's eyes gave Marilla strength.

"Rachel is coming back after supper and I want you all to be with me when I tell her. Saying I'm frightened sounds so silly," Marilla said, getting up to pace around the bedroom once more. "I'm almost eighteen. But after what happened at the church, and now with my father not here to stop her...and I know she'll be so furious. But if you're all here, surely to God she'll be reasonable."

"You're braver than I am, dear girl," Martha said, smiling at her niece. "Listen to me. Your father may be gone, but I'm still here. And I feel it's my duty to stand by your side. He always did and no matter what, I always will. It's what he would have wanted."

Marilla swiped at tears that had gathered and hugged her aunt. "Thank you, Aunt Martha."

From the kitchen below, they could hear Matthew stomping his muddied boots clean, then crossing to the stove to collect hot water on his way to the wash basin. They knew without having to see, so predictable was his routine.

"Marilla, speaking of your father, we need to discuss one more concern I have before we head downstairs." Aunt Martha's face became serious. "How will Matthew manage without him? We all miss him dearly, but the reality is, he worked as hard as any two men and now he's gone. Matthew may be able to handle the routine work of the farm along with you and your mother, but the potato harvest will begin soon and he's going to need help."

"Don't worry, Aunt Martha," Marilla said. "The neighbours will come. I know they will. We'll organize a bee. And don't you remember from your school days in Avonlea? When the boys were released to help with the harvest?"

"I do remember that," Martha said, smiling at the memories. For those few weeks every year, Martha could don a pair of boots and muck about the barn, doing all the chores her brother left behind. She felt freed from the restraints of being a girl, the restraints her mother imposed in preparing her daughter for the role of wife, and basked in the physical world of being a boy. Which felt like freedom. Freedom from a role she had no interest in.

"Well, regardless of how it gets done, I'm not leaving Green Gables until it is. I had planned to return to Halifax next week, but I do feel I'm needed here, and therefore, after giving it much thought, I've decided to stay."

Marilla breathed a sigh of relief. "Oh, thank you," she said, hugging her aunt tightly. With their roles as aunt and niece firmly back in place, they headed to the kitchen to prepare supper.

"A wedding," her aunt said, looping her arm through Marilla's. "Well now, won't that be lovely, unless of course I have to buy another dress!"

∽

The sun was leaning heavy in the west. As it made its way slowly toward the horizon, the clouds, left in its wake, gave up their innocent shades of white for shocking hues of pink and mauve. The gentle blue of daylight deepened, making way for the brilliance of the night sky. Marilla stopped washing the dishes to watch.

"This is my favourite time of day," she said to Rachel, who stood drying the dishes beside her. "Peaceful and pure."

"More like the calm before the storm, if you ask me."

Supper had been a quiet affair, with hardly a word spoken. Her brother rushed back to the barn as soon as it was over, the tension among the women so palpable he couldn't breathe. Her aunt had taken to the rocker on the front porch and her mother was dusting and rattling around in the front parlour, no doubt preparing for the meeting with the solicitor on Sunday. Rachel had quietly slipped through the back door into the kitchen just as Marilla was clearing the table.

"I'm not sure I should stay," Rachel said, her previous enthusiasm to witness Mrs. Cuthbert's comeuppance dissolving into fear with each passing minute.

"Rachel, you're my best friend. I need you here."

"You have your brother and your aunt. They're family. I'm not. Maybe I should just leave."

"Aren't maids of honour family?" The moment would have been serious if not for the look on Rachel's face. Her hands covered her mouth but did little to prevent the squeal that escaped. Marilla couldn't help but laugh.

"Oh, Marilla, I'm going to be a bridesmaid?" The fantasies they'd shared and played out as little girls suddenly came to life. "I'm going to be your bridesmaid."

Marilla was suddenly serious. "It's what I've always wanted, Rachel. You are the sister I never had. To me, you've always been family."

"What is all this nonsense about?" Mrs. Cuthbert's voice startled them and they turned to see her glaring from the doorway, arms folded.

"I need to talk to you," Marilla said. "Rachel, will you please ask Aunt Martha and Matthew to join us?" She pulled out a kitchen chair and spoke firmly to her mother. "Mother, please sit down."

"I will do no such thing." Her mother stood watching as Rachel ran down the hall toward the front of the house. "Why is she getting Martha?"

Marilla stood waiting, not willing to answer her mother's question until her aunt was present. When she heard the rustling of skirts from the front hall and the sound of Matthew banging the door shut, Marilla pulled out a chair and sat down. Aunt Martha and Rachel followed her lead. Matthew stood in the porch, looking terrified. His discomfort with any conversation was great; in a gathering of women, it was almost overwhelming, especially when it included his mother.

"Mother, I need to talk to you about something very important to me," Marilla began.

"If this is to be a private conversation, I suggest we move into the front parlour." Nora turned her back on the room and began walking away. Her condescending tone and abrupt departure made it clear she wanted to gain the upper hand.

"No, Mother, this is not private. They are all here because I asked them...and because I need them." Marilla rushed on, heedless of her mother's refusal to sit. "I've had a letter from William."

Her mother bristled. Matthew crossed the kitchen and settled quickly on a stool by the woodbox.

"He's left the Island."

"Well, thank goodness for that."

"But he'll be back at the end of October."

"It won't matter. By then, John will have forgiven all your foolishness and taken you back."

"It doesn't matter what John does or doesn't do," Marilla snapped, "because William and I are getting married."

Her mother, instantly enraged, lunged toward her. "You are not!"

Matthew stepped so quickly into his mother's path that she stumbled backward and would have fallen had Aunt Martha not reached out, held her arm, and guided her into a chair.

"How dare you?" her mother yelled at Matthew. "Let go of me," she hissed at Martha. "I forbid you to marry that uneducated, good-for-nothing labourer from Halifax. John Blythe is a respected businessman in this community, like his father. And you will be his wife—do you hear me?"

"You mean he'll become wealthy, don't you, Mother? That's what this has always been about." Marilla stood and stared down at her mother. "His family and all their property and all their success. You've always wanted to be part of their world, haven't you? Our father was never enough." Marilla began to shout. "We were never enough. You always wanted more!"

"How dare you speak to me this way?" her mother shouted back.

"And having me marry into the Blythe family was how you were going to get it. Well, that's never going to happen." Marilla folded her arms and stood her ground. "I don't love John Blythe. I love William Baker."

"Love," her mother scoffed. "Making a fool of yourself more like it. I heard all about the goings on at that dance, don't think I didn't. So you listen to me, you ungrateful little harlot—"

"That's enough! How dare you speak to Marilla that way?" Matthew shouted.

She continued as if he hadn't spoken. "This house and all this property belongs to me now, and I, not your father, get to say what happens and doesn't happen under this roof."

The pound of Marilla's mother's fist on the tabletop startled Rachel; she flinched and started to cry. Nora rose from the table, ending the discussion. She spun on her heels, walked to her bedroom down the hall, and slammed the door.

The silence that followed was heavy with dread.

Aunt Martha spoke first. "Marilla, please escort Rachel back to her home. Matthew, close up the barn and bring in some wood for the stove."

Everyone began to move as if from shock.

"I will speak with your mother first thing tomorrow," Martha, always the peacemaker, continued. "I'm sure she'll regret her words and perhaps, in the light of day, I can make her see reason."

Rachel and Marilla walked arm in arm down the lane heading away from Green Gables. Rachel, who'd witnessed Mrs. Cuthbert's anger but had never seen her so full of rage, trembled and sniffed.

Marilla held her friend close, and when they reached the main road and could no longer see the house, she spoke. "The only comfort I have right now, Rachel, is knowing that one day soon, with William by my side, I'll walk down this lane away from her and never have to come back."

CHAPTER 6

*M*ARILLA STOOD BEFORE THE MIRROR. SHE PINNED HER hair up and away from her face and leaned in to look closer. The sun pouring in from the window illuminated the pale yellow bruise on her cheek. "How can one week change so much, Aunt Martha? I feel as if I've lived a lifetime!"

"It often happens that way. Life can go on day after day like it always does and then suddenly...it all changes."

"Last Saturday I was getting ready to go to a dance to see William. I felt young...alive. And now, a week later, I feel a hundred years old." Marilla plunked herself down on a chair beside the bed to lace up her boots.

Her aunt smiled patiently, tucking the quilt as she worked to make the bed.

"I buried my father. Then watched the man I'm completely in love with walk out of my life."

"He did not walk out of your life. He's coming back." Martha said, fluffing the pillows and tossing them into place. "Don't forget that."

Marilla rushed on as question after question filled her mind. "And now the relationship with my mother, the one we've always managed to keep cordial even while mostly silent, has been ripped wide open."

"She'll come around, you'll see."

"And what if he *doesn't* come back? And what if she *doesn't* come around?"

"Marilla, dear, would you please calm yourself. This has been a difficult week for all of us. Give it some time, you'll see. And remember what the minister said: This too shall pass."

Aunt Martha grabbed her sweater from the back of the chair and opened the door. "In the meantime, we have work to do. Your father is no longer here and Matthew requires our help. He needs to fix the fencing down along the road and we need to give him a hand moving the cows to the lower pasture before he can start, so let's not keep him waiting."

The physical work provided relief for Marilla's anxieties and helped put life back into perspective. Her father had loved Green Gables, had built it with his own hands, and working the farm, alongside Matthew and Aunt Martha, like they always had when she visited, paid homage to his memory.

By noon their morning chores were done and she and Martha had stopped by the spring to cool off and catch their breath. They could see Matthew off in the distance and watched as he bent to his task.

"Your father often remarked that he was never happier than when he was working side by side with Matthew."

Marilla nodded. "And Matthew was never happier than when they stood in the middle of a newly planted field."

Martha reached for Marilla's hand and held it. "And those fields will be planted again, Marilla. You wait and see. Life will go on. This land and this farm will see to that."

They stopped by the house and picked up the lunch Martha had packed that morning and sat with Matthew beneath a cluster of maples before continuing their work. He seemed quiet, and Marilla suspected that he too had been shaken by their mother's wrath.

Marilla had avoided her mother throughout the day and by its end, though exhausted from the physical excursion, felt a measure of contentment she hadn't thought possible. William would be back.

Of that she was sure. Knowing this in her heart took the sting from her mother's hateful words.

It was nearly five when Marilla stepped inside the barn to return the garden tools and remove her filthy apron before heading to the house to wash up. Matthew was spreading clean hay in the horse's stall. The air, pungent with manure in the morning, now held the freshness of sweet-smelling hay. He set the rake down when he saw her come in.

"What am I going to do, Marilla?" This was the first moment they'd had to talk about what happened the previous evening, and she wasn't surprised that Matthew was picking up the conversation exactly where it had so abruptly ended. "After what she said last night, how can I stay?"

"What do you mean, how can you stay? This is your home, Matthew. You live here. You work here."

"I always thought it would be mine someday. After Father was gone." Marilla could see the disappointment on his face. "But you heard what she said."

"I did, Matthew, but it's still your home."

"Not without him." Matthew stepped out of his overalls and hung them on a hook. "I've been thinking. After the harvest, maybe I'll go into Charlottetown and see if I can get on at the shipyards. They're looking for strong men who can work hard."

"But what about Green Gables? What about the farm?" Marilla pleaded. "Matthew, what about me? You can't leave me. I won't have it. We've just buried our father. William is gone, and mother is as lost to me as she's ever been…I can't lose you too."

"What do you mean you can't lose me?" Matthew started pacing. "You're the one leaving. In two months you'll be married and gone. Where does that leave me? Here with her," he said, pointing to the house. "And I swear to God, Marilla, I'd rather die!"

"You'd rather what?" Aunt Martha said, stepping into the barn. Her smile faded when she saw Matthew's face. "What's wrong?"

Matthew hurried past her and Marilla rushed to follow. Aunt

Martha reached out and caught her sleeve. "Whoa, slow down, tell me what's happened."

"He says he's going to leave. That he can't stay here with Mother. That he'd rather die. Dear God, Aunt Martha, what are we going to do?"

Martha, weary from the long day, sighed heavily. "Well, first we're going to get washed up. Then we're going to make a strong cup of tea. We've worked hard today, Marilla, and we're all tired. When our strength has been restored, we're going to sit down and talk it out. Surely there's a solution to all this."

Marilla took a breath before asking the question that had been on her mind all afternoon. "I saw you speaking to Mother on the front porch after lunch. Was she sorry for her words? Would she listen to you? How will we ever find a solution to all this when she's not even being reasonable?"

Aunt Martha shook her head. "No, she wouldn't listen. She is still so very angry with you and still determined that she will decide what's best."

"Well, if she's angry now," Marilla said, heading out of the barn, "just imagine how angry she'll be when she learns that Matthew is thinking of leaving."

Aunt Martha looked toward heaven, blessed herself, and followed Marilla to the house.

෨

Sunday morning dawned grey and overcast. Fog rolled in from the Gulf, filling the coves and inlets with billowing clouds of damp salt air. Marilla, who woke to an empty house, poured herself some tea and sat gazing through the kitchen window. The house, bereft of sound, unnerved her.

It seemed as if there was nothing beyond the fog. She couldn't see the forest, the sky, or the ocean. A feeling of doom washed over her and she was suddenly terrified. The world closed in until the only thing left was the space surrounding Green Gables. She couldn't breathe, and rose so quickly she tipped over her chair. She rushed to the front door, yanked it open, and ran, leaving it to bang shut in her wake.

She moved without direction, her skirt growing heavy with moisture as she ran across the grass. She found the outline of the lane and followed the red clay path to the road. Her footfalls landed heavy and her breathing seemed to echo in the eerie silence surrounding her.

"Where is everyone? Aunt Martha? Matthew? Where are you?"

The cloud cover grew thicker as she ran, increasing the darkness until she could no longer see beyond her hand. She spun around to see which direction to go and became disoriented. The heavy mist unfolded, revealing the black iron gates of the cemetery off to her left. The need to be with her father took over and she cried out his name and stumbled through the entrance.

"Father!" Frightened and confused, Marilla called out to him and ran until the wilted flowers laid at his grave came into view.

"Marilla?" The muffled sound of her name reached across the headstones.

Matthew was kneeling at the foot of the grave. She stumbled toward him, and he stood quickly and reached for her.

"What are you doing here?" he said, and like a spell broken, Marilla's confusion lifted and she held her brother and cried.

"I felt so alone, Matthew. So frightened. I was in the house and then I ran, and I couldn't find anyone." Tears streamed down her face. "William is gone and everything is changing and I'm not sure what the future holds anymore."

Matthew looked down at his father's grave. "I felt the same. So I came to ask him what he would want me to do. And all I feel is that he wants me to stay." He took a deep breath. "And the truth is, I would never leave Green Gables. And he knew that." Matthew slapped his hat against his thigh and cursed under his breath. "I was foolish to think I could. I was just…."

"I know, Matthew, you were just upset."

"But how can I stay, Marilla? And why didn't father leave the farm to me? I don't understand."

Marilla wiped her face, took a deep breath, and gathered her strength. "We may know more after the meeting this afternoon. Perhaps we'll understand better what he intended for both of us when we hear what his will has to say."

A hint of sunlight shone through the grey clouds as they made their way back to the house. Marilla tried her best to dispel the feeling that regardless of what the solicitor had to say, somewhere beyond the fog, in the middle of the ocean, on a ship heading to Boston, her future was already being decided.

CHAPTER 7

AT FOUR O'CLOCK ON SUNDAY AFTERNOON, THE SOUND OF wheels approaching brought everyone to the front of the house. Matthew, wearing his work clothes, stood off to the side. His mother made it clear that his presence at the reading of the will was not required. His choice to attend was entirely his own and he hadn't yet made it. Marilla stood with Aunt Martha in the hallway while her mother opened the door.

When the wagon came to a stop, two men stepped down and made their way across the yard. The taller of the two was dressed formally in black, the other in workaday trousers. Each carried a leather case tucked beneath their arms. The man in black led the way forward and reached her mother first.

"Good afternoon, Mrs. Cuthbert, I'm Joseph Mackenzie. You may not remember me. I'm the solicitor representing your husband. We only met once before, I believe, and that was a number of years ago now." He held out his hand. "I'm very sorry for your loss."

She peered past him and watched in surprise as the other man made his way directly to Matthew. She finally shook his extended hand. "Thank you, Mr. Mackenzie. Of course I remember you. And yes it was only the once, but I would hardly forget, would I."

Mr. Mackenzie looked taken aback and for a moment his hand stayed suspended until her mother stepped aside to allow him in.

Everyone made their way to the front parlour and waited until Mr. Mackenzie had chosen his seat before gathering around him. Matthew, and the man who Marilla assumed by now was the representative from the Agricultural Society, walked in and filled the remaining chairs. A pitcher of water sat on the lace-covered table in the centre of the room. Marilla rose to offer them a glass. When she finished, the representative stood and introduced himself.

"Mrs. Cuthbert, I'm Richard Fraser. I met with your husband on several occasions and your son about five years back." He extended his hand. "I'm very sorry for your loss. Your husband was a fine man."

"Thank you, Mr. Fraser. And although my husband did mention your name, you and I have never met, which of course made me wonder why your presence at this meeting was requested. But before we begin—" Mrs. Cuthbert raised her hand to stop Mr. Fraser from speaking—"there's a great deal of work, as you can imagine, to be done on this farm, so if Matthew is not needed, I suggest he continue with his chores." Mrs. Cuthbert stared in Matthew's direction and he stood, ready to leave.

"No, Mrs. Cuthbert. Matthew's presence is most certainly required."

Matthew sat back down while Mr. Mackenzie removed the contents of his case. The room became quiet and he waited until everyone was settled.

"As you are aware, Mrs. Cuthbert, in the event there is no will, by law, any property owned by your husband is automatically passed on to the eldest son. Changes to the law made it possible, through the proper execution of a last will and testament, to leave property to a spouse. Your husband signed such a document, of which you were made aware, ten years ago." He hesitated before continuing. "But unfortunately, Mrs. Cuthbert, that will is no longer valid."

Marilla watched as her mother's pallor turned ashen. She coughed and spluttered and tried to clear her throat but a spasm took hold and she began to choke. Aunt Martha grabbed a glass of water and placed it in her hand.

She gulped greedily, spilling droplets onto her dress, then swallowed and fought for air. She struggled to her feet and startled everyone when she shrieked, "What do you mean it's no longer valid?"

Mr. Mackenzie rifled through his papers and retrieved a slim document which he held for her to see. "Your husband met with me five years ago when Matthew turned twenty-one and rewrote it, making the previous will null and void. I know this is unexpected, Mrs. Cuthbert. I know because he chose, against my advice, to keep this from you.

Nora slumped heavily in her chair, and when the room had settled once more he continued. "Green Gables and all its property, now owned or acquired in the future, belongs to your son, Matthew Cuthbert." He turned then and spoke directly to Matthew. "Your father has bequeathed all lands and buildings, currently known as Green Gables, to you. All current or future monies owed or earned from the purchase of equipment or sale of crops, currently being held in trust by the Agricultural Society, will now fall under your sole discretion. With the following exceptions." Mr. Mackenzie looked up to gauge the tension in the room, then continued speaking.

"Current records show an operating balance of one thousand dollars with an annual income of one hundred and fifty dollars. Twenty-five dollars a year is to be disbursed to your mother, Nora Cuthbert, until her death, thereafter it is to be retained by the estate. Twenty-five dollars a year is to be disbursed to your sister, Marilla Cuthbert, until her death, and thereafter it is to be distributed equally among her heirs."

Mr. Mackenzie looked down at the document in his lap. "I'll read the rest as written: 'The property known as Green Gables is to remain a home in perpetuity for the sole use, comfort, and security of my children, Marilla and Matthew Cuthbert, their respective spouses, children, and heirs, and only at their discretion shall it remain a place for my wife, Nora Cuthbert, to live out the remaining years of her life.'"

Marilla's mother sat immobile.

"You must understand, Mr. Cuthbert's expectation at the time of signing was that this transfer of title would not take place for some years to come. That being said, and as you were aware, Mrs. Cuthbert, his health had diminished in recent years and he was determined to provide for his children in the event of his death."

The solicitor reached into his leather pouch, pulled out a scroll tied in blue ribbon, and stood. "This copy is for you, Matthew."

Matthew rose slowly, walked past where his mother sat, and glared down at the woman who had belittled him all his life. For the first time, it seemed to Marilla, he stood taller. He took the scroll from Mr. Mackenzie and shook his hand. "I appreciate you coming all the way out to Avonlea, Mr. Mackenzie, especially on a Sunday."

"Truth be told, I was coming to visit my sister and her family. Wouldn't think of passing up an invitation to dinner," he said with a wink. "So thought I'd deliver this today rather than making a second trip out next week."

"Thank you."

"Don't thank me, young man, thank your father; it's what he wanted. He wasn't sure you'd want to be a farmer like himself, that's what he told me, but when your love for Green Gables surpassed his, he knew."

Mr. Fraser, who'd sat quietly throughout the reading, led Matthew into the kitchen. He explained before they left the room that there were papers to be signed and a plan for the upcoming harvest to be made. Marilla reached for Aunt Martha's hand and held her breath.

Their mother, shocked into silence, finally rose from her chair. They watched as she walked down the hall, entered her bedroom, and quietly closed the door.

CHAPTER 8

September 19, 1841

SEPTEMBER CREPT SLOWLY INTO AVONLEA, COOLING THE AIR as it gently prepared the fields and forests for the change of season. Their mother had kept to herself, saying little and spending more time sitting in the parlour than in her rocker by the stove. She continued to prepare meals as before and they still ate together in the kitchen. But the awkward silences that filled the room often sent Aunt Martha to the porch with her tea and Matthew back to the barn before he'd even finished eating, leaving his tea to grow cold in his cup.

By mid-month, all thoughts turned to the upcoming harvest Aunt Martha kept to the garden, loving nothing more than to scratch in the dirt, weeding and picking through rows of vegetables. Marilla kept busy preparing jars for pickling, knitting socks, and mending shawls in preparation for cooler nights. She worked hard, but the familiar pain behind her eyes and the tell-tale signs of a headache sent her to bed more often than usual, leaving her exhausted and unable to eat.

With Matthew now in control of the finances, old equipment had been replaced with new, a field hand had been hired, and the barn was refurbished to increase the capacity to store hay.

Even with the changes, stepping into the barn, especially in the early morning, made Marilla blush. The image of her and William, entwined and breathless, remained vivid in her memory.

"Marilla...*Marilllllla!*" Rachel's voice, loud with excitement, reached Marilla as she daydreamed. Her thoughts scattered and she ran from the barn as if caught in the act she'd only just imagined. She watched as Rachel came into view. In her hand, an envelope, flapping high above her head, brought her longing for William to life and she ran to claim the connection to the man she loved. She reached Rachel and took the letter from her extended hand.

"I almost fainted when I saw where it was from," Rachel said, breathless and panting. "Addressed to me. Well, heaven knows what your mother would have done if he'd sent it to Green Gables. But I know it's for you—it's from Boston! It's from William! Hurry, open it!"

Marilla's hands shook as she unfolded the sealed envelope.

September 5, 1841
Dear Marilla,
Our work here is almost complete. Sea trials begin next week. We'll be docking in Charlottetown on October 15. Please be there when I arrive.
All my love, William.

The smile on Rachel's eager face vanished as she watched Marilla pale before her. "What did he say? What's wrong?"

"He's coming home," was all Marilla managed to whisper before she collapsed at Rachel's feet.

༄

Marilla heard voices in the distance and felt a cool cloth on her forehead. She slowly opened her eyes and was surprised to see the kitchen coming into view. She was lying on the daybed tucked in the corner and tried to sit up. The room began to spin and her stomach heaved. Aunt Martha rushed toward her while Matthew and Rachel looked on.

"Lie down, Marilla dear, you've had a spell. How is your head? Is it pounding?"

"No, but I'm so dizzy and my stomach—" Before she could finish, she lurched forward and gagged on the bile rising in her throat.

"Oh, you poor dear," Aunt Martha said and held the basin while Marilla retched. "Your headaches are getting so much worse." She spoke to Matthew, who stood awkwardly amid the privacy of what clearly was a female ailment. "Not to worry, Matthew, and certainly no need to get the doctor. She'll be fine now. Rachel and I will take good care of her."

Matthew, who'd run from the field when he heard the commotion and, with Rachel's help, had carried his sister to the house, retreated back to the comfort and solitude of the barn.

Rachel took Marilla's hand. "You scared me half to death. Did William say something to upset you? I thought I heard you say he's coming home, then you collapsed…then I wasn't sure."

"He *is* coming home. I was so happy when I saw his name, then everything went white. I remember falling and feeling sick, but I don't remember getting here. What happened?"

"You fainted," Aunt Martha said, stepping in and replacing the cloth on her forehead. "Not to worry, my dear, I was the same at your age. I never fainted, mind you, but headaches with your, you know, your monthly…are quite common." Martha looked back and forth between the two young women, who were clearly unfamiliar and utterly embarrassed in hearing anyone, let alone an aunt, talk about something so personal. She quickly changed the subject.

"What is this about William? Did I hear you say he's coming home?"

"Yes, I received a letter," Marilla said while Rachel rummaged through her pocket, found it, and placed it back in her hand.

Marilla's eyes welled with tears as she pressed it to her heart "He says he will arrive in Charlottetown on October 15th. Isn't that wonderful?"

Martha, skeptical she'd ever use the word *wonderful* to describe William's return to Avonlea, was none the less pleased to see colour back in Marilla's cheeks at the mention of his name.

Rachel, relieved that all was well and with the mystery of the message finally revealed, was overcome with joy for her best friend. "You're really getting married."

The two young women clasped hands and beamed with excitement.

"Well now, why don't I leave you two to talk and I'll make a fresh pot of tea. That should help settle your stomach. Marilla dear, your mother will be returning shortly so if you feel able, why don't you make your way upstairs and I'll bring the tea to you there."

Marilla rose slowly and Martha watched as they left the kitchen. Though her niece had recovered quickly from her fainting spell, she wasn't at all convinced her illness was over, and the less her mother knew of the incident the better.

Nora had not missed one opportunity in the past few weeks to mention John Blythe or his parents and had even suggested having them over for tea. Most conversations ended with cupboards banging and doors slamming as Marilla stood her ground, insisting that William was the man she loved and that he would soon return. And as maudlin as Nora had been since she'd buried her husband, Martha knew her well enough to know she was not going to give up. And without his presence to provide buffer, Nora Cuthbert's long held plan to have their daughter marry into the Blythe family was now what she lived for.

Martha hated to think what would happen if even a whiff of what *she* suspected was wrong with Marilla hit Nora's nose the same as it had hers.

∽

Matthew watched from the doorway of the barn as his mother made her way down the lane leading home. Her gait was slow and her shoulders were slumped forward. She passed the rose garden, planted when she was first married, and he watched as she bent forward and touched the faded white petals of the one remaining rose. Seeing her there surprised him, as did the pain he felt when the memories blurred his vision. He could see the brilliant white blossoms trailing up and over the fence and her, face aglow, bending to kiss his cheek as he held her basket.

Matthew blinked and the ragweed, now growing among the bent and twisted stems, came into view. When her hope of being loved slowly died, so did her love for the garden. He knew her grief was not only for the loss of his father but for the loss of her dreams, which had died a long time ago.

His mother had been two months pregnant when his father married her at the town hall in Charlottetown. He'd only buried his first wife, the love of his life, six months before and the quiet ceremony was meant to quell the rumours. And even though their baby had been conceived on a night when his father's broken heart had found solace in his mother's arms, love had never blossomed.

Tears ran down Matthew's face. As a young boy, he'd heard it all. The fights, the weeping, the pleading and accusations. He still carried the hurt. His father was a respected man, a good man in so many ways. He'd agreed to marry his mother, had secretly rejoiced at the thought of a child, but he never loved her. Over the years, they'd blamed each other and eventually grew cold and resentful that neither'd had the life they'd hoped for.

As a little boy, Matthew had watched the light in his mother's eyes eventually go out while her affection for everyone and everything turned to anger and bitterness.

The final blow, delivered by the solicitor, had cut his mother deep, and though Matthew felt grateful for the security it provided, it did little to mend the hurt she'd inflicted. The image of staring down at her as she sat in shock the day of the reading was one he'd never forget. The pain in her eyes mirrored his own as a child and he wished in that moment, when the tables were finally turned, that he could have erased a lifetime of loss, for both of them, and embraced her.

❧

Nora could see Matthew watching from the barn and somehow knew he understood. The garden had been their treasure, and she'd poured everything into believing it held the key to lasting love. The white rose of Scotland was her mother's favourite and soon after she'd married, she'd brought shrubs from her mother's garden to start her own. And it flourished. The bushes had filled the little garden and roses drooped from every branch, filling the air with their sweetness. But they didn't last. They withered and died along with the love she'd held for a man she once adored.

She bent forward and touched the only one foolish enough to keep trying. Its silky petals, nearly choked by weeds and twisted branches, crumbled between her fingers. Like her, there was nothing left for it to hold on to.

Nora made her way across the yard. She could see Marilla in the upstairs window, and though she'd lost the power to enforce her will, she did not lose her belief that one way or another, Marilla was going to marry John Blythe. She would see to that. Marilla was too young to understand the importance of status in a small community and Nora was too hurt to explain the futility of love.

She stopped at the back door and looked around at the place she'd called home for the past twenty-six years. She would not have what happened to her happen to her daughter. To be left with nothing but the charity of her children after a lifetime of sacrifice.

❧

Marilla heard the tap on her bedroom door and looked away from the window where she'd glimpsed her mother bending to touch a rose in the small patch behind the house. Rachel had left a few minutes before and Marilla sat, sipping the last of her tea.

"Come in."

The door opened and Aunt Martha made her way across the room.

"Your mother is back from visiting her cousin and lunch should be ready soon." Martha sat on the bed and gathered her thoughts. "How are you feeling, Marilla?"

"Much better, thank you. The tea must have worked its magic." Martha watched as Marilla grew pensive.

"What happened, Aunt Martha? What happened to make Mother the way she is. I just saw her now, standing by that old patch of roses at the back of the house. She looked so wretched, so alone." Marilla, unexpectantly started to cry. "There's so much I don't know about her and even though she's been horrible for so long, I feel terribly sad."

The sudden change of emotions did not surprise Martha and she held her niece as she cried. *She's a woman now*, Martha thought, *more than she even knows*. And though this was not what she planned to discuss, this was as good a time as any to tell her the truth.

"I know this will be difficult to understand, but at one time, she loved your father very much, but he just wasn't in love with her. He broke her heart and married another woman."

"He what?" Marilla stood and stared in disbelief.

"However," Martha said holding up her hand, "that woman died a few months later. And when your mother came to comfort your father, to console him, well, like any other man, he needed someone, and I suppose he cared for her, but getting pregnant was definitely not what he wanted."

"She got pregnant? My mother?"

"Yes, and he did marry her, and I suppose he did try, but she knew he never really loved her."

Marilla slowly sat back in her chair and wiped her eyes. "Does Matthew know?"

Martha nodded slowly. "Yes."

"Did she blame him? Is that why she has always been so hard on him?"

"That, and her own bitterness. She felt trapped I suppose."

"And what about me? I wasn't even born until eight years later. Why have I always felt like she resents my very presence?"

"Because your father adored you. Instead of being the child she thought would bring him closer, your father's affection for you drove a bigger wedge between them. Jealousy is a soul-crushing emotion, Marilla, especially for a mother."

Marilla set her teacup down then met her aunt's eyes, which held the possibility of tears. "Why are you telling me this now?"

"Because you're not a child anymore. It's time you knew more about life and the consequences of love." Martha took Marilla's hands and held them as she spoke. "You say you love William and I'm sure he has shown you, in so many ways, that he loves you too. But if one of those ways was of a more intimate nature...."

.Marilla blushed. "Aunt Martha, why would you say that?"

"Listen to me, Marilla. I know this is embarrassing for you to discuss, but it is very important."

Marilla stopped fidgeting with her handkerchief and listened.

"When was your last monthly cycle?"

"Good heavens, Aunt Martha." Marilla stood and began pacing. "I don't remember. Why are you asking me about that? And what does *that* have to do with anything we've been talking about?"

"Marilla, it has everything to do with what we've been talking about. You didn't have a headache today did you?"

Marilla slowly shook her head "Well, no."

"And not only were you sick to your stomach, you fainted. And putting all the emotional turmoil and tears aside, you now tell me you don't remember when your last cycle was."

Marilla became tearful again. "What are you saying?"

Martha rose from the side of the bed and gently placed her hands on Marilla's arms. "What I'm trying to say is that all love has consequences. And you, my dear girl, like your mother back then, are carrying the greatest one of all."

CHAPTER 9

❧❦❧

"*I*'M CARRYING WHAT?"

Martha smiled and waited, giving her niece time to comprehend. She watched while the words slowly sank in and Marilla's expression changed from irritation to shock.

Marilla's eyes slowly widened. "No."

"Yes."

"But I can't be. Not now. I'm not even married." The urge to vomit overcame her and Marilla bent forward and covered her mouth.

Martha reacted quickly and guided Marilla back to her chair. "Sit down. Take a deep breath. Good, that's it, just stay calm."

"Oh my God, Aunt Martha, what am I going to do?"

"Nothing. You don't have to do anything. William will be here in less than a month and believe me, my dear, you won't be the first girl to walk down the aisle in your condition. And you certainly won't be the last."

"But—"

They startled when they heard the door from the kitchen below bang shut and Matthew stomp the dirt from his boots. When Marilla's mother shouted "Lunch is ready" from the foot of the back staircase, reality set in. The two women stared at each other silently, while in their heads they quickly formed a plan.

"Not one word, Aunt Martha," Marilla said. "Not one. She doesn't need to know."

Martha stared at her niece, hesitated for a moment, then spoke. "She may be more understanding than you think."

Marilla's expression hardened and Martha backed away. "But only if you want to, of course."

Marilla kept her voice low. "No, that's the last thing I want. I don't want anyone to know."

"Then no one needs to. You'll be married as soon as William returns and no one will be any the wiser."

Marilla was relieved. She hugged her Aunt and only then did she realize that Martha, her stoic, unflappable aunt, was trembling. "I'm so sorry, Aunt Martha."

"Don't be sorry." She took a deep breath. "The coming days may be difficult. We'll both need to be strong, but then you have your whole life to look forward to, Marilla. You're marrying a man who loves you very much." Tears stung Martha's eyes as she spoke. "And my dear sweet girl, you're bringing new life into the world, into this family, into this home. Don't ever be sorry for that."

∾

The following weeks were difficult. But they passed quickly. Between harvesting the biggest potato crop Green Gables had seen in years and planning for a November wedding, Marilla had little time to think. Her mother had slowly come around and though tensions had eased, her watchful eye and nosy nature made it difficult for Aunt Martha to speak and share time with Marilla in private, as they altered skirts and corsets for her ever-expanding waist.

Marilla sat now waiting for Rachel to arrive. The wedding invitations, spread over the kitchen table, needed to be addressed and taken to the post office. Marilla sipped her tea slowly and forced dry toast past her lips. Hiding her morning sickness was not nearly as difficult as hiding the truth. Especially from Rachel. But everyone who lived in Avonlea knew that when scandal touched one woman, it tainted, by association, the lives of those close to her. And Marilla wouldn't do that to Rachel. Especially at a time when she and Thomas were so obviously falling in love.

"Where has the time gone?"

Marilla looked up from where she sat and saw Aunt Martha staring at the calendar hanging on the wall. "Can you believe it's been almost two months since I left Halifax? Look at that," she said pointing to the date. "It's the end of September already."

Marilla's mother entered the kitchen carrying a bowl filled with green beans still moist from the garden. "That's when you originally planned to leave, wasn't it?"

"It was," Aunt Martha answered. She hesitated before continuing. "But that was before I knew anything about a wedding." She looked over at her niece and smiled. "And I wouldn't miss that for the world."

"Neither, it seems, would anyone else in Avonlea. It's all I hear about," her mother muttered before heading for the sink. "How many do you plan to invite?" she said, looking at the stack of envelopes on the table.

Marilla was surprised by her mother's expression of interest. "It's only a small wedding, Mother. Perhaps thirty-five."

"I see. Will his parents be attending?"

"He doesn't have any. They died when he was young."

Her mother spun around and pinned Marilla with her stare. "Well, who raised him, for heaven's sake? A man with no family. What kind of husband is that?"

"The kind of man that would likely value family above all else," Aunt Martha said, coming to Marilla's defense.

"He was raised in an orphanage in Halifax," Marilla explained.

Marilla had never had a chance to tell her mother anything about William, as she would never listen, and now without hesitation, it all poured out. "And he did very well at school… and he's hardworking and ambitious and, imagine this, he was hired as an apprentice when he was only fifteen. And he's smart and brave and soon we'll have our own—"

Aunt Martha's sudden coughing spell stopped Marilla from saying more. She blushed and lowered her head.

"Well, we'll see." Her mother wiped her hands and walked to the table. "Time will tell, won't it? I've tried talking sense into you, Marilla. But it's no use." Mrs. Cuthbert placed her hands on her hips and leaned in close. "But there's a lot of planning and a lot of dreaming going on right now and no man in sight. You best be careful is all I'm saying." Her mother's eyes grew moist and she struggled to speak. "Not all dreams come true."

Marilla understood her mother more now than she ever had before. When their eyes met it was as if they were seeing each other, really seeing each other, for the first time. She'd changed since her father passed away, they'd all noticed it. Whether from resignation or brokenness, Marilla wasn't sure, but she was grateful nonetheless for the softening that emerged.

Rachel suddenly appeared at the back door and when she entered the kitchen, it was as if a spell had been broken. All three women moved into action. Aunt Martha excused herself and went upstairs, moved beyond words by what she had just witnessed. Marilla's mother headed to her bedroom down the hall and gently closed the door. Marilla stood, swallowed the lump in her throat, and headed to the stove.

Rachel, whose senses had been on alert since witnessing Mrs. Cuthbert's outrage the month before, stopped just inside the door. "Marilla...what's happened?"

"Nothing has happened, Rachel. We were just having a discussion about the invitations."

"And...are they still being mailed?"

"Yes, of course. Come and sit. I'll pour some tea."

Rachel made her way across the room and sat in her usual spot at the table.

"It's just that mother asked questions and showed interest and I was so surprised." Marilla carried the teapot to the table to let it steep and sat down across from Rachel. "I can't explain it, but...so much has changed and she seems different. That's all."

"No need to explain," Rachel said reassuringly. "I'm just happy it's come about before the wedding. Do you think she'll want to be there now? She was so adamant that she wanted nothing to do with it."

Marilla brushed aside a few invitations to make room for their teacups. "Maybe. I wish I could talk to William. I miss him terribly and there is so much I need to tell him and we'll have so little time together before the wedding...."

"Speaking of which," Rachel said, looking at the invitations piled on the table. "Let's get started on these or there might not be a wedding at all."

Marilla smiled at Rachel as she filled their cups. *Such a dear friend*, she thought. Always there to help cheer her on and lighten the mood whenever it got heavy. Thoughts of her new life with William had consumed her these past weeks, but now the thought of how much she was going to miss her best friend finally sank in.

"I'm going to miss you."

"Oh don't be silly." Rachel said lifting her cup and taking a sip. "You're only going to Halifax, not the ends of the earth. And besides, you'll be back for my wedding next summer, won't you?" The look on Marilla's face was well worth the wait in telling her, Rachel thought, and she started to laugh.

"What did you say?" Marilla stared. "Wedding? You and Thomas? Why didn't you tell me? Am I not your best friend?"

Rachel reached for her hands. "Marilla, you have been rather preoccupied lately, but yes, you are my best friend, no matter what. After all, I will need a bridesmaid, won't I?"

A squeal suddenly erupted, and just as suddenly Marilla started to cry. "When did this happen? When is the wedding?"

"We will discuss all this later. I have a year to plan. You have a month. At this moment we have invitations to mail." Rachel winked and gathered a pile of envelopes. "So now, wipe those tears...and start writing."

∾

In looking back, the walk to the post office was the very beginning of the end. In her mind, Marilla could still see the sun sparkling off the water as they headed down the road. The archway of golden trees, whose leaves ruffled in the autumn air, watched over them but could do nothing to protect them from what was to come. Arm in arm, she and Rachel, innocent to what lay ahead, laughed and dreamed and planned. Only when they got closer to town did a stirring of something amiss penetrate their awareness and quiet their talk.

Small groups of shipyard workers were gathered along the road, deep in conversation. Other workers were sitting on the wide front porch of the general store, shaking their heads and shouting questions. Across the street, people filled the front porch of the post office and spilled out into the yard, while inside the sound of a woman's pleading cry could be heard.

"What's happened?" Rachel said, clinging to Marilla's arm.

Mrs. Webber, the postmistress, was standing in the front window, and when she saw Marilla her hand flew to her mouth. She turned away from where she stood and in the next moment was at the front door. Marilla, unable to move, watched Mrs. Webber fight her way through the crowd and run to where she and Rachel stood.

When Rachel let go of her arm to run and meet Mrs. Webber, the sudden movement made Marilla dizzy and she stumbled sideways, spilling the invitations over the road. She watched as they spoke and when Mrs. Webber turned her face, wet with tears, towards Marilla, she knew it was about William and her knees buckled.

Mrs. Webber reached Marilla as she fought for air, and held her tight. "You poor dear girl. I'm so sorry. There's been an accident at the shipyard in Boston and I wanted to send word but then everyone arrived and I couldn't leave."

Marilla's legs collapsed beneath her and Rachel rushed forward to help Mrs. Webber lower her to the ground. Marilla listened as if through a fog. The words *William, shipyard,* and *explosion* sounded muffled and distant. When the words *no survivors* reached her, she cradled her womb and fell into the darkness that closed in around her.

CHAPTER 10

❦

October 15, 1841

Avonlea, PEI

MARILLA STOOD LOOKING OUT OVER THE WATER. She'd slipped out the back door while everyone slept and made her way to the beach. The air was cold and she pulled her shawl tighter around her shoulders. The pungent smell of kelp and seaweed hung heavy in the air. Left behind by the ebbing tide, it lay in patches along the sand as she made her way to the water's edge. In the distance, the dawn of another day broke the line separating sea from sky.

Thinking she'd find answers to the questions that had haunted her for the past two weeks, she breathed the sharp salt air and raised her head skyward.

Marilla's voice, plaintive at first, pushed past the tears welling in her throat and began to rise: "Why? Why have you done this? What kind of God are you?"

She laid her hand over the slight swell at her middle and swayed with the weight of her decision. In less than a week, she would leave Avonlea for Halifax. Not as a bride with William by her side, but with Aunt Martha. There was no other choice. William was gone and, though she'd struggled and argued through every possible choice, she simply couldn't keep the baby. And so the decision was made. She would stay with Aunt Martha until the baby was born using "a change of scenery is good for the soul" as explanation to anyone who asked.

But the truth of what she was really going to do broke her heart. Losing William was terrible enough, but giving up her only connection to him, their baby, was unspeakable. A sob broke loose and she fell to her knees in the sand and wept.

Movement from down the beach caught her eye and she watched as someone ran toward her. *God almighty*, she thought. *Not now.*

"Marilla, is that you? Are you all right? I was walking and I saw someone fall." John Blythe reached out his hand. "Here, let me help you."

Marilla took John's hand as he helped her to her feet. She'd rather tell him to leave her alone, but at that moment she had neither the strength nor inclination to do so. She stumbled in the sand and fell against him. John caught and held her until she gained her balance.

"You are nearly frozen," he said holding her hand. "Come, Marilla, let me get you home."

"I don't need your help, John." Marilla bristled at his assumption that she would and walked away. "I'm perfectly capable of getting myself home."

John followed. "I came to Green Gables, you know, when I heard, to say how sorry I was."

She remembered him showing up. Remembered her mother's pleas at her bedroom door.

"He's come to pay his respects, Marilla. You must come down and show him the same."

"It is not respect he's come to pay, Mother. Don't you understand? It's to gloat and take advantage of my...situation."

"Very well then. I will tell him to come another time, when perhaps you've had a chance to rest...and reconsider."

"Reconsider what?" she'd shouted through the door, but her mother had already left.

"None of that matters now, John. Just leave me be."

"Marilla, please. I heard you were leaving Avonlea...and I need you to understand that no matter what happened between us, I would never have wished this for you." John's voice faltered. "Because, the truth is...I've never stopped loving you."

Marilla stopped in her retreat across the beach and faced him as he continued.

"My behaviour last summer was inexcusable, and I want you to know that when you return, I hope we can put this year behind us and perhaps start anew."

Here was her chance. The one her mother begged her to consider. When John came by, after the accident, her mother's hope had flared. She quickly supported Aunt Martha's plan to take Marilla back with her to Halifax with the idea that once she returned, a life with John would once again be possible. What no one understood was that this year would never be behind her. She would carry it for the rest of her life. Along with the truth. A truth that would send John and the highly respected Blythe family running if they knew.

Without another word, Marilla walked away from John, and a life that was never meant to be, toward the shattered remains of a life she only hoped to survive.

෨

By the time Marilla strolled down the lane leading home, the sun had fully risen, warming the morning air as it moved across the sky. She could see the farmhand heading out across the field while Matthew leaned against the doorway of the barn enjoying his first glimpse of the day. She'd avoided Matthew during the business of preparing to leave because his eyes were the only ones, aside from her aunt's, who knew the truth. After all, he was the one who found the pink corset ribbon on the floor of the barn.

But she needed her brother, now more than ever. She'd lost her father and William and though Matthew was the quietest, gentlest man she ever knew, his strength had always held their family up. And since her talk with Aunt Martha, she now knew just how much he'd shielded her.

"Good morning, little sister," Matthew said as she approached. "You were up and out early this morning. Taking a last look around, were you, before heading off to the mainland?" He looked down at her skirt and Marilla followed his gaze. "Playing in the sand were you?"

Marilla knew this Matthew. The one who avoided discomfort by making a joke. She punched his arm and he started laughing. The sound reminded her of all that they'd shared and suddenly tears filled her eyes and she wrapped her arms around him.

"I'm going to miss you," Marilla said, sniffling against his shirt.

"Ah, don't be foolish. You'll be getting so high and mighty over there in Halifax, you won't give us farmers another thought." He squeezed Marilla as he spoke and she held him tight, sealing a memory she never wanted to forget.

"I really don't have a choice, Matthew", she whispered and felt his arms tighten around her. "Do I? Please tell me you understand. If I keep the baby and stay here, they'd call it a bastard, wouldn't they? And what kind of life would that be?" Her face grew hot with tears as she felt again the anguish of the decision she and Aunt Martha had come to. Her long-time friend, Etta Byers, would see to the arrangements when they arrived in Halifax. "I could keep the baby and remain in Halifax, but then I could never come back here."

Matthew stepped back and Marilla watched him struggle to speak. "Green Gables is your home, Marilla. It will always be your home. You're just as much a part of this place as I am." Tears filled his eyes even as he tried to smile. "We're as much a part of this farm as the cows."

Marilla smiled through her tears and felt relief in her chest. "If not as good-looking."

The sound of his laughter dispelled the sadness in his eyes. "Go on now, you need to finish packing your travel trunk. And I need to start the milking."

When Marilla reached the house, she looked back and saw Matthew standing just inside the barn, his face etched in grief for a child he would never know.

∽

"I don't understand, Marilla. Why do you have to leave?"

No amount of explanation was ever going to be enough for Rachel and so she stood, even now, as the wagon prepared to leave, pleading with Marilla. The weather had turned cold. Marilla and Aunt Martha were bundled in heavy coats and covered with blankets for the trip into Charlottetown, where they would catch the afternoon ferry that would take them to Nova Scotia. Mr. Webber drove mail from the post office to the ferry every week and had agreed to take them along.

"I'll be back, Rachel. It's only for a little while."

The lie tasted bitter on her tongue. She wouldn't be back for Christmas as they'd all been told. Only she and Aunt Martha knew she wouldn't be back until next summer, but all that would come later.

Marilla's mother stood on the front porch, her shawl wrapped tightly around her. Their goodbyes had taken place in the kitchen.

"Life goes on, Marilla. Though you don't believe it now, you'll survive this." She'd passed Marilla a basket filled with cold chicken and biscuits for the journey. "Hurry along now, Mr. Webber's waiting. We'll see you at Christmas. And I hope by then, you'll be more open to what John Blythe has to offer."

The wagon pulled away, and Marilla watched her mother head back into the house while Thomas, the rock on which Rachel now leaned, placed his arm around her shoulder and led her home. Matthew gathered his tools and headed to the pasture to continue repairs on the fence. Tomorrow morning would dawn on them as it always did, and life in Avonlea would go on as it always had.

As the lane leading away from Green Gables disappeared behind her, Marilla whispered goodbye and wiped the tears from her cheek. Today was her eighteenth birthday. Her mother had not said a word. Rachel, tearful and sniffling, had tucked a small package in her hand before she walked away. Matthew, her dear sweet brother, had spoken the words quietly as he tucked blankets around her, knowing this was not what she'd planned.

"Happy birthday, Marilla."

His eyes had glistened with tears as the wagon started to move and he'd winked before turning to leave. "I guess that means you're all grown up."

Martha reached for Marilla's hand beneath the blanket and held it tight. "Matthew is right. You are all grown up now."

Marilla nodded but kept her thoughts to herself. Because unlike most young women who stepped lightly over the threshold from young girl to grown woman, she, instead, had fallen headlong into the abyss.

∽

Nurse Browne closed the curtain and marvelled at her young patient. She'd worked at the Mass General Hospital for ten years and had never seen a man fight as hard to live as this one. Except for a heart that refused to stop beating, there was little else working. He'd been rendered deaf from the explosion and his eyes, injured in the blast, were wrapped in gauze. Though his chest heaved, and tortured sounds escaped, he'd yet to come round.

"Any change in his condition?"

"None, Doctor. And he won't last long at this rate. He might have been sent to the morgue by mistake the first time, but he's not far from being sent back."

"Bloody shame. They think he died along with the rest of them." The doctor ran his hands through his hair, frustrated and tired. "And we can't even send word to say otherwise because we don't know who he is." He leaned closer. "And by the looks of it, we may never."

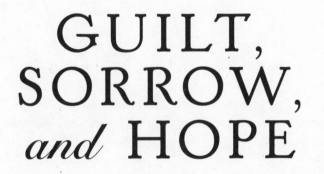

PART II

GUILT, SORROW, and HOPE

CHAPTER 11

April 21, 1842

Halifax, NS

THE RAIN LASHED AGAINST THE WINDOW WHILE A nor'easter, blowing straight up from the harbour, rattled the panes. It was only when the darkness of a long, fretful night faded to grey that Marilla's strength gave out. Beads of sweat dampened her hair and she gripped the sheets. A guttural moan filled the room, drowning out the storm. She rode the wave of pain that arched her back and screamed as it ripped through her.

"Marilla, listen to me. The baby is coming. You need to breathe now and prepare yourself to push."

"I can't."

"You must."

Marilla lifted her head and peered down at Doris, the midwife, whose arms were buried beneath the sheet draped over her knees. Illuminated by the glow of kerosene, she raised her head and smiled weakly.

Marilla squinted into the dimness of the room. "Where's Aunt Martha? I need her here."

"She's gone to get more towels."

"When will Miss Byers be here?"

"Not till later, Marilla. Don't think about that now."

The next wave of pain gripped Marilla and her body arched. The need to bear down pulled her upright. She bent forward, clutching her thighs, while the primal need to push took possession of her body. Marilla heard the door open. Heard her aunt's footsteps cross to the bed. Heard her intake of breath and the whispered rebuke of the midwife. The contraction released its grip and Marilla opened her eyes. The sheet had fallen away and the midwife scrambled to cover the blood pooling at her feet.

Aunt Martha quickly grabbed the sheet and placed it over her niece's knees. She wouldn't meet Marilla's eyes and a prickle of panic made Marilla grab for her arm.

"What's wrong? Something's wrong. Tell me."

The words pushed out in a scream as her body folded in pain. Marilla felt the room and everything in it fade away. Time was lost as she pushed and groaned and gasped.

From a distance, Marilla could hear the midwife, her voice calm and firm. "Listen to me, Marilla. There is nothing wrong. It's coming fast, that's all. I can see the baby's crown, so when I say push, I want you to push with everything you have."

Marilla felt the baby move down through her body and though the pain was unbearable and the need to push overwhelming, she wanted to hold back. *My baby. William's baby.* She'd carried both of them close to her heart for months and now, they soon would be gone. And she couldn't bear that.

The midwife's hands moved quickly beneath the sheet. "Push, Marilla…push. Martha, grab that towel…one more, Marilla…push now, push."

The feeling of being emptied came as her baby slipped out, awash in blood and water. Marilla collapsed back on the pillow and fought for air. When the sheet fell away she raised her head.

The baby, a tiny little girl, lay at her feet. Marilla watched as the cord was severed, and held her own breath as the baby wriggled and fought for air. The mewling sounds soon turned to healthy cries and she reached to hold her baby girl. The midwife cleaned and swaddled her quickly then placed her in Marilla's arms.

The baby fussed then settled against the warmth of her mother.

"My baby," Marilla whispered. "Oh, Aunt Martha...look at my beautiful baby."

Marilla looked over to where her aunt stood beside the bed. Her face, veiled in the gloom of early morning, glistened with tears. The joy Marilla felt was suddenly pierced by the pain in her aunt's eyes. All the preparation, all the details of what would happen next, Marilla had, for one brief moment, completely forgotten.

She stared at her aunt and pleaded, "No, Aunt Martha, I can't. Please, don't take her. Not now. Please, just let me hold her."

Martha knelt on the floor and leaned across the bed, placing her hand gently on the sleeping infant. She gave a weak smile to Marilla. "She is beautiful. And she will always be your daughter, Marilla. But...*you*...can't be...*her* mother."

Panic stole Marilla's breath and her chest began to heave.

"No, Aunt Martha. I can't do this. She's mine."

Marilla pulled the baby away from Martha's outstretched hands and pressed her close. "Tell Miss Byers that I have changed my mind."

"Oh, Marilla, my dear sweet girl, you know I can't. You said it yourself, this baby needs a family."

The midwife stood. Her arms held the bundled towels and blood-ied remains of yet another love story. She'd witnessed it all before.

"Marilla, listen to your aunt. It is the only choice you have right now. But you're young, you've got your whole life ahead of you."

The sound of knocking from the front door below startled them into silence. Marilla's eyes widened and she began to panic. The midwife glanced back and forth between the two women and watched as Martha rose slowly from the floor.

"No," Marilla shouted, gasping for air.

"Doris, please go down and let Miss Byers in."

The baby stirred and began to cry. "No, Aunt Martha. Don't do this!"

Martha reached down to lift the baby from her arms and Marilla lashed out: "Noooo!"

"Marilla, you will only make this worse. Let me take her…let me be the one to pass her over, not you. It will be better this way, I promise."

Martha choked on her own tears as she wrestled the baby from Marilla's arms. Marilla's scream filled the room as her baby was pulled away. Martha hurried across the room and out into the hallway, slipping past the midwife just as she entered. Doris shut the door and leaned heavily against it. She needed a moment to fortify her strength.

She'd been delivering babies for years. Watched as other young women like Marilla struggled, pushed, and screamed their way to motherhood. The only thing missing that could stop this tearing apart of a young heart and soul and turn it into a joyful celebration was a small gold wedding band.

❧

The rooming house in the North End of Halifax was clean and well run. Shipyard workers had for years found a tidy bed and a warm meal waiting for them at the end of a long hard day. It was, however, watched over with an iron fist by Mrs. Murphy. Rules were strictly enforced. The list hung on the wall at each landing of the three-storey building. At the top of the list was the number-one rule: "No overnight guests," followed by the only other one that mattered, "No noise after dark."

Duncan grabbed his pants, opened the door, and stepped onto the third-floor landing. He heard doors opening and closing from the two floors below and looked down over the side of the railing. Heads, tousled from sleep, peered up through the stairwell toward the top floor.

·"For the love of God…would someone go up there and shut him up?"

"And who in the name of Jesus is Marilla? He's been screaming for her half the bloody night."

"I'll see to him," Duncan yelled. "Go back to bed, the lot of you."

Duncan moved down the hall toward the ruckus and banged on the door. "William, wake up. Open the door. It's me. Duncan. Let me in."

The noise stopped and in the silence Duncan could hear murmurings and mutterings from the floors below.

"Thank God for that. Between the wind and rain and him bellowing, how's a man supposed to get a goddamn night's sleep?"

"He might have been mistaken for dead once, but by the Christ if I'd had to go up there."

"And I'd sure like to clap eyes on that Marilla...she must be a hell of a looker."

The laughter faded as one by one the men walked back to their rooms and closed the doors.

Duncan paced until William, bleary-eyed and disoriented, unlocked the door. He then stepped inside and led William to a chair in the corner, stumbling over boots and clothes left where they'd been dropped. The smell of his body, rank with the sweat and grime of a hard day's work, hung in the air. He lit the lamp and turned up the wick. The sight of William, pale and glassy-eyed, shocked Duncan and he stepped back and stared. "Christ... you look terrible."

"I thought I heard Marilla. She was screaming and I ran to find her. But it was dark and...then there was a flash."

"That's just the storm you're hearing. You must have had a bad dream, that's all."

Duncan found a bottle of rye sitting on the dresser. He sloshed some in a glass and passed it to William.

"Here, drink this. You woke up half the house, for Christ's sake."

They both turned as Mrs. Murphy, clad in robe and slippers, ran breathless through the door.

"What's happened? I don't appreciate being dragged out of bed this hour of the night, let alone have to climb all this way—"

She stopped when she saw William. The poor man. God love him. He'd been through hell and back before he arrived in Halifax, and by the looks of him he'd been drug right back through.

"I'm sorry, Mrs. Murphy." William tried to stand but lost his balance. Duncan grabbed his arm and led him to the bed. "I got a bit unsettled with the storm…I guess. It was so loud…."

"It can sound louder up here, close to the attic." Mrs. Murphy helped get William back to bed. "There's a room on the first floor that'll be vacant in two weeks. I'll move you down there."

William's eyes closed when his head met the pillow. And just like that, the storm that had held him in its clutches blew over and he lay spent and calm. Mrs. Murphy pulled the blanket to his chin. Duncan doused the lamp and they stepped out into the hallway.

"It's a damn shame what happened," Mrs. Murphy whispered, hugging herself against the chill.

Duncan, who'd been there from the beginning, sighed heavily. "That it is."

"And he can't get hold of this girl?"

"He's tried for months. Sends letter after letter, but nothing. Not a word. She's gotten married, he supposes. After all, she'd been told he was dead."

"Such a shame," Mrs. Murphy repeated, tutting and muttering as she shook her head.

They reached Duncan's room and he stood, his hand on the doorknob.

"She had no way to know, you see? And it's as plain as the nose on your face, those letters from Boston never got to her. But he won't listen. No sir. And now it's too late."

Mrs. Murphy bristled. "Too late for her maybe, but he's a young man; he needs to look to the future."

"He says he's going back," Duncan said lowering his voice.

Mrs. Murphy leaned in. "Going back to where?"

"To Avonlea."

"No!" Mrs. Murphy clamped her hand over her mouth and hissed through her fingers. "When?"

"This summer," Duncan said, shaking his head in utter bewilderment. "Says until he looks her straight in the eye, he can't let go."

"Dear God in heaven," Mrs. Murphy said, blessing herself and looking skyward. "Will the young never learn?" She turned and shuffled toward the stairs. "Goodnight, Duncan. Get some sleep."

Duncan opened his door and headed back to bed. "Goodnight, Mrs. Murphy."

◦～

Mrs. Cuthbert ran across the yard through the pouring rain and pulled open the back door. She placed her dripping raincoat on a hook above the woodbox and stepped into the warmth of the kitchen. She peered through the window above the sink, watching to see if Matthew was heading back from the pasture. He wasn't, and she breathed a sigh of relief.

From the pocket of her skirt she removed the letter. The first ones had come from Boston. This one said Halifax. *Damn.* This needed to stop. *Damn him to hell.*

She walked to her bedroom and closed the door. She removed the pillowcase from her bottom drawer and dumped the contents on the bed. *Damn him.* Marilla was coming back in two months and John Blythe was patiently waiting.

"And you, you bastard," Mrs. Cuthbert hissed, "you will not destroy her chances this time." She shook the letter in her hand. "No matter how many you send. To Marilla, you will always be dead."

CHAPTER 12

May 5, 1842

Halifax, NS

MARTHA LEFT THE PITCHER OF WARM WATER ON THE commode next to Marilla's bed and hurried downstairs to answer the front door.

"Good morning, Etta. Come in, come in. My, but it's wet out there."

Etta Byers, Ladies' Auxiliary president for St. Paul's Anglican Church, lowered her umbrella and stepped inside. A tall, handsome woman, she often intimidated men and women alike. But Martha and she had been friends for years and only Martha knew the insecurity that lay beneath the surface. The secrets hidden behind the facade.

A kettle boiling in the kitchen at the back of the house began to whistle. "Etta, be a dear…make your way into the parlour and let me catch that before it wakes Marilla."

Martha hurried down the hall. "I'll make us tea, will I?"

"That would be lovely, Martha. And if there's a biscuit left in your pantry, I wouldn't say no to it."

Etta removed her coat, hung it on a peg inside the porch, and made her way to the front room, to the place that felt more like home than her own. A fire was lit, and the room felt warm and cozy. Wood smoke scented the air, and Etta sat with a sigh in her favourite armchair. She loved nothing more than a visit with Martha, the only person she could truly be herself with, and this chair, like Martha, had always been there over the years when she needed it.

Martha returned from the kitchen carrying a tray laden with tea and fresh biscuits. She placed it on the table by the window.

"How is Marilla faring?" Etta asked.

"Not good, I'm afraid. She hardly eats. She won't leave the bed and there's not been a peaceful night's sleep in almost two weeks. Even when letters arrive, those from Rachel and the few that Matthew sends, which have always brought such comfort, she says nothing…not a word. And they are simply left unopened on her bureau. It's not like her." Martha began to cry and pulled a hankie from beneath her sleeve. "I'm so worried, Etta. You know what can happen. She'll not survive, if this goes on much longer."

Etta stood and led Martha to her chair, knelt before her and held her hand. "And you are hopeful, Martha, that once she sees me, talks to me, knows more about how the baby is doing, she'll improve?"

"Yes, I do. It was too sudden, you see," Martha said sitting back and shaking her head. "You came that night…and I know it is best they not get attached, and when we discussed it, Marilla said she understood, but she simply wasn't prepared. I wasn't prepared."

Martha's eyes brimmed with tears and she choked on her next words. "Who…in the name of God…can ever be ready for that?"

"No one," Etta said tenderly. "And I do understand. You *know* I understand." She returned to her chair, pulled a handkerchief from her pocket, and dabbed at her own eyes.

"Dear lord…look at the two of us," Martha said, rising to serve the tea.

"A lot of good we'll do her if we don't shore up our own strength first."

She passed a steaming cup to Etta then offered her a plate of warm buttered biscuits. "Drink your tea, dear. Then go up."

∾

Etta stood outside Marilla's room. She felt hesitant only because she knew that what she was about to do was against all the rules. Rules, she hated to admit, that served no one but the church. She knocked gently. "Marilla, it's Miss Byers. May I come in?"

The answer did not come immediately, and its absence filled Etta with concern. When she raised her hand to knock once more, she heard footsteps and the door slowly opened. Marilla, pale and sullen, stood aside to let her in. Etta eased her way through, closed the door, and watched as Marilla made her way back to bed. Shocked at the sight of this young woman dragging herself as someone might at eighty with a rats' nest of greasy hair spreading like nettle around her head, Etta reached for a chair in the corner of the room and placed it next to the bed.

The room would have been grey enough with the rain and fog of early May hanging heavy over Halifax, but with the curtains drawn, the gloom felt suffocating. The air held the pungent odour of a body not bathed and the sickly smell of a chamber pot not emptied. Etta placed her handkerchief over her mouth and waited till her stomach settled.

"Marilla, your aunt has asked me here, hoping that I can provide some comfort."

Marilla's head rose slowly, and even in the gloom Etta could see her angry glare.

"You? Who took my baby? Who carried her out into a godawful storm?" Marilla spat and her anger flared. "What kind of people are you? You and your holier-than-thou church. What comfort could *you* possibly offer *me*?"

Maybe it was the tone, or hearing the truth, or maybe even the guilt, but something inside Etta snapped. She rose from her chair, crossed the room, and pulled the curtains wide open.

"Get out of bed, Marilla. Enough is enough."

Marilla stared. "What are you doing?"

"I'm not doing anything," Etta said, reaching for Marilla's robe and slippers crumpled in a pile on the floor. "You, on the other hand, are taking a bath."

"What?"

Etta tossed the robe on the bed, crossed the room, and opened the door. "I'll put the water on to boil, and you can get out of that filthy nightgown and meet me downstairs."

Marilla crossed her arms and shouted, "How dare you?"

"No, Marilla, how dare you?" Etta straightened her shoulders. "You think you're the only woman who ever lost her baby? Well, you're not!" Her voice trembled, then broke. "And I sure as hell don't make the rules, but what choice do *we* have but to follow them and somehow find the strength to get up and keep going?"

The door slammed, leaving Marilla too stunned to speak. She slumped against the pillows and wanted nothing more than to bury her head beneath the quilt. But something in Etta's tone stilled her anger and made her reach for the robe. The words *what choice do we have* hung in the air and for the first time, Marilla realized she wasn't alone in this. Etta knew how she felt.

Minutes later, Marilla walked hesitantly into the kitchen. The large washtub was sitting in the centre of the room. A clean towel and bar of soap sat on the chair beside it. Steam rose lazily, clouding the windows as Martha and Etta tipped pitchers and kettles filled with hot water into the tub.

Etta moved brusquely about the room, averting her eyes while Aunt Martha reached for Marilla and held her close. "I'm so relieved to see you up and about, my dear girl. And having a bath is such a wonderful idea. I know how much you enjoy them. I should have thought of it myself. But no matter, have a nice hot soak now and then after, I'll fix you a plate. You must be famished."

Martha and Etta closed the kitchen door behind them and left Marilla facing the tub. She removed her robe, then stared at her body. She touched the skin at her waist and cradled the emptiness beneath her hand. Stepping over the edge of the washtub, she lowered her body, still tender from the birth, into the steaming water and almost cried, so soothing was its touch against her skin.

She hadn't wanted to feel anything at all, had wanted only to die. Had wept and panicked whenever she thought of her baby and cursed and spat whenever she thought of them taking her away. But the warmth of the water loosened her ire and a feeling of gratitude began to surface. Marilla had known the purpose for Miss Byers's visit. She and her aunt had talked it through and Marilla had promised to listen.

She took a deep breath, wiped her tears, reached for the soap, and started to bathe. By the time her hair was washed and her skin was pink from scrubbing, she began to feel better and more like herself than she thought she ever would.

Marilla dried off and hung her towel behind the stove to dry. She pulled a clean nightie over her head, tied her robe in place, and joined her aunt and Miss Byers in the parlour.

When she entered, they both spoke at once.

"Well now, there she is," Martha said as she stood and gathered the tea tray.

Etta finally met her eyes. "Are you feeling better?"

"Marilla dear, you sit here," her aunt said, pointing to her own chair. "I'll fix us something to eat."

Marilla sat and waited until Martha's footsteps receded down the hall before speaking. "Miss Byers…?"

"Please, Marilla, call me Etta. I realize this is the first time we've actually met but I've known your aunt for a long time and from stories she's told over the years of you and your family, calling me Miss Byers feels a bit formal."

The smile that warmed Etta's face at the mention of her family touched Marilla, and she nodded, surprised again by this woman for whom she'd harboured such hate.

"Yes, I am feeling better. Thank you." Marilla hesitated, then leaned forward. "Etta?" Marilla said, feeling the formality between them soften at the use of her name. "My aunt explained to me the work that you do…for women in my situation. What did you mean when you said…what choice do *we* have?"

Just at that moment, her aunt stepped back into the room carrying a tray piled high with food, and by the look she shared with Etta, it was obvious she'd heard the question. Etta stood quickly and helped Martha with the tray while Marilla began pulling chairs toward the small table by the window. The question hung in the air while they busied themselves setting out bowls and pouring cups of tea, and not until they finally settled did Etta begin.

But before she did, Aunt Martha surprised Marilla by reaching out and squeezing Etta's hand, a gesture that spoke of comfort and support for a friend. She thought of Rachel in that moment and wished so much that she were there. But when Etta smiled, acknowledging her gratitude, the affection shared in that one glance spoke of something deeper.

"When I said that you were not the only one, what I meant was that I, too, had been a…woman in your situation."

No one spoke as the words settled around them, confirming for Marilla what she'd felt earlier.

"What happened to *your* baby?"

Etta spoke quietly: "I don't know. She was taken…and I was never told."

"You had a baby girl? Like me?"

Etta straightened and held Marilla's gaze. "Yes. And that's why I agreed to help. Not only because I have the authority to do so, but because your aunt asked me."

Aunt Martha looked relieved, perhaps thinking this might have been a tearful, difficult conversation for Etta to have. She cleared her throat and spoke to them both. "We have a great deal more to discuss, but what I would like to suggest is that perhaps, before the chowder gets cold, we finish eating first."

Marilla never forgot the comfort or the feeling of belonging she felt as they each, with heartaches of their own, sat around the table drinking cups of tea and talking till it was almost dark, forging a bond that would hold Marilla in its embrace until she could stand on her own.

By the end of the evening, the plan for the next day was made. Etta would take Marilla to the home of Mrs. MacDonald, who lived two blocks away on Spring Garden Road. A lovely woman, Etta assured Marilla, who at present was caring for the baby until the couple who were adopting her, a Mr. and Mrs. Willis, arrived from Stewiacke to take her home.

"The day they arrive, Marilla, you will need to meet with them and sign papers. It's a private affair, you understand, but they need assurance that you will not seek guardianship of your daughter at a later date. And I could have done that on your behalf, but they have expressed a desire to meet you."

"Why?" Marilla asked.

"I'm not certain. I only know this from Mrs. MacDonald, who's been corresponding with them. It is very unusual."

"But a blessing for you," Aunt Martha said, "in that you will have an opportunity to meet the people who will raise your daughter. There's comfort in that, isn't there?"

"Yes, there is. And I'll have time to say goodbye…properly." Marilla grew sad. "I didn't get that chance the night she was born."

Etta spoke, her voice now heavy with responsibility. "But you do understand that what we're undertaking is deemed not appropriate under these circumstances or believed to be helpful. So I need assurance from you that you are prepared, this time, to accept what needs to be done."

"I am," Marilla said and reached for Etta's hands. "Thank you for all that you've done. I appreciate it beyond words. Please forgive me for my harsh words earlier. I didn't know about…about your loss."

"Until today, Marilla, no one except your aunt did."

"And you do promise you'll write from time to time and let me know how she's doing?"

"I will, Marilla. And only because I wish someone had done that for me."

☙

Etta arrived early the next morning as planned. It was a short walk
from Aunt Martha's house on Barrington Street to Spring Garden
Road, and it took everything Marilla had not to fling aside social
decorum and run wildly down the street. She had promised to rein
in her emotions, and so she did.

The house where the MacDonalds lived with their four small
children was built in the same manner as her aunt's, but instead of
being set back from the street, as they were in the South End, it sat,
or so it seemed to Marilla, directly on the cobblestones.

Etta tapped the knocker and Marilla held her breath. Mrs.
MacDonald opened the door carrying a small boy on her hip while
a little girl tugged at her skirt. Her face was warm and open and her
eyes never left Marilla's even as she greeted Etta.

"Thank goodness the rain has finally ceased," she said,
sticking her head out the door. "Another day and I would have
gone mad." She laughed and nuzzled her son. "The children get
restless. My poor little darlings," she said. "Confined indoors all
day."

The little girl reached for her shoes. "Walk, Mommy? Walk?"

"And they especially miss our walks to the Public Gardens.
Don't you, darling?"

A voice from across the street made them turn. "Yoo-hoo, Mrs.
MacDonald, are you off to the Gardens for a walk?"

"No, Mrs. Murphy, not this morning."

Marilla could see tension crease Mrs. MacDonald's forehead
as the older woman quickly made her way across the street.

"A house full of babies and still time for visitors," she said
when she reached them.

"I'm sorry, Mrs. Murphy, but I really must get the children
out of the chill." She ignored Mrs. Murphy's inquisitive face. "Miss
Byers, Marilla, please do come in. Goodbye, Mrs. Murphy, enjoy
your walk."

The door closed in her face and Mrs. Murphy stood without moving, surprised by the abrupt greeting. She walked away, muttering under her breath, her brow creased in thought at what she'd heard.

Marilla and Etta followed behind the small entourage as Mrs. MacDonald, with children in tow, made her way to the kitchen. She quickly produced two large sugar cookies and settled the children in a large crib full of toys by the window.

"Oh, that Mrs. Murphy. She is a gossip if ever I saw one. Runs a boarding house up in the North End. Poor woman, surrounded by men. It's no wonder she likes to talk. Here, let me take your coats, ladies."

She placed them in the back porch then walked to the stove where she raised the lid and stoked the fire. "My oldest is at school and the babies, bless them, are both sleeping, so we should have a few minutes' peace. Come," she beckoned. "Sit down and I'll make some tea."

Marilla stood, unable to move, while her aunt pulled out a chair. When Mrs. MacDonald turned around, her smile faded and she quickly set the teapot down and walked directly to Marilla.

"Oh, Marilla, please forgive me. I've been prattling on and on and here you are, all anxious and wanting nothing more than to see your baby."

When Marilla nodded her head, tears that had pooled and blurred her vision slid down her cheek.

"Miss Byers, please help yourself. The cups are in the pantry. And keep an eye on those two, will you, while I take Marilla upstairs."

Mrs. MacDonald placed her arm around Marilla's shoulder and gently led her upstairs. "She's a darling baby. Healthy as a horse. Eats and sleeps no problem. I can't imagine your situation, Marilla. But if seeing her and knowing she's doing well gives you some peace, I'm only too happy to oblige."

They reached the top of the stairs, stepped quietly forward, and stopped in front of a door at the end of the hall. The pounding of her heart stole Marilla's breath and panic engulfed her. When Mrs. MacDonald opened the door, Marilla's thoughts began to swirl.

She hesitated. *What if I can't do this? What if I can't let go? What if it breaks me?*

"Marilla. Are you sure this is what you want?"

"No. This is not what I want, Mrs. MacDonald. This is not at *all* what I want. But this, right now, even if it's all I ever have…is what I need."

Marilla stepped into the baby-scented warmth of a tiny bedroom and crossed to the bassinet. Tears prickled at the sight of her baby nestled beneath the folds of a pink blanket, with only her head and the small curve of her back creating a bump in the middle of its softness. Marilla gently pulled the blanket back and marvelled at her tiny body, made all the more precious by having tucked her knees beneath her.

Marilla reached in and lifted her sleeping daughter, wrapped from head to toe in flannel, and watched in wonder as she stretched and yawned and settled into place against her breasts. She reached out and touched the softness of her daughter's hair, traced the outline of her nose, and when she bent to kiss her lashes, her eyes suddenly fluttered open and Marilla stared in awe at the image of William looking straight into her heart.

From somewhere deep inside, the gentle sway of motherhood began its rhythmic motion. Marilla, whose empty breasts ached with longing, rocked back and forth, back and forth, cradling her baby, her own flesh and blood, while she breathed in her sweetness and gently kissed her face.

CHAPTER 13

❧⟡❧

MRS. MURPHY RUSHED ALONG THE STREET TOWARD HOME. She was late getting supper ready. And heaven forbid they have to wait. If their plates weren't piled high and in front of them by five o'clock, you would swear to God it was the end of the world. She rummaged through her pocket, found the key, and unlocked the door.

The shipyard whistle blew at exactly four every day and the sound, heard by the entire North End of Halifax, chased Mrs. Murphy down the hall and into her kitchen. Thank heavens the corned beef was already cooked. By the time the front door opened and they all fell in, the cabbage and potatoes would be done.

By four thirty, with pots bubbling and the dining table set, Mrs. Murphy lowered herself into the rocker beside the stove. She removed her shoes and took advantage of the few remaining minutes to rest her feet and drink some tea before the lumbering sound of workboots shattered the peace.

Her feelings were still smarting from how abruptly Mrs. MacDonald had spoken to her. "Imagine," Mrs. Murphy said aloud. The need to voice her thoughts often overcame her and though she'd been observed on more than one occasion talking to herself, she paid no mind.

"And not so much as an introduction. How rude."

Mrs. Murphy sipped her tea and tried her best to remember the name she'd heard.

"Stella? Marcella? Marilla! That's it, Marilla."

William, who'd arrived home ahead of the others and slipped quietly in the front door, stopped in his climb up the stairs and headed to the kitchen.

"Did I hear you say Marilla?"

Mrs. Murphy's jaw dropped and she stared at William. "You scared the life out of me. I didn't hear you come in. Where's Duncan and the others?"

"Did I hear you say Marilla?"

"Yes. Why?"

"Where did you hear it?"

"I was heading for a walk today, down to the Gardens and I passed Mrs. MacDonald's. Lovely woman, four children. We walk together sometimes you see."

"Where, Mrs. Murphy? Just tell me where."

William's face had clouded over and Mrs. Murphy started to feel anxious.

"Mrs. MacDonald was at her front door on Spring Garden Road, and there were two women standing outside. She said their names and that's when I heard it. I heard her say Marilla."

William's body tensed and he reached up and pulled a hand roughly through his hair."

"Why, William? What does that mean?"

"What did she look like?"

"Well, she was only young. A skinny little thing, though rather tall for a lady. Hair piled high, reddish brown I think. She had a bonnet on of course, but she did look my way and her eyes were the brightest blue."

Mrs. Murphy reached for her apron and walked to the stove. "She looked a bit sad though, I must say. And I've been so curious all day, wondering who they could possibly be and what they were doing there."

"Mrs. Murphy, you need to take me there."

"What? Why would I...?"

"Because I need to see her. Now. I need to know."

"Know what?"

The front door opened and voices loud with laughter filled the entryway.

"I need to know if she's *my* Marilla."

Mrs. Murphy yelped: "*Your* Marilla! That's where I heard the name. The night of the storm. You don't think? No, it can't be. What would be the chances?"

The stomp of boots and the sound of doors opening and closing propelled Mrs. Murphy into action.

"William, this will just have to wait. I can't leave now. You know that. Let me get the men fed and then we'll go."

William, teeth clenched and hands curled into fists, stormed out of the kitchen, taking whatever air was left in the room with him.

Anger, simmering since the night of the storm, gathered in each step he took. By the time he reached his room, the force behind the slamming door rattled the house.

"Damn her."

His hands shook trying to pour a drink and he sat down on the edge of the bed. After all these months, after all the letters, why hadn't she had the decency to write him? And now she was here? In Halifax? Had he meant nothing to her?

A knock interrupted his thoughts and the door slowly opened.

"Safe to come in?" Duncan said, holding the door partially open and poking his head through.

William gestured with his hand and Duncan stepped in, his eyes creased with humour and ready to tease.

"I heard the slam from the first floor. I came to check the hinges. They best be in tact or Mrs. Murphy will have your hide."

"She's here. Marilla. Right here in Halifax."

"Whoa, slow down. What are you talking about?" Duncan pulled a chair over and sat next to William.

"Mrs. Murphy saw her today. Down on Spring Garden Road. She was standing on the doorstep in front of a house."

"And what made Mrs. Murphy, who's never laid eyes on your Marilla, think it was her?"

"She heard her name. The woman at the door said Marilla."

"For the love of God, William, she's surely not the only Marilla in the entire city of Halifax."

"Yes, I know, but she described her." William stood and started pacing. "She told me what she looked like. Said she was tall like my Marilla, and that her eyes were blue."

"Oh well, that's it then. That's her." Duncan rolled his eyes and stood. "And what now? "You're off to chase down the only tall, blue-eyed woman in Halifax?"

"I need to see her," William spat. "I need to look her right in the eye and have her tell me…after all these months, after all the goddamn letters, why she never so much as said what happened. Did she marry? Or maybe the truth is that she never loved me at all? Jesus Christ!" William shouted. "I just need to know."

"What you need…is to let this go."

The two men stood, staring down the other, while anger, pride, and reason wrestled with the bonds of friendship. Without a word, Duncan turned his back on William and left the room.

∽

The air was cold and the wind had gathered strength as the sun began its slide toward dusk. Mrs. Murphy clutched at her scarf and William knew she was trying her best to keep up with him, but even he could not control the pace. He buried his hands deep inside his pockets and held tightly to the letter he'd prepared. That it might not be his Marilla and here he was doing nothing more than making a damn fool of himself, fuelled his footsteps. But the truth was that, the thought of seeing her after all these months, of coming face to face, scared the hell out of him.

As if reading his mind, Mrs. Murphy, who'd stopped to catch her breath, said, "You do realize that we may be on a fool's errand, William, and that she might not be there at all. Or that it might not even be her."

"Yes, I am perfectly aware, Mrs. Murphy, but I must at least try.

She has an aunt who lives in Halifax, I met her last summer, and we have to determine if your Mrs. MacDonald somehow knows her. It does seem a coincidence doesn't it?"

"Well, yes, I suppose. Marilla is certainly not a common name. Well, it's no matter what the outcome, we're here now."

Mrs. Murphy stopped walking and William, surprised they had arrived so soon, held his breath as she approached the door and knocked. They could hear voices from inside, along with the thump and patter of feet. The door swung open and a large, flustered man carrying a crying baby swaddled in pink stared at them while he yelled into the house, where the sound of a child's wailing could be heard.

"Mary, put your brother down, he's not a toy." He stood in the porch and scowled at William and Mrs. Murphy. "What do you two want? If you're looking for the missus, she'll be up at the church." He deftly swung the baby up and over his shoulder. "Another meeting if I had to guess."

William found his voice and spoke. "This is Mrs. Murphy, my landlady from up on North Street."

Mrs. Murphy nodded and mumbled, "Nice to meet you, Mr. MacDonald."

"And this morning she saw your wife speaking to a young woman out here…on your steps."

"I was on my way to the Gardens, you see. I sometimes walk there with your missus and the little ones."

"She heard her say the name Marilla. And I just want to know—"

"Can't help you there. Likely some woman from the church. They're here all the time for one thing or another." He started to close the door.

William reached into his pocket and pulled out the letter. "Please, sir, could you pass this along to your wife and see that it gets to Marilla? It's very important."

Mr. MacDonald grabbed the letter, shifted the baby in his arms, and closed the door. They could hear his voice trail off as he walked further into the house and William stood unable to move.

The urge to pound the door down and cry out in frustration left him weak.

Mrs. Murphy, horrified her boarder would make a scene in the middle of Spring Garden Road, looped her arm through William's and urged him on.

"Come, William, let's head back to the house. There's nothing more to be done tonight. But I promise I'll come back, first chance I get tomorrow, and straighten this all out."

Mr. MacDonald gently placed the baby girl back in her bassinet. When he raced to the kitchen to wash up the children, he tossed the letter on the sideboard, already overflowing with papers, where his wife could see to it when she got home.

CHAPTER 14

❧❧❧

May 20, 1842

Halifax, NS

MARILLA WOKE SCREAMING. ONLY WHEN SHE OPENED HER eyes did the last broken fragments of her dream drift away. She was holding her baby and running, the sound of surf guiding her steps through the dark, along the beach toward the light. Before she reached it, a woman, arms outstretched and grey with mist, emerged through the fog and snatched the baby from her. Marilla screamed but she couldn't move, couldn't run.

"Nooo!" Marilla yelled, tearing and searching through the blankets piled around her. As she opened her eyes, the lace curtains came into view and the sunlight jarred her awake. She fell back panting and began to sob.

The bedroom door swung open and Martha rushed in. "Good heavens, Marilla. Are you all right? What's happened?" She hurried across the room, sat on the edge of the bed, and gently pried Marilla's hands from her face. "Oh, Marilla, what is it? Sh, don't cry now. I'm here."

Marilla, struggling to catch her breath, sat up and moved into Martha's arms. "I had an awful dream. I was on the beach in Avonlea and I was taking her home and then someone took her. Just took her." Marilla leaned back and held out her arms. "Right from my arms."

"Sh, Marilla, it was just a dream. Settle down now, don't get yourself all upset."

"But it was not just a dream, was it? Marilla pushed her legs over the side of the bed and stood. "It is what actually happened."

Martha let out a sigh and her shoulders slumped forward. "Marilla dear, we've been over this. What good will it do to torture yourself?" She stood and faced her niece. "I can see you're upset. And if you feel you are not prepared to meet with Mr. and Mrs. Willis today then so be it. As Etta has said before, she will meet with them on your behalf and sign the adoption papers. You do not need to be there. And we will *all* understand if that's what you choose."

Martha headed toward the door. "Etta and I had hoped that seeing the baby for yourself last week would have eased your mind, but I must be honest with you, Marilla, I'm starting to regret that decision. I love you dearly, you know that, but it's time to pull yourself together, take care of what needs to be done to set things right. Only then can you finally put this dreadful chapter of your life behind you."

Marilla watched her aunt leave the room and squelched the impulse to lash out and accuse her of being terribly unkind. But Aunt Martha was right. Marilla had to face the truth. William was dead, and it didn't matter that she still loved him, he was never coming back. And she knew, though it nearly broke her heart, that without him she could never keep the baby. She dressed, pinned her hair in place, and headed downstairs. It was time.

∾

Mrs. MacDonald wiped her hands on the dishtowel and rushed to answer the front door. She welcomed Mr. and Mrs. Willis, hung up their coats, and led them to the parlour. A fire, lit by her husband that morning before he left, welcomed them.

"Oh, how lovely. We're staying at an inn just outside of Halifax and left very early, so we can certainly use some warming up." The couple, older than she was expecting, settled in chairs facing the fireplace.

"Please, make yourselves comfortable and I'll bring you some tea. Miss Cuthbert will be here shortly, along with Miss Byers."

"When can I see the baby, Mrs. MacDonald? I am ever so anxious to hold her."

"Yes, of course. Perhaps once you've warmed a bit. She was sleeping, last I looked. But no matter, she's off to her new home today. So as soon as you feel ready, I'll bring her down."

A tender smile passed between the couple and Mrs. Willis reached for her husband's hand. He took it and began to rub. "Your hands are very cold, Catherine. I think Mrs. MacDonald is right, it's best to warm up a bit first."

The door knocker stopped the conversation and Mrs. MacDonald could feel the tension in the room rise; she was grateful she'd sent the children to her sister's for the morning. This was never easy, and no matter the planning and preparation, it often did not go well.

"That'll be Miss Byers and Miss Cuthbert now. I'll show them in and we'll join you in a few moments."

Mrs. MacDonald opened the front door and was pleased to see a very composed Marilla standing beside Etta. "Good morning, Etta. Good morning, Marilla. Please, come in." She stepped back so they could enter. "The Willises have arrived and are waiting in the parlour." Mrs. MacDonald reached for Marilla's hands. "Are you ready, my dear?"

"Yes," Marilla said, though she trembled slightly. "I'm ready."

"Well then, let me take you in straight away. I'm sure you're as anxious to meet them as they are you."

They followed as Mrs. MacDonald led the way. When they reached the parlour, Marilla hesitated for a moment then stepped through the doorway. And there she sat. The woman who would be her little girl's mother. A warm, gentle face smiled back. She looked at Mr. Willis and immediately sensed his strength, his kindness.

Mrs. MacDonald and Etta sat perched on the edge of their chairs, holding their breath, while Marilla stood and stared.

Mr. Willis rose first and extended his hand. "I'm Charles Willis and this is my wife, Catherine. We came to find out about your, uh." He coughed and cleared his throat. "Your situation and your little girl from Miss Byers here. And I want you to know that she'll be well looked after."

They watched as Mrs. Willis rose and stood next to her husband. "And she'll be loved. So very loved."

Marilla's throat closed over and her eyes filled with tears. She wasn't sure who reached out first, but in the next moment the kind of mother she had never had, the kind of mother she would never be, wrapped her arms around Marilla and held her.

As she cried, Mrs. Willis whispered, "I want to thank you from the bottom of my heart for this gift…of your baby girl. We will treasure her always and treasure you for the giving."

The room was quiet but for the crackling fire and gentle weeping of the two women, lost in their joy and grief, until the whimpering of a baby pulled them apart.

Mrs. MacDonald stood quickly. "Well, there she is. I'll give you both a moment to gather yourselves. In the meantime, I'll change her nappy and freshen her up. Etta, could you please prepare the paperwork and perhaps set out the tea while I tend to the baby?"

Etta quickly made her way to the kitchen, leaving Marilla and the Willises behind to talk. She breathed a sigh of relief as she filled the kettle. She felt a quiet confidence that the next hour or so would go well.

Etta looked over at the sideboard and rolled her eyes. As lovely a caregiver as Mrs. MacDonald was, her tendency toward clutter could be a nuisance. She rifled through the papers, looking for the document she'd prepared a week ago and left with Mrs. MacDonald to complete. She could see the tail end sticking out from under a newspaper and tugged.

Papers shifted and an envelope fell to the floor. "Oh, for heaven's sake," Etta whispered as she bent and picked it up. She placed the crumpled envelope back on the pile and started to walk away until the name *Marilla Cuthbert*, scrawled across the front, caught her eye. She reached back and picked it up. There was no return address nor any indication who it was from.

"That's strange."

At that moment Mrs. MacDonald walked into the kitchen carrying the baby and saw the envelope in Etta's hand.

"Oh, don't pay any attention to that," Mrs. MacDonald said, placing the baby in the bassinet. "Mrs. Murphy, you know, that woman, or dare I say busybody, who you and Marilla saw when you arrived for your visit last week?"

"Yes, of course, I remember."

"Well, that evening she dropped it off for Marilla. Always recruiting for the Irish Society that one, pay no mind. Poor John, his hands full with the kids and two strangers on the doorstep. Some man from the boarding house was with her and he passed John the envelope just before he closed the door."

"But how would they know her name?"

"Oh don't you worry, busybodies have their way. You can give it to Marilla after we've dealt with all this. She doesn't need to worry about that now."

A faint flicker of apprehension tugged at Etta's thoughts, but she placed the envelope in her pocket and laid the adoption papers out on the table.

When the tea was ready and the baby dressed, Mrs. MacDonald and Etta walked into the parlour. Etta set the tray down on the table and waited while Mrs. MacDonald crossed the room. She walked to the settee where Marilla and Mrs. Willis sat side by side and placed the baby in Mrs. Willis's outstretched arms. Marilla sat ramrod straight and held her hands tightly on her lap.

"Oh my, she is a darling," Mrs. Willis said as she pulled the blanket away from the baby's face and gazed at her soft downy head. Mr. Willis rose from his chair and knelt before his wife. He touched the tiny hand clutched under her chin and smiled at his wife as tears filled his eyes.

Marilla's baby was now a part of their world and the intimacy of the moment tore at her heart. She rose quickly and walked to the hallway where her breath caught in her chest. She heaved, gulping in air as tears flowed down her cheeks. Etta's arms were suddenly around her and together they headed toward the kitchen.

"She says her name is Bertha," Marilla said between sobs. "She's their Bertha now. Not my Anne. She would have been my Anne. Mine and William's."

Marilla stood and paced the room then clutched desperately at Etta's hands. "But she promised me they would baptize her as Bertha Anne, you see. So some part of me will always be with her. Won't it, Etta? Some part of her will always be mine."

Etta steered Marilla toward a chair, praying she could settle her before she was gripped with hysteria. "Yes, Marilla, of course. Calm down now and catch your breath. We're almost done here."

Etta pushed the adoption papers toward Marilla and placed a quill between her fingers.

THIS INDENTURE MADE THE TWENTIETH day of MAY IN THE YEAR OF OUR LORD ONE THOUSAND EIGHT HUNDRED AND FORTY-TWO BETWEEN CATHERINE WILLIS OF STEWIACKE, NOVA SCOTIA, OF THE ONE PART AND MARILLA CUTHBERT OF AVONLEA, PRINCE EDWARD ISLAND, OF THE OTHER PART, THAT WHEREAS THE AFORESAID MARILLA CUTHBERT IS AT PRESENT UNMARRIED, SHE HEREBY RELINQUISH AND GIVE UP ALL FUTURE CLAIM OF ANY KIND TO THE SAID CHILD FOR ALL TIME.

She held Marilla's shaking hand as it dipped in the ink and pointed to the place beneath her name. A tear dripped and blurred the edges where she signed.

"There, that is all you need to do. It's over now, Marilla, and you have done the right thing. We're going to leave like we discussed, and Mrs. MacDonald will finish up with the Willises and see them off."

Marilla stood on unsteady legs and Etta held her arm as they made their way to the front door. Mrs. MacDonald joined them just as Etta was helping Marilla into her coat.

"Take care of yourself, Marilla my dear. I would surely like to know how you're getting on so please stay in touch. And perhaps we'll meet again the next time you visit Halifax." She opened her arms and Marilla stepped into her embrace.

They then said goodbye, stepped out onto the street, and watched the door close behind them. They got only as far as the entrance to the Gardens when Marilla's legs gave out. A gentleman stepped forward and helped Etta get Marilla to a bench where she assured him they would be fine. They sat quiet, sheltered from the wind, and felt the sun's warmth on their faces while birds overhead spoke of a spring that had finally arrived.

Etta reached inside her coat and pulled out the envelope she'd tucked away. Thinking a diversion at that moment might help lighten Marilla's grief, she handed her the letter. Marilla held it without moving.

"Remember that funny little lady we saw last week when we first visited with Mrs. MacDonald, the one she often walks with through these gardens? Well, apparently she dropped that off for you."

Marilla turned it over in her hand.

"Mrs. MacDonald says she's always recruiting new members for the Irish Society she belongs to, so I guess she thought you being young and all, would make a good member. Of course, she had no idea you'll be leaving. Anyway, Mrs. MacDonald hung onto it for you. I thought you might like to open it now.

The handwriting looked familiar and Marilla felt her heart begin to race. She tore open the envelope and unfolded the letter.

If this letter is being opened by anyone other than Marilla Cuthbert of Avonlea, just throw it away.

Marilla shrieked and jumped to her feet. "This is from William. My William."

"Marilla, what on earth are you talking about?"

She held the letter and skimmed the words. *I survived the explosion in Boston. I'm living back here in Halifax. At Mrs. Murphy's boarding house. Please let me know what happened.*

For a moment Etta couldn't breathe. "No! That's not possible… there's been a—"

Before she could say another word, Marilla screamed and started to run: "My baby."

Etta took chase. "No, Marilla, it's too late. She's gone." Etta caught her sleeve and pulled her to a stop.

"But we can get married just like we planned," Marilla said, shaking her arm free. "And then we can take our baby home to Avonlea."

"No Marilla you can't. The papers are already signed. Remember? It's too late."

The words stopped Marilla cold in her tracks. She fell to her knees, slumped forward, and pressed the letter to her chest. For a moment, Etta thought she'd fainted until her head tilted skyward. And for as long as she lived, Etta knew, she would never forget the sound that rose from the depths of Marilla's heart.

CHAPTER 15

MARTHA QUIETLY CLOSED THE BEDROOM DOOR AND walked with the doctor as they made their way downstairs. "The medication I administered will help her rest. I'll leave a tablet with you in the event she requires it this evening. Try and get her up to eat later in the day. She's weak and needs to gain her strength."

"She's had a terrible shock," Etta said, joining them in the front porch. Martha opened the door and the doctor stepped out. "Thank you for coming, we didn't know what else to do."

"You did the right thing. But not to worry. She's young. Whatever misfortune has befallen her, it will certainly not diminish her spirit for long." He smiled reassuringly "My experience has shown me it is the young who, more often than not, recover the quickest."

Etta and Martha made their way to the parlour and sat down, breathing a sigh of relief.

"What a day. Martha, if you could have seen her, it would have broken your heart. Did she show you the letter?"

"No, it's still clutched in her hand and she wouldn't release it. When I tried, she became so agitated I had to let it be."

"What in the name of heavens will she do?"

"Well, I expect she'll go see him. Won't she? What else can she do?" Martha shook her head. "How is this even possible? I was there, Etta, when the news was delivered. They said he'd died. Why did no one write? I just don't understand."

"Neither does she," Etta said, dabbing at her eyes. "What a cruel thing, Martha. The day she signs the adoption paper and hands over her baby. Hands over *their* baby. It is beyond cruel."

They sat together the rest of the afternoon, drinking tea and waiting for Marilla to rouse. Martha peered in once or twice, making sure she remained settled, then closed the door and quietly crept downstairs.

⁓

Marilla heard the door close but didn't stir. She felt heavy, weighed down. Her thoughts began to scatter, spreading the images, floating behind her eyes, around the room. William's body, mangled and burnt. The wagon ride out of Avonlea. Her baby's face. The words *give up for all times*. Her name scrawled on a letter. The letter! The numbness in her limbs receded and she felt the crumpled letter in her hand. She struggled to sit up.

The paper was crushed, and she gently unfolded it and read his name signed at the bottom. "*William Baker.* You're alive. You're alive and living in Halifax. But how?" The strength of her voice surprised her and with it came a surge of anger. "Why didn't you write to me? Why didn't you let me know?" Anger lifted her from the bed and fuelled her forward. "How could you do that to me? To us?"

She stumbled to the wash basin and splashed cold water on her face. Determined to get the answers, she fumbled with her clothes and headed downstairs.

Startled to hear footsteps on the stairs, Martha sat up straight in her chair. When Marilla rounded the corner and entered the room, her expression defiant and determined, both she and Etta stood.

"Marilla dear, what are you doing up? You need to rest."

"I'm feeling better, Aunt Martha. But I can no longer just lie here and rest."

"Well, let me heat some soup then. The doctor said you needed to eat. And look at the time," Martha said, gesturing to the clock on the mantle. "You haven't eaten all day and it's almost four." She looked at Etta. "You'll stay and join us?"

"Thank you, Martha, but no. Now that Marilla is up and on the mend, I think it best I leave. There's much for you to discuss and I don't feel it's my place nor would it be helpful for me to stay." She reached for Marilla's hands and held them as she spoke. "Take care of yourself, Marilla. I know we'll meet again, and I pray the circumstances are happier than they are at present. If I don't see you before you leave, have a safe journey back to Avonlea."

Marilla had no words for Etta Byers. She understood on some level that she was being entirely unfair, but her simmering resentment of Etta's unwillingness to revoke the document in the face of what they now knew left her unable to speak. She headed to the kitchen while her aunt showed Etta to the door.

Martha entered the kitchen, grabbed her apron from the back of the pantry door, and walked to the stove. "You could have said goodbye, Marilla. None of this is her fault. And I know you're well aware of that. You're angry, and I would be too, but it's not Etta you're angry with. Is it?"

Marilla could hear the sense behind the words but couldn't release the anger. Not yet, not till she knew the truth about William. She needed the anger to hold her up, push her forward, and give her the strength she needed to face him.

"Not really I suppose," Marilla said, flinging herself in a chair at the table. "I am angry with myself mostly...for being such a fool. And with William of course. But for what, Aunt Martha, for being alive?" Marilla stood and began to pace.

"Believe me, Marilla, Etta was as shocked as you to discover that the father of the baby whose adoption she helped arrange is in fact alive. After all, that would have altered everything."

"Everything," Marilla said, thinking of all that she'd lost. Her anger flared and she began to cry. "Why, then, did he not let me know? What happened? I cannot believe he didn't love me, I simply can't. Something's not right. I need to find out."

"And you will, but not till you have had something to eat," Martha said, setting bowls on the table. "And not without me. I have a few choice words of my own he needs to hear."

∾

They stood on the street outside the boarding house on North Street. Aunt Martha's neighbour, on his way to pick up a load of coal from the North End, provided a lift in his wagon, and promised to return before nightfall. It was just past six and with the sun hidden behind a stubborn layer of grey cloud, it would become dark soon.

Marilla walked up the short flight of steps and knocked on the door. She could hear footsteps, and when the door opened she recognized the smiling face of Mrs. Murphy.

Mrs. Murphy peered past Marilla to where her aunt stood, and they watched as the smile left her face and her eyes widened with recognition. "Well, if it isn't Miss Cuthbert herself right here on my doorstep. I must say it took you long enough. It's a good thing for you, miss, that poor William wasn't holding his breath."

"May I see him, please?"

"That'll be up to him."

Martha stepped forward and introduced herself. "Good evening, Mrs. Murphy, I'm Martha Cuthbert, Marilla's aunt. It is very important that we speak to William. There's been a terrible misunderstanding."

Mrs. Murphy responded to Martha's plea and led them into the front hall. Together they stared up the staircase and their eyes followed the steps as they wound their way to the top floor. Voices and footsteps sounded throughout the house as Mrs. Murphy led them into the small sitting room off the hallway. "I'll let William know you're here."

Martha crossed the room and sat on the edge of a well-worn armchair. Marilla stood and watched Mrs. Murphy climb the stairs.

She heard the knock on a door high above, the sound of muffled voices, and then suddenly the pounding of boots as they clambered down each flight. Her heart banged inside her chest when at last William stood on the bottom landing.

William stared, too afraid to move. He'd dreamed this moment so many times and was terrified he'd wake. But it was her. His Marilla. More woman now than the girl he'd left behind. He stared into her eyes, glistening with tears, and swayed with the memory of their passion. "It's you. It's really you."

And no matter the anger and hurt, the loss and regret, Marilla's legs moved unbidden toward the man she loved, whose body was not burnt and broken, but alive and moving toward her, past the months of grief and sorrow, to this moment. His arms enfolded her and she laid her face against his chest and breathed him in. He lifted her off her feet and buried his face in her hair.

"Marilla, my Marilla. Is it really you?" He lowered her, then stood and stared.

A ragged scar ran down his cheek and a patch of blotchy pink skin along his neck looked tender; Marilla instinctively reached to touch it, but instead she took a step back. "What happened, William? Why didn't you, or someone, write and let me know that you had survived?"

William looked shocked. "I *did* write you, Marilla. The first one was sent from the hospital in Boston, and I sent another as soon as I was able and two more since coming here. Why did *you* never write back?"

"I never wrote back because I never *received* any letters. What are you talking about?"

Aunt Martha, who William hadn't realized was sitting behind them, spoke. "Who did you mail them to?"

William whirled around. "Aunt Martha, I didn't see you there." He looked over at Marilla. "I knew your aunt lived in Halifax and when Mrs. Murphy said she saw you, I was hoping beyond hope that you were staying with her."

Martha's words, which held a note of suspicion, brought a sick feeling to Marilla's heart. "Did you send them to Rachel, as you had done before?"

"Well no, not this time, they were sent directly to Green Gables." William started to pace. "That was the only address the hospital had…it's what I gave the captain when we left. And I knew Mrs. Webber was there and would get them to you, so I didn't think…." William, aware that his words had caused a stir, looked back and forth between Marilla and her aunt. "What's wrong?"

"I never got them," Marilla said, reaching for a chair. "I left Avonlea soon after hearing that you'd been killed and came to stay with Aunt Martha, here in Halifax."

"You what?" William stared. "Why? Why did you leave?"

Marilla froze and Martha held her breath. "I was grieving, William. I couldn't bear to stay."

"So all this time, all these months, you thought I was dead?"

"Yes," Marilla whispered. "I didn't know you were alive until just this morning. When I finally got the letter you gave to Mrs. MacDonald.

"But surely your mother would have…" His voice trailed off.

Aunt Martha collapsed back in her chair. "No, she never sent them. Dear lord."

"Oh, Marilla, I'm so sorry," William said, running his hands through his hair. "I was so angry that you never wrote back. I thought by the time you received my first letter, you had been too hurt. And by the second letter, that you no longer loved me. As time went on I began to think that perhaps you *had* married John Blythe after all, and therefore couldn't write. So that's why I gave that letter to Mrs. MacDonald, because I just needed to know."

He kneeled in front of Marilla, whose shoulders shook while tears ran down her face. He lifted her chin so he could see her. The pain in her eyes tore at his heart and he gently took her hand. "I love you, Marilla. Please tell me you didn't marry."

Marilla shook her head and wiped her face. "No, I didn't marry. And I love you, William, more than you'll ever know."

LOUISE MICHALOS

William bent and kissed her hand. "Thank God, Marilla."

His face lifted and Marilla could see the William she loved. The sparkling brown eyes so filled with joy and a smile that had always melted her heart. "You have made me so happy."

He held her face between his hands and gently kissed her as she cried. First her eyes, then her face, till finally his mouth found hers and they tasted and clung to each other. How she'd longed for this moment. To have William return to her and be her husband. She looked into his eyes, so full of love, and imagined the light leaving them when he found out what she'd done. He would never believe she *ever* loved him if he knew the truth. That she gave away their baby girl, the very symbol of their love, would shatter any belief he ever held of a life they could share. And she never wanted to see that light go out. Not by her.

Marilla released her hold on William and stood. "I'm so sorry, William, but I have to go."

"You have to go? Marilla, I don't understand." William tensed. "We've only just found each other. We can finally be married like we'd planned. Where are you going? I'll come with you," he said, rushing to her side. "Marilla, I don't want to be without you ever again."

"It's too late, William. We can never be together. Not now." Marilla started walking away and her heart broke as he followed. She made her way to the front door where Martha was standing, waiting.

"Martha, please talk to her. I don't understand. Why is she leaving?"

Martha watched as Marilla rushed out the door and down the walkway toward the road. "Marilla, what's wrong?" she shouted. "What is William talking about? Why are you leaving?" She turned to William. "It's been a shock seeing you, William. Give her some time. I'll speak with her."

Martha caught up with Marilla as she rounded the corner and pulled her to a stop. "Marilla, talk to me. I thought this is what you wanted."

Marilla sobbed. "I did, until I looked into his eyes. Aunt Martha, you don't understand. I'm going to have to live the rest of my life hiding the truth, from everyone, about what I've done. With him, I would be living a lie."

"But Marilla, he loves you."

"And if I told him the truth? How much do you think he would love me then?" Marilla, torn by what she knew she had to do, took a shuddering breath and wiped at her face. "The truth will be burden enough to carry, Aunt Martha. I simply can't look into William's eyes, every day for the rest of my life, knowing I never told him the truth."

CHAPTER 16

May 30, 1842
Charlottetown, PEI

MARILLA STOOD ON THE DECK OF THE FERRY THAT HAD carried her home. Between the wharf in Halifax, where she'd left a weeping Aunt Martha, to the jetty in Charlottetown, where Rachel and Thomas stood waving in excitement at her arrival, lay the Northumberland Strait, an expanse of frigid grey ocean that now separated her two worlds. The one she left behind and the one she had to face.

She stepped down the gangplank, marvelling at the green grass and red mud that embraced the waves as they splashed ashore. The sun sparkled on the water and the smell of salt brine filled her lungs. When Rachel reached her, with skirt flying and bonnet flapping, the warmth of her embrace and whispered welcome brought tears to Marilla's eyes.

"Marilla, my dearest friend, I've missed you beyond words." Rachel stepped back, held Marilla's hands, and teased, "I thought all this time in the big city of Halifax would have changed you somehow, but you look exactly the same. Doesn't she, Thomas?"

Thomas had finally reached them and stood smiling beside his wife-to-be. "Doesn't she what?"

"Doesn't she look just the same as when she left?"

"Well for heaven's sake, Rachel, she's only been gone a few months. What did you expect?"

"Men," Rachel said, looping her arm through Marilla's while Thomas picked up her baggage and followed behind. "Really...what do *they* know?"

Rachel led the way to the wagon and Marilla listened as she prattled on. Though they were not yet married, Rachel's tone and manner were that of someone married for years and Marilla felt a tug of longing at the banter she and Thomas shared. She'd missed the sound of Rachel's voice and even though she was her dearest friend, and always would be, a distance existed between them now. Marilla, who'd loved nothing more than sharing everything she felt and hoped for and dreamed about with Rachel, struggled against saying what was in her heart: *I may look the same, Rachel, but I'm not the Marilla you once knew.*

When the wagon reached the lane leading to Green Gables, Marilla began to feel anxious and needed some time to prepare herself for what lay ahead. "Thomas, could you please stop here? I'd like to walk the rest of the way."

Rachel reacted with surprise. "Are you all right, Marilla? You've been so quiet this whole ride home, you've hardly said a word."

"Not much chance of that," Thomas muttered then winked.

"I'm fine, really," Marilla said, patting Rachel's hand. "I'd just like to stretch my legs and take a look around."

"Why of course, Marilla. I understand. Thomas and I will go on ahead and put your bags in the porch."

Marilla stepped down and watched the wagon pull ahead. The sun felt warm on her back and there was comfort in having the red clay once more beneath her feet. Summer was her favourite time of year and she gazed at the row of silver maples, heavy with tender green leaves that lined the path. The pungent smell of soil, freshly plowed and ready for planting, filled the air. She could see cows grazing in the lower pasture and hear chickens clucking in their pen beside the barn.

The house stood solid against the blue sky. The freshly painted gables that edged the roofline were bold against the gleaming white walls, and in spite of all she had been through, she felt a lifting of her heart. "I'm home," she said aloud.

The approaching wagon had brought Matthew from the barn. He waved as Rachel and Thomas made their way to the house, then stood watching as Marilla made her way down the lane. She could see him hesitate. In Avonlea, he alone carried the knowledge of her loss, and for the first time realized how much that loss was his as well. They reached for each other and Matthew's shoulders shook as Marilla whispered, "I had a little girl, Matthew. A beautiful baby girl. And you are her uncle...you *would* have been her uncle. I'm so sorry."

Matthew straightened, pulled a handkerchief from his overalls and blew his nose. "No need to say more, Marilla. What's done is done. You're home now, that's all that matters."

Marilla knew there would be nothing more ever said about her baby, so she quickly changed the subject as they walked together toward the house, "It's good to be home, Matthew. How have you been?"

"Had a good winter all in all."

"How's mother?"

"Same as ever I suppose. Not much new around here, Marilla. Except for John Blythe. I have to warn you, she's got him convinced you'd be ready to marry soon as you're back."

"What do you mean, warn me?"

They'd reached the back door and Matthew held it open. "You'll see."

They stepped around the bags sitting where Thomas had placed them and walked into the kitchen. Thomas leaned awkwardly against the door frame while Rachel stood, looking unsure where to sit. Around the table, which had been set with cake and teacups, sat John Blythe and her mother, looking for all the world like the barn cat who'd proudly brought home her catch.

John's face broke into a smile and he rose from where he sat. "Marilla, it's so nice to have you back. I trust your time in Halifax was restful and that you've returned fully restored."

Marilla completely ignored John and instead glared at her mother. "What is the meaning of this? Why is he here?"

"He's here, like the rest of us, to welcome you home, of course." Mrs. Cuthbert stood and walked to the stove. "Now, please sit down, all of you, while I pour the tea. I'm sure you young people have a great deal to talk about."

Nobody moved and an awkward silence filled the room.

Rachel spoke first. "I was not aware that John had been invited to join us for tea."

John's smile faded and he looked at Mrs. Cuthbert. "You didn't tell any of them—including Marilla, by the looks of it—that I would be here?"

"Well, what is the good of a surprise if everyone knows?" She looked at Marilla. "I thought it would be nice to have familiar faces greet you on your return. And John is as familiar to you as anyone. For heaven's sake, Marilla, don't make such a fuss." She waved her arm to the others. "Come now, all of you, have a seat. We don't want the tea to get cold."

"Did you really imagine you would get away with it?" Marilla said.

Her mother answered impatiently, "Get away with what? What on earth are you on about now?"

"The letters, Mother. William's letters. The ones you never sent to me."

Her mother whirled around, mouth agape, then sank heavily into the rocker beside the stove while Rachel rushed to Marilla's side. "William wrote you letters? He's alive? How can that be?"

"Mrs. Cuthbert," John demanded, "what is Marilla talking about?"

"Tell him, Mother. Tell them all. How you kept the letters sent to me from Boston. Letters from William, telling me he had survived the explosion on the ship and was very much alive."

Her mother's face paled. "How did you...?"

"Find out?" Marilla leaned toward her mother and shouted: "Because he told me himself. In Halifax. Where he lives." She whirled around to face John. "So I guess the surprise is on you. She obviously led you to believe we'd marry when I returned. Tell me, John, is that what you still want?"

The flush in John's face deepened and his jaw clenched. "It's what I wanted, yes...but not like this, Marilla. I was never party to this, nor would I ever have wanted to be." He glared at her mother. "You deceived me—and lied to her!" The kitchen door slammed behind John as he stormed out, and for the first time since entering the kitchen, Matthew spoke. "Thomas, I appreciate you picking Marilla up at the ferry and bringing her home."

Thomas understood the unspoken message behind the words and moved into action. "Come, Rachel, let's go home now."

"But Marilla, what happened?" Rachel pleaded as he led her across the room.

"This is a private family matter." Thomas looked at Matthew and Marilla as he opened the door. "And you can rest assured that as far as we're concerned, it will remain that way."

Marilla and Matthew sat at the table, stunned into silence, and watched their mother, humiliated and petulant, push back and forth in the rocker. The sun began to slip toward the horizon and in the gathering gloom Matthew lit the lantern. Marilla sat, spent and strangely calm, and gazed out the window.

A line had finally been drawn. One her mother would never cross again. Marilla had left Green Gables as a young woman filled with grief and cradling a secret. Too innocent then to understand the events that were to follow. She was no longer that woman. She'd suffered losses too great to ever live as others wanted.

She stared at her mother. A year ago Marilla had wanted nothing more than to leave Green Gables. To start a new life in Halifax and be free of her mother's suffocating presence. Not now. Marilla saw her mother for who she was. A woman whose shameful behaviour diminished any authority she would ever wield again.

In the distance, Marilla watched as the last rays of sunlight danced on the water and a thought settled deep in her heart and held her firm. This was her life now. And it would be lived as she saw fit. Tomorrow she would gather the broken pieces of that life, along with the letters from William, and try her best to put it back together.

CHAPTER 17

MARILLA WALKED TO THE BEACH AND FOUND HER favourite rock nestled in the outcropping at the edge of the sand. She'd climbed it many times over the years and she sat there now, as she had then, searching for peace among the waves. She unlaced her boots and removed her stockings. She placed her feet on the cold wet sand and walked to the edge of the water. The icy ripples lapped at her feet and she quickly stepped back.

The scene in the kitchen that morning with her mother had been awful, and it continued to play over and over in her mind. She'd screamed and shouted and tried to make her mother understand, but there was no point. She wouldn't listen and, having recovered from the shock of her deceit being exposed, was completely incapable of apologizing.

"I know you don't believe me, Marilla, but I was only doing what I thought was best for you." Her mother had gone to her bedroom, retrieved the letters, and threw them in Marilla's lap. "There. Take them. And no, I never opened them. I would *never* do that. So who knew how crippled and maimed he might have been and I thought it best for you not to know. What kind of life would you have had?" She slammed and banged around the kitchen as she spoke. "The only sensible thing to do, in my mind, was to put all that in the past and start fresh."

"But you don't understand," Marilla yelled. "I *needed* to know. It would have made all the difference in the world. You had no right to decide what was best for me."

"You might be eighteen years old now, Marilla, but regardless of your age, I am still your mother. Go on," she'd said, waving Marilla away, "read the letters if that's what you want, but what's done is done."

Marilla glared at her mother. "You have no idea what you've done." She'd then stormed out of the house and headed to the beach to be alone.

Marilla walked back to where she'd left her shoes, climbed on the rock, and reached into her skirt pocket for the letters. There were four, just as William had said. By the time she got through the second letter, Marilla could hear his frustration. When she hadn't written back, after he'd sent two more, he'd begun to assume she had married and then by the fourth, to believe she had never loved him at all.

How could anything have gone so wrong? If she had only stayed, if she had only known. She cried for William and their baby. She cried till there were no more tears, then gathered herself and headed back to the house. Knowing what she knew now couldn't turn back the clock or change what happened. Her mother's words rang in her ears. "What's done is done."

༠༄

The room was bright when Marilla woke, and she could hear Matthew and her mother downstairs in the kitchen. *It must be Sunday*, she thought, *or else Matthew would be out in the fields by now.* She'd been back for three weeks, and other than visiting her father's grave and having tea with Rachel and her family, she'd stayed close to home.

Her mother shouted from the foot of the steps. "Marilla, church starts in an hour. If you plan to attend, I suggest you get yourself ready. Matthew and I will be leaving soon."

The thought of going to church and facing everyone made her cringe. As her father often said, the door to the church was always open; it was the hearts and minds of those inside that sometimes weren't. But something was missing and Marilla desperately needed to find it. Whether it was compassion or forgiveness, she wasn't certain. She only hoped the comfort she used to feel stepping into the sanctuary was still there. She pulled back the covers and prepared herself to find out.

The bell sounded just as they made it down the bumpy path leading to the church. Matthew settled the horses and tied the wagon while Marilla and her mother quickly made their way inside. People stared and whispered as they walked down the aisle. Matthew followed in behind and reached them just as the organ struck the first note of the opening hymn and the congregation rose.

Marilla wasn't surprised to see that John was absent from the Blythe family, gathered in their usual place across the aisle. After his humiliation at the hands of her mother, he'd left for Charlottetown and hadn't been seen since. She felt a hand on her shoulder and turned to see Rachel and Thomas in the pew behind. Their wedding was three weeks away and they glowed with excitement.

The choir began to sing and the new minister, hidden at first from Marilla's view, stepped forward and joined them. His voice rose with exuberance, surprising Marilla and filling the church and her heart with unexpected joy. She craned to see him and when he glanced in her direction, he nodded as if in recognition.

"Is that the new minister?" Marilla asked Matthew.

"That's him. Reverend Smith. All the way from Halifax," Matthew whispered.

Her mother leaned closer. "Entirely too liberal for my liking. Singing and cavorting with the choir. It is simply unheard of."

This was the new minister? She would never have guessed that. Ministers were stodgy, pious, and very reserved. Though silver-haired and middle-aged, he certainly seemed none of those. Something like hope bubbled up inside her.

"He's wonderful," Rachel said over her shoulder. "And the best thing that's ever happened to Avonlea."

During his sermon, Reverend Smith beamed from his pulpit while the congregation hung on his every word. "This church is not for the holiest or most righteous," he said. "This church is not for those who have never strayed. This church, this space we call the sanctuary, is just that. A sanctuary. Not for those with the nicest clothes or the biggest donation. Although the latter is always very much appreciated." The congregation murmured with laughter. "But for those burdened with loss and sorrow. For those who seek forgiveness, not damnation. We must open our hearts. We must reach out to those who suffer. This is our church. This is what God asks of us. So, please, everyone stand."

The congregation, who were as surprised as Marilla by the request, whispered and fussed but eventually stood.

"I want you to turn to the people around you, your neighbours, your friends, and offer them your hand."

The congregation stood frozen in place. Never before had there been such a request. Reverend Smith stepped out from behind the pulpit and began shaking the hands of the choir members, who in turn did the same. And so it began until the sound of voices and laughter filled the church.

Marilla's mother huffed beside her. "Well, I never in all my life saw the likes of this!"

When Reverend Smith reached Marilla, he held her hand gently and surprised her again when he whispered, "I assume you're Marilla, the prodigal daughter?"

"Yes, I am."

"Welcome back. Whatever troubles took you away, my dear child, I'm happy you've returned."

The simple act of holding her hand felt like acceptance. It was as if her own father, whom she missed terribly, had reached out and assured her that all would be fine. Tears prickled and her heart swelled. This stranger, who knew nothing of the shame she carried or the guilt she felt, had welcomed her back to the only place that could truly restore her soul.

Marilla smiled at Rachel and Thomas and awkwardly offered her hand. They hugged and laughed and smiled. Neighbours whom she hadn't seen in months or spoken to in years welcomed her home. When she reached for Matthew's hand, she was pleased to see that it was being held by a beautiful young woman, the one he'd written to her about, who stood gazing shyly up at her brother while he blushed to his very roots.

"You must be Violet," Marilla said. She reached for her hand but Violet surprised her by wrapping her arms around Marilla and giving her a hug instead. "I'm so happy to meet you, Marilla. Matthew's told me so much about you."

As the congregation continued to greet each other, Marilla turned to face the front where the stained-glass window cast a warm yellow glow across the altar. Her mother stood beside her, stiff and unmoving at first, then ever so slowly, she looked at Marilla. For a brief moment, their eyes met and Marilla could see sorrow and regret glistening on her mother's lashes, and when her fingers reached across the space between them and encircled her own, Marilla held them. She accepted what could never be spoken aloud, and though forgiveness was not yet possible, offered a small measure of compassion in return.

The service ended and everyone made their way to the church hall for tea, where Rachel's wedding plans were being discussed in excited detail.

The minister introduced Marilla to his wife, and between promises to teach Sunday school in the fall and plans for Rachel's wedding well underway, it was if she'd never left, and by the time they climbed back into the wagon and made for home, the feeling she'd had since returning to Avonlea, that something was missing, began to fade.

∾

The weeks leading up to the wedding kept Marilla busy. She made alterations to the dress she'd worn when she and William had danced until morning and where Rachel and Thomas had rekindled their long-held affection for each other. Trying it on brought back the memory of his fingers on the buttons. And held within the fabric, his scent still lingered. She wanted him with her, and this was the only way.

The day of the wedding finally arrived, and though thick grey fog hugged the coastline most of the morning, by two that afternoon the waters surrounding Avonlea were sparkling under a brilliant blue sky. Marilla, holding a fresh bouquet of lilacs, stood at the back of the church as everyone settled into place. She could see her mother sitting with Matthew and Violet in their pew near the front. Violet, sensing her presence, turned and smiled. Only she afforded Marilla a small measure of sympathy, knowing now the story of Marilla's lost chance at marriage. Many others had none, thinking she was a fool for turning down a second chance with John Blythe.

The organ music began, and everyone stood. Marilla felt her chest tighten and stepped forward, down an aisle she would never walk as William's bride. She stopped at the front, smiled at Thomas, so handsome in his suit, and turned with everyone to watch. When Rachel stepped into the vestibule and the sunlight fell across her beautiful white dress, the congregation drew in a collective breath. Thomas beamed with pride and Marilla, eyes brimming with tears, smiled for her best friend.

As Rachel made her way toward the altar, and even as her heart ached, Marilla knew one thing for sure: She would not let the past year of her life, in which she'd lost so much, define the rest. Or let bitterness consume her as it had her mother. She would hold William and their baby in her heart for the rest of her life. A life lived right here in Avonlea, where their memory would always be treasured and where new ones, like the joy on Rachel's face, would be made.

CHAPTER 18

⚬⚬⚬⚬⚬

April 21, 1843

Avonlea, PEI

*I*N THE WEEKS AND MONTHS THAT FOLLOWED, MARILLA
found solace in the rhythm and routine of farm life. She
worked hard during the day and fell exhausted into bed each night,
welcoming the nothingness of sleep. Except for whispered snippets
of speculation, no one spoke of her time away, and so she practiced
the long-held tradition of simply pretending the past year of her life
had never happened.

And it almost worked. Until the last of the heavy winter snow
left the fields and April arrived. Marilla became restless and more
agitated as the twenty-first got closer, and no amount of work could
smother the memories as they inched ever closer to the surface.

Rachel had announced in November she was having a baby,
and with her belly now swollen beneath her apron, Marilla was
haunted by the memory of her own. Without knowing, she'd find
herself cradling the emptiness beneath her hand and remembering the life she once held. As Rachel got closer to the day when she
would hold her child, Marilla pulled further away.

After supper she cleaned the kitchen and set the bread to rise.
The gloom of dusk began to close around the house, and she carried
a candle to light the way upstairs. She could feel her grief gathering

like a storm within her and her hand shook as she closed the bed-room door.

Marilla placed the candle on her bureau and opened the top drawer. Her baby would be one year old today. She removed the small flat box tucked beneath a shawl, held it gently in her arms, and crawled onto the bed. With legs tucked beneath her she rocked back and forth, cradling what was left of all that she once had.

She gently removed the lid and allowed the memories, held like prisoners, to escape, and with them was carried back in time. She closed her eyes and swayed while the storm around her heart gathered strength. She reached into the box and picked up a small pink ribbon. It had loosened from her corset when William's hands, desperate to feel her skin, had torn the last of the buttons away. Beneath the ribbon lay his letters, folded and grey. His words, sent unheeded, had died on the paper and Marilla held them to her face and mourned their loss.

At the bottom of the box lay a tiny flannel blanket. She raised it slowly to her face and breathed in the lingering sweetness of her baby. Her daughter had been swaddled in it the night she was born, and Aunt Martha had given it to her the day she left Halifax.

"This did happen," Marilla said pressing it tightly against her chest and curling her body around it. "You did happen."

She cradled and rocked and sobbed, releasing tears she'd been keeping to herself and feeling grief she pretended not to have. "My baby," she whimpered over and over. "My baby girl."

∾

Nora's hand, poised to knock, flew to cover her mouth "Dear God in heaven," she whispered, then tiptoed down the staircase leading to the kitchen. She placed the pitcher of water intended for Marilla's commode back in the pantry and collapsed in the rocker by the stove. The words *you have no idea what you've done* echoed back to her and the mystery of why Marilla had stayed in Halifax beyond Christmas fell into place.

"Dear God," she cried again as the enormity of what she'd done took hold. Marilla was pregnant when she left Avonlea. And she left believing William was dead. She gave up her baby because she thought he was dead. She gave up her *daughter. My granddaughter.* Tears prickled, her heart ached and she hung her head in shame while the words *what's done is done* rose like bile in her throat. She covered her face and cried, "God forgive me...I didn't know. I just didn't know."

When the tears finally stopped, Nora straightened her back, wiped her face, and stood. Darkness had fallen and she walked to the table and turned up the wick. Matthew would be back soon—he was already late—and would be looking for his tea.

She looked around the kitchen. How could nothing have changed...when in truth, everything had? She lifted the tea towel covering the bowl Marilla prepared. The dough had risen and was ready for the pans. And though she wanted nothing more than to crawl under her quilt and shut out the world, life had to go on. What choice did she or Marilla, or anyone for that matter have, but to carry on?

"This bread will not bake itself," she muttered while gathering the pans from the pantry.

And Nora Cuthbert knew for one thing for certain as she kneaded and pounded and folded the dough. She would never forgive herself. Never. She also knew that the burden of carrying what she'd done with her to her grave would never be punishment enough.

∾

The back door opened, and Matthew stepped into the porch just as Marilla descended the stairs and entered the kitchen. Their mother looked startled, as if she'd been found out, and all three stood staring at the face of the other. Each one held a secret, it was obvious in their eyes, and each one wondered what secret the other held.

"What's happened?" Matthew asked, stepping into the room.

"Nothing's happened," his mother said, waving his concern aside and reaching for the kettle. "Why are you so late?"

Marilla, grateful for the diversion, started setting the table for their evening tea. "Where were you?"

"It's neither of your concern where I was or why I'm late."

Marilla and her mother stopped in their labour and stared. Matthew, embarrassed at his outburst and flustered by their attention, plunked himself down at the table with a look that dared them to argue. They suspected it had to do with Violet, but said not a word.

The kettle whistled and the tea was poured. Plates of gingerbread were set in place and they ate in silence while the lantern flickered and glowed. The clock ticked and the wood crackled in the stove.

Something caught Marilla's eye and she peered out the window. She could see a light, bobbing and swaying across the pasture, heading toward the house. "Matthew?" she asked "Why would Billy be out in the fields this time of night? Has the horse gotten loose again?"

Matthew stood and looked closer. "What's the good of a farmhand if he can't even secure the barn? For the love of Pete," he cursed and headed to the door. Before he reached it, Thomas rushed through, breathless and panicked, and without a word to Matthew headed straight into the kitchen.

Marilla rose quickly and rushed to his side. "Thomas, what is it? What's happened?"

"It's Rachel. Marilla, you need to come." He began to shake. "She's screaming. There's blood everywhere." He struggled to catch his breath and collapsed in a chair. "The midwife is over in Carmody delivering twins and I didn't know what else to do."

Marilla grabbed her shawl and headed for the door. "Matthew, go get the doctor. Mother, you come with me."

Mrs. Cuthbert grabbed the lantern from the table and followed them outside. The chill in the air quickened their pace. They made it to the end of the lane and were turning left toward the Lynde house when Matthew, riding bareback, passed them at full gallop. They were only steps from the Lyndes' front door when a scream stopped them dead. The sound reached them from deep inside the house and rose unabated, filling the air and Marilla with dread. Leaving Thomas in the kitchen to prepare water and gather towels, they made their way upstairs to where Rachel, seven months into her first pregnancy, lay splayed and panting.

By the time Matthew returned with Dr. Timmins, it was over. The body of a baby girl, too small to face a world she wasn't yet meant to enter, slithered lifeless from Rachel's womb. Dr. Timmins quickly severed the cord, wrapped the infant in a towel, and headed toward the door. Rachel, unaware of what was happening, cried out as he left the room.

"Where are you going? Give me my baby! I want my baby! Thomas?" she asked raising her head weakly and looking around, "Where is he taking my baby?"

Thomas reached his wife's side and buried his sobs in her empty outstretched arms. Mrs. Cuthbert led Marilla, shaken and dazed, from the room and followed the doctor downstairs. Marilla watched as he gently placed the small bundle inside his black leather satchel.

When he straightened and turned to speak, Marilla could see how tired he was and she watched as sorrow glistened in his eyes. "I'm sorry I couldn't get here any sooner." He coughed to clear his throat. "Not that it would have made any difference. But I know what a comfort it was for Rachel to have you here." He headed to the wash basin in the corner. "You and your mother head on home now. I'll stay a while, at least till she's settled."

They headed home, letting the fresh air wash over them, releasing the smells of life and death from their clothes. Rachel's anguished screams and pleadings for her baby rose from behind and floated toward Marilla as if in a dream. She became disoriented and frightened. Not until she and her mother reached the lane leading home did the image of her own baby being wrenched from her arms begin to fade. The darkness gave way to the first hint of morning and Green Gables came into view. She stopped, suddenly aware of her surroundings.

"My baby," Marilla whispered, pressing her fingers to her lips.

"That's all she kept saying. Wasn't it? Poor Rachel...what a shame." Her mother, aware Marilla was no longer walking beside her, turned around. Mrs. Cuthbert would never forget the pain etched on her daughter's face and rushed to reassure. "But she's young, Marilla. And strong. You both are. There will be other babies. I promise."

Marilla stared at her mother and wondered at the innocence of her words. Other babies. She would never know how deeply those words, meant for Rachel, had touched her. Nor could she ever say, but when her mother reached out and tenderly wiped away her tears, it was as if she knew.

CHAPTER 19

⁂

*O*F COURSE, NO ONE KNEW THEN THAT THOMAS AND RACHEL Lynde would go on to have eleven more children. But it would have made no difference if they had. No one came to offer sympathy. No one knew how. The death of an infant was a hushed and hidden affair within small communities like Avonlea.

Rachel, exhausted and inconsolable, remained in bed while Thomas retreated to the barn. The minister arrived at the Lynde house later that morning and retrieved the tiny wooden box that Thomas had built in haste. They went together to collect the infant's remains from Dr. Timmins, then walked slowly to the cemetery, where the minister lowered the tiny box into a small grave, shaded by oak and pine, at the far end of the cemetery. Thomas placed a carved wooden cross to mark the place and headed home alone to comfort his wife. And with that, life in Avonlea very quickly returned to normal.

∾

The morning sun, high overhead, shone its way through the heavy lace curtains and woke Marilla from a fitful sleep. She gazed around the room. Her clothes, piled in the corner, brought back images of the night before. Exhausted, she'd dropped them, bloodied and damp, on the spot where she stood, pulled a nightdress over her head, and fell into bed. And if not for the need to slide the chamber pail from under the bed, she would have remained there for the rest of the day. It was that, and her promise to Rachel that she would be back to check on her, that propelled her forward, and once up, she moved quickly. The dampness of early spring hung in the air and she shivered while she washed and dressed.

The kitchen was quiet and the fire was low in the stove. Marilla lifted the grate, dropped a log, and watched the embers scatter as it settled into place. Three pans of bread dough, left overnight to rise, billowed high in the centre of the table, and when she peered down the hall Marilla was surprised, at this hour, to see her mother's bedroom door still closed. But before she could see to any of this she needed to find Matthew. She grabbed her sweater and headed to the barn.

Matthew stood knee-deep in hay he'd thrown from the loft above. He plunged his pitchfork and tossed what he'd speared into the horse's stall. Marilla entered the barn and he waited for what he knew she'd come to say. The night before, he'd stood in the kitchen of the Lyndes' home, relayed the message that Dr. Timmins was in the midst of delivering twins and couldn't come, then quickly left. The close proximity to such a private affair and the sounds emanating throughout the house sent him stumbling out the door and onto his horse.

"It was too small, Matthew. It didn't survive."

Matthew kicked the dust at his feet. "The minister rode past 'bout an hour ago. Figured that's what happened."

Nothing more would ever be said about Thomas and Rachel's sorrow, but looking into her brother's eyes, Marilla could see his own. She remembered his outburst the evening before. It was so unlike him and she'd known then that something was bothering him.

"Matthew, what's happened? Is this about Violet?"

He stomped away from Marilla and stabbed the pitchfork deep into a mound of hay. "Nothing's happened. Now just *leave* it."

Marilla knew not to push. "I'll leave it for now, Matthew, 'cause there's work to be done, but we will discuss this, you know we will."

Matthew ignored her as she walked away. His frustration mounted knowing she was right. They would talk. They always did. But this time would be different because no amount of talk could give him something he just didn't have. A goddamn backbone. The pitchfork stuck where he'd stabbed it and he cursed while struggling to pull it loose. He staggered backwards when it released, lost his balance, and fell. He flailed with frustration and cursed aloud.

"You useless, clumsy moron. You simpleton. What kind of man are you?" He struggled to his feet. Matthew bent forward to catch his breath and winced once again at the pain crushing his chest. "Sure as hell not the kind a woman wants for a husband." Tears stung and he rubbed his sleeve roughly across his eyes. "Sorry, Violet," he whispered into the empty barn. "But I just can't do it."

And therein lay the problem. She needed more of him. More than walking quietly along wooded paths. More than picnics for two by the shore. She'd come from Charlottetown the previous summer to visit her aunt, had stood beside him in church every Sunday since that first awkward greeting, and with nothing more than a kiss on the cheek, had completely stolen his heart.

But now it was time. Her reputation and his reluctance to ask for her hand had become grist for the gossip mill, and time was running out. Hers was not a question of love but of honour. His was not a question of commitment but of self-preservation. His crippling shyness, his discomfort with anything and anyone outside of Avonlea made it impossible for him to meet her family and attend all the expected social events, let alone stand in front of a congregation in Charlottetown and get married. He became ill at the thought of it. But that's exactly what she wanted. And the only thing he would never be able to give her.

The line had been drawn long before this moment. He'd carried the weight of his mother's wrath his entire life, and the only place and the only time he felt safe was when his feet stood on the red clay soil of Green Gables. No matter he was twenty-seven. No matter that Violet brought him the kind of joy he'd always longed for.

Matthew stood in the doorway of the barn and looked out across the fields and pastures that stretched to the water's edge, to where the line that encompassed his world ended. He could never, would never, go further. The time had come. He had to let her go.

∽

It was later that afternoon when Marilla, carrying a fresh loaf of bread wrapped in a tea towel, knocked on the back door of Rachel Lynde's home. Her husband opened it and beckoned her inside.

"I'm so sorry," Marilla started to say, but Thomas, too emotional and too embarrassed to be seen so, waved her words away. "She's waiting for you."

He carried the bread into the pantry, leaving Marilla to make her own way upstairs. The house was quiet, the curtains were drawn, and though the afternoon was bright with sunshine, the hallway was heavy with gloom. Marilla stopped to gather her strength. All through the night she had been tormented by guilt at having pulled away from Rachel in recent weeks. But the very thought of seeing the baby nestled in her arms had filled Marilla with such hate, it nearly took her breath away. And now she could not dispel the awful feeling that somehow her resentment at having to watch Rachel and Thomas live the life she'd lost had somehow caused this.

She knocked before pushing the door open and stepped inside. When her eyes adjusted to the light, she could see quilts piled high on the bed and the faint outline of Rachel's head, where clumps of dark brown hair fell across the pillow.

"Rachel. It's me, Marilla."

The quilts moved and a hand reached out. Marilla walked to the side of the bed and gently held it.

"I'm so sorry, Rachel. I know how difficult this must be for you."

The blankets shifted and Rachel struggled to sit up. "How would *you* know?"

Surprised by the unexpected tone in Rachel's voice, Marilla stood motionless and stared.

"How could you possibly know? You never carried a child inside you." Rachel held back tears while her rage mounted. "You never had to bury *your* baby girl," she shouted.

The word *bury* hung in the air between them and Marilla watched as it made its way into Rachel's heart, turning the unimaginable suddenly very real. Her face registered the truth and she started to panic. "Oh my God, she's in the ground. My baby is in the ground." She pushed back the blankets and started to flail, getting more tangled with each movement. "I need to hold her."

Marilla reached for Rachel and tried to soothe her. "You can't, Rachel, she's gone."

"But you don't understand. I never got to hold her...I never got to kiss her." Rachel struggled and started to scream. Marilla held her back while Thomas's footfalls pounded on the stairs. He rushed through the door, gathered Rachel, screaming and flailing, and laid her back on the bed.

She watched from the doorway as Thomas rocked and hushed and whispered tenderly to his wife, then stepped into the hallway, closed the door, and hurried downstairs. With every step, Marilla's guilt lessened, and in its place simmering anger, unleashed by the shock of Rachel's words, filled her chest. Instead of heading toward the lane home, Marilla gathered her skirt and started to run, the fury of having to swallow the truth and not hurl it in Rachel's face making her stumble and lurch, pushing her forward and ripping at her heart.

She didn't stop till she cleared the trees and she fell to her knees while her lungs screamed for air. When she looked up, the gates to the cemetery off in the distance stood black against the sky. Her voice broke the silence of the empty fields: "I do know what it's like. I *do*." Marilla struggled to her feet and headed toward the pines at the edge of the clearing. "How dare you think you're the only one?" Tears blurred her way and she walked aimlessly along the fence bordering the cemetery that led to the road.

The pungent smell of newly turned sod filled the air. A small patch close to the fence drew her close. When the tiny cross came into view, Marilla stumbled backward. She hadn't meant to come this close, wasn't aware she had. It was only ever the minister, along with grieving parents, who came to this section of the graveyard. Too frightened to look, she smothered a scream and ran.

Matthew, returning from town, pulled the wagon onto the lane leading home. The surplus potatoes from last fall were now completely sold, and the wagon rattled over the ruts left by the spring rain. The horse startled and pulled back on the reins, its front legs pawing at the dirt. Marilla, heedless of their presence, had pushed her way through the low brush and ran as if being chased.

Matthew shouted and drew the wagon alongside. Only then did she slow and turn to look.

"What's the hurry? Did Webber's bull chase you across the field again?" Matthew stopped grinning when he finally saw his sister's face. He pulled the wagon to a stop and jumped down.

"Marilla, what is it? What happened?"

She spun around, squinting into the sun. "I'm going back."

"Back to where? To Rachel's?"

"No, I'm going back to Halifax."

Stunned into silence, Matthew stood waiting.

"Don't look at me like that. I'm going. And I'm going to find William and tell him everything." Marilla wanted to push hard against his protests, but none came. "Say something."

Matthew shrugged his shoulders and stuffed his hands into his overalls.

"And then we're going to get married like we planned." Her fury began to wane and her desperation surfaced. "And then we're going to get our baby back…and bring her home. Because she's not dead, Matthew. *She's* alive. Not like Rachel's baby." The memory of the grave made Marilla shudder. "Rachel can never get her daughter back. She can never hold her. But I can. Don't you see?"

Matthew could see the fear on Marilla's face and in her eyes saw the answer she so desperately wanted to hear. "Yes, Marilla, I do."

From her bedroom window Mrs. Cuthbert watched as Marilla fell against Matthew and wept. *Must have brought it all back, I suppose. Seeing Rachel and the baby and all*, she thought to herself. She envied their closeness. They didn't need her anymore, never really had. *I'll not live long enough to fix all that I've ruined or ever know that kind of love.*

She gathered her arms around her own grief and knelt before the window. Tears blurred the edges of her world and her heart cried out, *But I would have dearly loved a granddaughter.*

CHAPTER 20

May 15, 1843

Halifax, NS

MARTHA OPENED THE DOOR TO THE FRONT PORCH AND gathered the mail scattered on the floor. She headed to the kitchen, dropped the letters on the table, and reached for the kettle. Etta was on her way home for lunch and Martha wanted to have the tea ready when she arrived. The lunchtime routine had been in place for as long as they could remember. And there was no need to change it now, though Etta, God love her, had offered. Martha smiled as she hurried about setting the table and peering into the oven. They each knew their strengths, and cooking was not one of Etta's.

At first it may have seemed odd: Martha a widow and Etta a single woman who'd refused any opportunity of marriage, until it was too late. Only they knew the truth. That neither had ever wanted to marry. The kind of comfort and devotion they sought could not be found within the confines of a marriage nor, as they'd always known, in the suffocating circle of a man's arms. They'd discovered together that what they needed and what they wanted most was each other.

And as time passed, those who may have cared were so busy with their own lives and their own problems that two unremarkable women living quiet, unremarkable lives received no notice at all.

And so, the decision was made. Grief for her brother had started it, perhaps. Then when Marilla left, the strain of caring for her niece and seeing her through those awful winter months finally took its toll. Her need for comfort and the loss of family made her reach out. And Etta was there as always. She sold her house and moved into the place she'd always considered home anyway. There wasn't a name for what they shared. The ones that existed were foul and completely void of love, so they simply let it be.

Martha poured the boiling water over the tea leaves, set the cozy over the pot while it steeped, and sat down to read her mail. The letter from Prince Edward Island caught her eye and she tore it open. Her excitement grew as she scanned the words.

"Oh, how lovely! Marilla's coming for a visit."

Etta, who'd entered the back porch unnoticed, walked into the kitchen. "Who's coming for a visit?"

"There you are," Martha said, rising from her chair. She reached for Etta and their lips pressed warmly together as they exchanged a tender kiss.

"Marilla's coming." She shook the letter in her hand. "She'll arrive at the end of May and stay for a few weeks. Isn't that wonderful?"

Etta's expression remained unchanged. "Did she say why?"

"Well, for a visit of course. To see Halifax again, I suppose. And to see me, her favourite aunt."

Etta could see the joy in Martha's eyes and so kept her concern to herself. But they had both been there the day Marilla left Halifax, when she swore she would never be back.

"What is it? What are you not saying? I know you, Etta, and you have that look."

Etta lifted the cover from the pot simmering on the stove. "The look of a hungry woman, perhaps?"

Martha placed her hands on her hips. "Very well then. Let's eat, but I know there's something on your mind. Perhaps once you've eaten your favourite dessert."

Etta brightened. "Rhubarb pie? You made me rhubarb pie?"

"Yes I did. And maybe *then* you'll be ready to tell me what it is."

ೢ

Marilla stood on the deck of the ferry boat *Charles* and watched as it pulled alongside the wharf in Halifax. The early morning fog had burned off, revealing a sun that now warmed her back. The air was fresh and she breathed deeply. A crewman tossed a heavy rope high in the air and it was caught and secured in place. A small group was gathered on the pier to welcome the newest ferry from Charlottetown, and when the gangplank was lowered, they cheered. Marilla disembarked amid the excitement and scanned the faces in search of her aunt.

Marilla stood, savouring the feeling of solid ground after a full day of motion. Martha was never one for punctuality, and Marilla wasn't surprised to see that she was not among the people waiting. She approached the steward who was busy sorting baggage.

"Excuse me, sir, my aunt does not appear to be here just yet. Where might I wait until her arrival?"

He pointed over her shoulder. "Follow that lot over there, miss."

Marilla turned and saw a group of people heading toward a tall stone building. A sign with the words *Pontack Inn* swung over a neat doorway, and planters filled with pine branches welcomed the guests as they entered. She gathered her bags and headed inside with the others.

With a seat secured by the window and breakfast ordered, Marilla sat and waited, keeping an eye on the dock for when her aunt arrived. Now that she was here, the weight of her decision and the planning it required felt heavy on her shoulders. And the energy that had fuelled the resolve to reclaim her life began to wane.

A week after her baby's funeral, Rachel, back on her feet, had of course, apologized for her outburst. Memory of that day, and the holding back of a truth she could never share, still pained Marilla. She'd gone to tell her friend of her plans to visit Aunt Martha in Halifax and together had pinned clothes on the line.

"Calving season is now upon us and Thomas has visited every farm from here to Carmody. But honestly, how many pairs of over-alls does one man need?" She moved through the row of pant legs flapping in the breeze and smiled at Marilla. An attempt Marilla knew to ease the tension that hung between them. "I appreciate you coming by to help." She'd lowered her head then and spoke quietly. "I certainly don't deserve it. I'm so sorry, Marilla, for what I said on that morning…after…."

"You were not yourself, Rachel."

"But I said some terrible things…."

Marilla bristled at the reminder. "Yes, you did. You said I couldn't possibly know what it was like. Why would you think I wouldn't know?" Marilla grabbed the empty laundry basket to keep from shouting, *I do know what it's like to carry a baby. I carried my own!*, and instead headed toward the house. "I am a woman, after all."

Rachel followed behind. "Please forgive me, Marilla. Please. Before you leave for Halifax, I need to know that…that you forgive me…and that we are still good friends."

Marilla swallowed the tears that rimmed her eyes and turned to face Rachel. Oh, how she wanted to tell her. Tell her everything! But she couldn't. Not even her plan to find William. There would be too many questions, and Marilla wasn't sure she'd have the answers.

Instead she took a deep breath and tried her best to smile. "Yes, I forgive you. But don't ever forget that each of us has suffered…in our own way."

Rachel brightened. "I won't, Marilla. I promise. And thank you."

"Well, you're welcome, but all gratitude aside, I could really use a cup of tea." Rachel linked her arm through Marilla's as they made their way to the kitchen, and in that one moment they were able to step together across the chasm that separated their lives.

Up until a few days before Marilla left, only Matthew knew her plans. Nora had kept to her room in the days following the death of

Rachel's baby. But by then the wheels were in motion and Marilla's determination to get William and her baby back grew stronger. To their surprise, her mother hadn't protested when she was told—in part, Marilla supposed, by the fact that John Blythe had left the Island for Upper Canada, and with no other prospects in sight, marrying William was better than no marriage at all, a fate considered worse than death.

The question she'd refused to consider before leaving was whether or not William would still be in Halifax. And if he was, would he still want her. And the one that scared her the most was whether or not he perhaps had already married. The boarding house was so close to where she now sat and the realization of all that could go wrong plagued her.

The sight of Aunt Martha, skirt gathered and rushing along the pier, caught her eye and she banged on the window. Her aunt stopped and when she saw Marilla waving, her expression of panic, brought on no doubt by being late, turned to delight.

Martha made her way inside, and when she reached the table where Marilla stood waiting, she gathered her into the familiar embrace of her open arms. "Oh, Marilla. My dear, sweet girl. You've no idea how happy I am to see you." She stepped back. "Let me look at you."

Marilla warmed at the unabashed attention her aunt always gave and felt her strength return. Whatever happened, her aunt would see her through. The tenderness she felt for Martha at that moment brought tears to her eyes, and she tried to hide them from the scrutiny she was under.

The server approached and took Martha's order, and they settled across from each other.

"Marilla dear, what is this all about? You're tearful and anxious and I'm quite certain, as happy as you may be to see your old aunt, that I alone am not the cause of such excitement."

Aside from Matthew, there was no one else who knew the extent of her plan. Coming back for William hadn't really surprised her mother but beyond that, she knew nothing. Marilla hesitated, straining against words that had justified her return to Halifax but whose utterance at this moment may very well sound foolish.

"I've come back, Aunt Martha, to find William and tell him everything."

Martha's eyes widened and her hand covered her mouth. Marilla rushed on before she could speak.

"And then we're going to be married like we planned."

The server arrived and Marilla waited until she was out of earshot before continuing. She leaned in close. "And then we're going to get our baby back."

∾

The distance to Aunt Martha's house wasn't long, and since each could carry a bag, they made the decision to walk. The silence between them stretched on till Marilla felt she would scream.

"Please, Aunt Martha, say something…anything."

"What can I say, Marilla?" She stopped walking and faced her niece. "Besides, why do you want to discuss it now? Sounds to me like you've made up your mind."

"Well yes, I have, but what do you think?"

"What does it matter?"

"It matters because you've been with me from the very beginning and I need to know if you understand."

They'd reached the house and Martha unlocked the door. "Take your bags upstairs, Marilla, and I'll gather some towels so you can wash up." With the subject quickly changed, Aunt Martha headed to the kitchen.

Knowing her aunt would say nothing more till she was good and ready, Marilla made her way upstairs. The bedroom door at the end of the hall stood open and rays of sunlight danced across the bed, brightening the soft pink roses of the quilt. The lace curtains moved gently at the open window, sending speckles of light across the rose-patterned walls.

This was not how Marilla remembered this room, and for a moment she couldn't connect it to the images in her mind. What she remembered was the gloom of endless rain and fog, the days of drawn curtains and deep sorrow. The reality startled her and for a moment she questioned what was real. Time had passed and life had moved on for everyone. Even for her baby. Why did she think she could come back and simply pick up where she left off?

She dropped the bags at her feet. "What, in the name of God, am I doing?"

Her aunt, carrying an armful of towels, stepped onto the landing and made her way down the hall to where she stood.

"I don't know, Marilla, but before you rip your world and everyone else's wide open, including that dear little child's, you'd better find out."

CHAPTER 21

❦

*M*ARILLA SPENT THE REST OF THE DAY SETTLING IN AND
preparing herself for the visit to the boarding house planned
for the following morning. Aunt Martha reluctantly agreed to
accompany her, but only because she didn't want Marilla walking
alone in a city she barely knew.

Etta was working that day from her small office at the church,
and Martha left shortly after lunch to meet with her and explain
the situation. Etta's involvement would be necessary if Marilla were
to carry out her plan. As far as Martha knew, the cancellation of
an adoption agreement had only ever happened once before, but
she assured Marilla that the circumstances were completely different than hers and all the parties involved were in agreement.
But Marilla, far from being discouraged by this news, took it as a
hopeful sign that it was indeed possible.

"Yes, Marilla, it's possible, but not very likely."

"Why? What were the circumstances of that other mother?"

"Well, I don't know, Etta never said. I just remember her being
concerned for the child."

"But—"

"Enough, Marilla. It's not me you need to convince, it's Etta.
And if you think dealing with her on this subject will be difficult,
it will be nothing compared to the Willises. Have you thought of

that?" The door had slammed behind her, leaving Marilla alone to wash the dishes and tidy the kitchen.

It was close to four when Marilla heard the front door open and the sound of voices filling the hallway. She was upstairs hanging clothes in the closet and tucking things away when she stopped to listen.

"But this *can't* wait, Martha, surely you can see that?"

"I know, Etta, but she's just arrived."

"The sooner we do it, the better. Waiting will only make it worse."

"Mrs. MacDonald, are you sure about this?"

Marilla's knees weakened and she sank to the bed. *Why is Mrs. MacDonald here?* She could hear Aunt Martha settling them in the parlour, and she waited till her heart stopped pounding before she made her way downstairs. The voices quieted as she approached and they stared, wary and anxious, when she entered the room.

Marilla looked around the room. She hadn't seen Etta since leaving Halifax a year ago, when Marilla's petulant attitude toward her had prevented them from saying a proper goodbye, and she nodded now to show that it had passed. She then looked at her aunt. "What is this about, Aunt Martha? Why is Mrs. MacDonald here?"

"I'm here because I have a letter for you from the Willises. It arrived two days ago and when I took it over to Etta's office today, your aunt was visiting and when she explained the reason for your visit—"

Martha cut in. "Why don't I put the kettle on and make us all a nice cup of tea?"

"Thank you, Martha, that would be lovely," Etta said, then pointed to the settee by the window. "Marilla, why don't you come and sit down?"

Aunt Martha headed to the kitchen and Marilla, anxious for the truth, crossed the room and perched on the edge of the seat. "Has something happened to the baby?"

"Oh no, not at all," Mrs. MacDonald said. "She's just fine. And God love Mrs. Willis, she promised she'd stay in touch. And here it is, a year later, and your first letter."

She seemed pleased by this fact and for a moment Marilla was confused. "Thank you, Mrs. MacDonald, I'm happy to hear that, so why then are you all so...I don't know. I mean, I understand that what I'm asking is very unusual and it won't be easy, but once the Willises know the truth about what happened, about the letters I never got, about William and I..."

Marilla felt the tension rise in the room and lost her patience. "Would someone please tell me what is going on?"

At that moment Aunt Martha breezed through the doorway carrying a tray heavy with cups and biscuits and Etta sighed with relief at having the moment they dreaded delayed.

Mrs. MacDonald got up from her chair, sat beside Marilla, and held her hands. "Do you remember Mrs. Murphy?

Marilla nodded as the scowling face of William's landlady came to mind. Her pulse quickened and the hairs on her neck prickled.

"Well, I still see her from time to time when I'm out walking with the children and—"

"Here's your tea, Marilla. It's nice and sweet, the way you like it."

Marilla sat motionless, ignoring the offered cup, and her aunt, embarrassed now by the feebleness of her gesture, set the rattling cup and saucer back on the tray.

"About two months back, she mentioned that your young man—"

"William?" Marilla said.

"Yes, William. Well, according to her...he is very sick."

Marilla looked at her aunt and when she saw tears glisten in her eyes, she panicked, pulled her hands free, and stood.

"Tell me. Tell me what you're all not saying."

Martha struggled for words. "Oh, Marilla. I'm so sorry. There is no easy way to say this. William is not just sick. He's dying."

ⱸ

And from there, it all began to unravel. The only thing she had never considered, had never even imagined, was that William would be dying. The words that floated to her from across the room made no sense. *Damaged lungs. Explosion debris. Coughing blood.*

When at last she breathed and the rushing sounds receded, she spoke. "He was fine, I saw him. Aunt Martha, you were there."

Martha nodded, bewildered. "Yes I was, and I'm as shocked as you." She looked at Mrs. MacDonald and tried once more to express her disbelief. "He *did* seem fine. He nearly flew down the stairs when Mrs. Murphy told him you were there. Remember, Marilla?"

Marilla nodded.

"But that was over a year ago," Mrs. MacDonald said. "And apparently he caught a terrible cold sometime in January. We had a miserable winter, we surely did, and the poor man just never recovered. Mrs. Murphy was right there with him when the doctor came. Said he suffered too much damage to his lungs. The explosion and all, he suspects."

Marilla stood. "I want to see him."

Everyone spoke at once.

"Not today, Marilla, you must get some rest," Aunt Martha said.

"It's been a terrible shock, you need to give yourself some time," Etta agreed.

Mrs. MacDonald dug into her pocket. "Marilla, what about the letter?" she said, holding it up. "From Mrs. Willis. Do you still want to see it?"

Forgotten amidst the shock of hearing such devastating news, Marilla stared at the lifeline to the one remaining piece of her shattered plans, her baby girl.

She clutched at the envelope and the room began to sway. Hands guided her to the chair by the window where the sash was opened wide. The curtains swayed and Marilla welcomed the breeze while Aunt Martha and Etta ushered Mrs. MacDonald to the door.

"Thank you for coming," Marilla heard her whisper, "but she really does need some rest. She's been travelling since yesterday and with all this…good lord, who would have thought."

The front door closed and they returned to the parlour. Martha poured tea, still warm beneath the cozy, and handed one to Marilla. "Whenever you're ready, my dear."

Marilla sat up, grateful for their presence, opened the envelope, and began.

May 1, 1843
Dear Miss Cuthbert,

I hope this letter finds you well. Birthdays are the best way to mark the passing of time, and so I waited until Bertha celebrated her first before I wrote as I promised I would. She was baptized when she was three months old and, respecting your request, was given the middle name Anne. She is doing well and grows bigger every day. And whether it's from the undivided attention she receives as an only child or because her father adores her beyond words, either way, she is the happiest child I have ever known. She has brought us so much joy and we continue to be ever grateful for the gift of her in our lives. I wish you happiness and hope that one day you'll find the courage to love again.

With kindest regards,
Mrs. Catherine Willis

Marilla looked up and met their steady gaze, and without uttering a single word, watched the remaining threads that had bound her determination to reclaim her life unravel at her feet.

CHAPTER 22

*T*HE HALLWAY WAS HUSHED AS SHE FOLLOWED BEHIND
Mrs. Murphy. Surprised and irritated to find Marilla and her
aunt standing at her door the following morning, she had reluctantly agreed, after both had pleaded, to take Marilla to see William.

"Why didn't someone write and tell me he was sick?"

Mrs. Murphy glared. "The gall of you. He wrote you letters
before. Remember? And a lot of good that did him." She leaned in
closer and hissed, "His lungs might be what's killing him, but it was
you who broke his heart."

She opened the door to William's room, and without any
warning of what was to come, stepped aside. The air, heavy with
the pall of death, made Marilla's stomach lurch. She covered her
mouth and entered. When the door closed behind her, she felt her
legs go weak.

A lamp flickered, illuminating a small bed in the middle of the
room. The shrunken shape of a man lay still beneath the sheets and
Marilla stepped closer to look. She didn't recognize him as the man
she knew. His once beautiful thick hair lay damp and limp against
his forehead. The arms that held her in their strong embrace looked
boney and pale.

Marilla swallowed her fear, uncovered her mouth, and leaned
forward. "William, it's me Marilla."

The blankets stirred and his hand reached out. Marilla took it in her own and tried to rub away the chill. She sat down beside him on the bed and held it to her heart. "William, I'm so sorry. I didn't know."

When his eyes opened, Marilla inhaled sharply. There he was. The man she loved. The man who'd held her and her whole world within his arms. His hand, clasping hers, rose to his lips. He tried to talk but a rasping sound deep in his chest made him wheeze. "Marilla. You came. I prayed you would." He pressed her hand against his cheek and held it tight. "I loved you, Marilla, I still do. Why did you leave me?"

This was the moment she'd waited for. When he would finally know the truth and the plans for the rest of their life would unfold.

But there was no life for them. Not now, not ever. Marilla struggled to find the right words.

Would it be a comfort to know of the legacy he left behind? Or cruel to be told of a child he would never live to see? She remembered the letter and Catherine's words, *the gift of her in our lives* and knew their child would never, could never, be theirs. So she did what she had to do even though the truth, held within her, tore at her heart.

She held him and spoke of their time together and how much his love had meant to her. They both spoke of regret and all they'd hoped to do. When his weeping ebbed he lay spent and quiet, clinging to Marilla. She felt his heart beneath her as she lay across his chest, dampened now by her tears. She burrowed deeper into the place that once was hers but knew it was gone. His fingers touched her face, caressed her hair, then rested on her back.

"I will always love you, William, and I promise to remember you, not as you are now but as you were when you were mine."

"That's all I ask."

When Marilla heard the door open, she pressed her face against his cheek and whispered. "I have to leave now, William, you need your rest, but I'll be back first thing tomorrow."

His eyes found hers as she rose to leave, and they told her what she already feared. She gently wiped his tears and kissed him goodbye. She tucked the blankets around him and slowly retreated, leaving Mrs. Murphy to douse the light and shut the door.

"He's the most peaceful I've seen him in days," she said, leading Marilla down the staircase. "I mightn't agree with you showing up like you did, but if you've settled his mind, then who am I to say."

"I'm sorry, Mrs. Murphy, truly I am." Marilla stopped and reached into her handbag. "And ever so grateful." She slipped a fold of money into Mrs. Murphy's hand and waved aside her objections. "Please, I want to do this for him. And for you. It's the least I can do."

They made their way downstairs where her aunt was waiting. Mrs. Murphy led them to the front door, and with her anger finally defused, hugged Marilla tightly, then bade them good day.

They stood on the stoop, staring at the closed door, and said not a word. Marilla pressed her hand against it and sealed the image in her mind. She'd done what she had to do and there was no turning back.

"Did you tell him?"

Marilla shook her head, unable to speak, and started for home.

∾

She awoke early, startled, though from what she wasn't sure. Dreams had merged throughout the night with her own tortured thoughts, so much so that the quilts were flung about the bed and scattered on the floor. Her head ached and her mouth was parched. She pulled her robe from the tangle of bedclothes and headed to the kitchen for water.

It was dim in the hallway. The sun had yet to break through the early morning fog. She crept down the back stairwell, careful not to wake her aunt whose bedroom was down a narrow hall on the other side of the kitchen.

Marilla filled a glass from the pail of water sitting in the pantry and sat at the table. Her heart was heavy with loss and her body ached with the weight of it. She'd lost everything. Her baby, her plans, even her William. How could it have gone so wrong? She thought back to the night she escaped through her bedroom window and ran, without heed, straight into William's arms. When the dream of a new life sat perched on the edge of her old one and all she had to do was reach out and claim it. "What a fool I was," she said, scolding herself. Tears stung and she swallowed hard.

Marilla would always remember this moment. When her heart gave out. When it hardened and ceased to feel. She was not yet twenty and though she knew she'd live for many more years, in that moment her battered and bruised heart shored itself up against love. *Like my mother*, she thought.

Marilla heard the bedroom door open down the hall. She mopped at her face and hurried to the pantry to refill her glass, avoiding the moment she had to face her aunt. When she turned to make her way back to the table, it was Etta, with robe and hair dishevelled, who entered the kitchen, not her aunt. Marilla was so startled, she dropped her glass.

Etta, half asleep and thinking she was alone, shrieked and clutched her nightdress. "Dear lord, Marilla, you frightened the life out of me."

Her aunt, hearing the commotion, rushed to the kitchen. "What is it? Etta, what's happened?" When she saw Marilla standing just outside the pantry, a shocked look on her face at having found Etta coming from her bedroom, she stared, unable to speak.

Marilla looked back and forth from one woman to the other, trying to make sense of what she was seeing. Etta had often been a houseguest of her aunt. They'd been friends for years. And she knew that Etta had sold her house the previous year and moved in. Her mind began to race. She knew they'd always been very close, but they would never under any circumstances share the same bed. Would they? Unless. Marilla shrieked and stumbled backward.

"Marilla dear, please let me explain."

"But...but Aunt Martha, explain what? I don't understand."

"I know, and I'm sorry." Martha grabbed a broom from behind the door and began to sweep. "Be careful where you step, you two, there's glass everywhere.

Etta, composed now after her initial fright, walked to the table, raised the wick on the lamp, and pulled out a chair. Marilla, surprised by their ease with one another, stepped hesitantly over the shards of glass and joined her. Martha swept the pile into the corner, and without another word, dropped a stick of wood into the stove and set the kettle to boil.

When her aunt joined them at the table, Marilla stared from one to the other. Etta reached for Martha's hand and held it while she spoke. "Remember the day I came to see you, after your baby was born, when you couldn't get out of bed and you were so angry?"

"Yes, of course I do. How could I forget?"

"Do you remember what I told you? About how we don't make the rules?"

Marilla nodded.

"Well, we don't. We don't make any of the rules. Right now, all the rules are made by men, and they suit them, not us. I told you about my own baby then, how I had no choice." Martha patted Etta's hand as she continued. "What I didn't tell you was that I was only seventeen. And he, a friend of my own father, was a brute of a man." Tears emerged along with the memory, and Etta swallowed hard. "I had no choice in it, you see? And then when she was taken from me, I had no choice in that either. There's so much we don't get to choose, Marilla. Look at what's happened to you."

Afraid she may have gone too far, Etta leaned back in her chair and sighed. "But who we love? That's our choice." She smiled tenderly at Martha. "Can you understand that?"

"Well...yes, I suppose I can. But what about marriage? What about what people would say?"

Martha spoke up. "I was married once. Briefly."

"What?" Marilla said staring in disbelief.

"You never met him. Not many people did. And I never kept his name. This was all before you were born. Even your father, thought it would be a good marriage. And I tried, but it was horrible." Martha folded her arms against the suddenness of her anger. "And the only thing that saved me from living the rest of my life trying to be someone I'm not was that he died."

Marilla flinched at the harshness in her aunt's voice.

"I'm sorry. I hate to say it that way, Marilla, but it's true. I couldn't have said then what I truly wanted, but I knew I did not want that!"

"And we've always been friends," Etta said gently. "Your aunt has seen me through so much."

"And Etta's visits always brought such comfort. We understood each other and wanted the same kind of life."

"But aren't you the least bit concerned about what would happen if people found out?"

The kettle whistled and Martha rose to make their tea. Though it was not yet seven, the grey skies were giving way to sunshine and Etta stood, blew out the lantern, and turned down the wick.

The harsh sound of the doorbell so early in the morning startled them, and Marilla watched as Etta and her aunt answered the question, without having to say a word.

"It's okay, Etta," Martha said, though her hand trembled as she poured the water over the tea. "You two sit, I'll see to the door." It rang again before she reached the porch and Marilla watched as her aunt stopped to settle her nerves before opening it.

Mrs. MacDonald, pale and anxious, stood clasping her shawl against the chill. Mrs. Murphy stood beside her, wiping at her face with a crumpled handkerchief while catching her breath. "Pardon us, Martha, for calling on you so early," Mrs. MacDonald began, "but we need to see Marilla." And with that, Mrs Murphy burst into tears.

Before Martha could usher them inside, Marilla's footsteps sounded behind her. When Mrs. Murphy saw her, she pushed her way passed Martha into the hallway and threw her arms around Marilla.

"He's gone, Marilla. Your William's gone." The sound of crying brought Etta from the kitchen and they stood watching as the two women clung to each other. "He didn't last the night, my girl." Mrs. Murphy spluttered. "Waited till you came, I swear...then went as peaceful as could be."

It was only when her aunt began ushering them down the hall and into the kitchen that Mrs. Murphy released Marilla from her grasp.

"I can't stay, my love, the men will be up and looking for their breakfast. I have to get back."

"I can't stay either, Martha, I just brought Mrs. Murphy over. She didn't know where you lived. And my own household will be up by now and the children will be howling for *their* breakfast."

"Yes of course, I understand."

Marilla saw them to the door. "Thank you, Mrs. Murphy, for letting me know. And thank you, Mrs. MacDonald. I appreciate all that you've done." Marilla swallowed her tears. "Both of you."

She closed the door behind them and leaned against it to gather her strength. William was gone. How foolish she'd been to believe she could simply come back and claim what was hers. She knew now what they'd known all along.

When all the rules get broken, these are the women who pick up the pieces. Who understand and forgive. Who keep secrets and bear wrongs. Women like Mrs. MacDonald, and Mrs. Murphy, even Etta and Aunt Martha. The women who'd kept *her* secrets and bore *her* wrongs.

Marilla wiped her face, straightened her shoulders, and headed to the kitchen. When she entered, Etta was tenderly holding her aunt, and when she looked into their eyes and saw the pain that breaking the rules and keeping secrets had caused, she knew, without question, that she would always keep theirs.

CHAPTER 23

HE FUNERAL TOOK PLACE TWO DAYS LATER. WILLIAM WAS laid out in the parlour of the boarding house, the only home he'd ever really known. Shipyard workers, those close to William who'd watched him suffer and those who'd shown up to pay their respects, filled the hall and stairways, while others spilled out into the yard, clapping shoulders and shaking hands. Though none had ever seen her, when Marilla stepped off the street and onto the walkway, they quieted and stepped aside to let her through, removing hats and nodding heads as she passed.

Mrs. Murphy, sitting vigil, stood as they entered the room. With her aunt on one side and Etta on the other, Marilla stopped just inside the doorway and stared at the casket. She pressed a hand to her chest, took a deep shuddering breath, and stepped forward. He was resting in the only jacket he'd said he owned, and she cried out when she saw it. It was the one he'd worn the night of the dance, the one he'd laid beneath them in the barn. His body, ravaged by illness, lay shrivelled within its folds. She reached out and gently placed her hand on his, flinching when nothing more than cold flesh met her fingers. She bowed her head, letting the tears fall, and prayed for his soul.

The minister's words, soft in their attempt at comfort, touched those gathered in the hallway and around the room. He'd been with

William throughout his suffering, and when he spoke of William's love of life, he looked at Marilla and smiled. "He spoke of you often, Marilla. And of his hopes for the future and the children he'd longed to one day have."

Marilla's intake of breath stopped him and for a moment, with brow creased in concern, he waited. Martha reached for Marilla's hand and held it while he continued.

"He was raised in an orphanage, as most of you know, so family was very important to him, and when he knew he would not be recovering, it was that loss he grieved the most. And though his time on earth was short, it was full. Look around this room. At the friends he knew and the people he loved."

He then looked at Marilla and spoke words she knew were meant to comfort. "I want you to know that above all else, it was the gift of you in his life that brought our William the most joy."

She lowered her head to hide tears she couldn't stop. The minister would never know that instead of bringing comfort, his words were breaking her heart. What joy? His letters had gone unanswered, his words begging her not to leave had landed against her back as she walked away. And the words that she now knew would have brought him the most joy, knowing he had fathered a child, had died on her lips, the night she leaned down, looked straight into his eyes, and kissed him goodbye.

Guilt and regret gathered in every step to the cemetery and by the time William was lowered into his grave Marilla could bear it no more. She fell to her knees, while the damp, fetid smell of earth filled the air. Martha helped her to her feet while the minister spoke the words that would commit him to the ground.

Her words, desperate to be heard, mingled with the final prayer.

"I'm so sorry, William," she whispered. "I should have told you."

When the first shovelful of dirt hit the casket, her panic rose and she leaned closer and started to scream: "I'm sorry, William! Can you hear me? I said I'm sorry."

She struggled against the arms that pulled her back. "Please forgive me," she begged. "Tell me you forgive me. Tell me." Her sobs echoed across the graveyard as she was led away. "William! Tell me you forgive me."

∽

A week later Marilla stood, bags gathered at her feet, watching as the ferry boat from Charlottetown docked and prepared for passengers. Gulls screeched overhead, and when the noon cannon sounded, she flinched. She gathered her bags and followed the crowd as it pushed forward.

"Are you sure you can't stay longer?" Martha had said as she stood in the front porch waiting for her ride. It had rained for two solid days with no sign of letting up, and though it wasn't far, walking to the ferry was out of the question. "I hate to see you leave so soon. We'd hoped to show you around a bit. Once this rain stopped, of course."

"I know, Aunt Martha."

Martha stood, wringing her hands. "So your memories of Halifax wouldn't always be so...."

"I know, and I appreciate everything you and Etta have done. I'll never forget that."

"And you're so young, Marilla, and this—" She hesitated, looking down the hallway as Etta approached with a packed lunch. "Well, this has all been too much for anyone to cope with, let alone...."

"I'm fine, Aunt Martha," she said, squeezing her hand. "Really, it's fine."

Etta's smile warmed the air as she passed Marilla a small wicker basket. "There's cheese, buttered biscuits and"—she winked at Marilla—"one of your favourites."

Marilla smiled. Her bitterness toward Etta had been replaced with admiration for the life she'd chosen and the young women, like herself, that she'd bravely helped. "Molasses cake?"

Etta reached out and gently touched her hand, tears suddenly misting her eyes. "Take care, Marilla, we'll miss you."

"There he is now, Marilla," Martha said, and they peered out the door toward the road where Martha's neighbour, Mr. Roberts, riding high in his covered wagon, pulled into the yard. They picked up Marilla's baggage and headed outside.

"Morning, Martha, Etta. So this here's the little lady needs a lift to the dock, is it?"

"Yes, Mr. Roberts," Martha said, running ahead. "This is my niece, Marilla. I appreciate you dropping her off on your way to work."

"She'll be a mite bit early, but I dare say a whole lot dryer."

Marilla was bundled with hugs and kisses up into the wagon and the image of them, standing in the yard waving goodbye, brought tears to her eyes as she made her way on board.

She stood on the deck, tightened the scarf around her neck, and watched Halifax fade into the distance, its cold grey waters lapping against a shoreline that slowly disappeared into the fog. Though William was buried beneath its soil and its salt air was the first breath her baby ever drew, Halifax would never be her home. She reached into her handbag and pulled out the letter from Mrs. Willis. That's all she had now. All that was left. And she would carry it back to Green Gables and tuck it beneath the treasures already hidden inside her room. And that place, which held the memories of how much she had loved, would always be home. And in that moment she longed to be there, back to where she knew she belonged.

∾

The drizzle soon turned to showers and Marilla, struggling against the wind, pulled open the hatch and rushed inside. She found her way to her tiny overnight cabin down a narrow hall and placed her baggage in the overhead rack. *So like a train*, she thought, *except for the lap of waves against the hull.*

She shrugged out of her wet coat and was just placing it on a peg behind the door when it suddenly opened and the large backside of an elderly man, bent gathering his bags, pushed its way through. He grunted as he tugged them over the threshold, and when he stood, closing the door with his foot, Marilla, startled by the intrusion, fell against the bunks and he, wet and windblown, fell against the door.

"My dear good woman! What in the name of heavens are you doing here?"

"This is my cabin, sir. The more appropriate question is, what are *you* doing here?"

Marilla reached for her handbag and he his billfold, searching for the ticket that would provide the answer.

"It says right here, cabin twenty-four," he said.

Marilla shook her ticket. "And it says right here, cabin twenty-three."

They stared at each other, confident each was right, until a knock at the cabin door rattled them both. "Miss Cuthbert, do you need assistance with your baggage?"

Realizing his error, the man opened the door and, before Marilla could say a word, dragged his bags out into the hallway.

"My apologies, sir, I seem to have made a mistake."

Shocked at finding a man stepping from the room, the steward poked his head around the corner and stared at Marilla. "Miss Cuthbert, is this gentleman bothering you?"

"No, not at all. As he said, there's been a mistake. I believe his room is next door."

Marilla picked up the man's hat, passed it through the door, and closed it behind her. A snicker, unbidden and rare, forced its way through. She covered her face and bent forward. When she stood, the sound of laughter filled the room. She couldn't remember the last time she had laughed, and though guilty for its presence at a time so full of grief, she rejoiced at the sound and the lifting of her heart.

The following morning, lulled by the waves throughout the night and feeling content inside her bunk, Marilla hugged the blankets to her chest and thought of all that lay ahead. The man next door, Mr. Sullivan, a recent widow, unused to travelling without his wife, had apologized profusely for his intrusion. In the passenger lounge later that evening they'd shared a pot of tea then bade each other goodnight. She could still hear the sound of his laughter and the comfort in his words.

He'd leaned across the table soon after they were seated and said, "Please believe me when I say I do miss my wife, but I am so relieved she was not here to witness the sight of me stumbling backwards through your cabin door."

Marilla, surprised by the note of humour in his voice, tried not to smile.

"She would surely have died all over again," he said, then threw back his head and laughed, surprising those who had gathered for a quiet evening tea.

He'd pulled a hankie from his pocket and wiped his eyes, and only then did Marilla see the sorrow the memory had evoked. "Please don't think me heartless, but if she were here, my Rosie, she would have laughed with me. We shared everything, you see. That's what I miss the most." He stopped and took a deep breath. "I loved her very much."

He'd looked embarrassed then, the exposure of his pain to a stranger, unheard of under normal circumstances, deepening the colour beneath his collar. His hands trembled as he reached for his cup.

Marilla understood his pain and felt her own grief fill her chest. "I too lost someone I loved very much…and never imagined it was even possible to laugh again, when for just a moment I could forget. But I did, so I thank you for that."

Mr. Sullivan leaned in and spoke words Marilla would never forget. "Remember, Miss Cuthbert, love is not taken to the grave along with those we love. It lives on in each of us. Don't ever stop living the life you've been given, and like my Rosie, don't ever stop seeing the joy."

The laughter had been a gift. A reminder that even as she grieved, her heart would mend. She would carry her burden of loss, as others do, but life was for the living, he'd told her. She was young and she'd survive.

Marilla reached for the letter she'd tucked beneath her pillow and pressed it to her heart. William was gone, but his child, their child, was very much alive.

Amid the loss and sadness, guilt and sorrow, there was, for the first time in a long time, a feeling of hope.

PART III

NEVER
LOOK
BACK

CHAPTER 24

April 28, 1852

Stewiacke, NS

"*B*ERTHA, PLEASE SLOW DOWN. YOU KNOW I CAN'T KEEP UP."
"But Mommy, we need to hurry, I can hear the wagon."

The lane leading from the house to the main road seemed to be getting longer, Catherine thought as she stopped, pressed a hand to her heart, and struggled to catch her breath. She'd been sick on and off throughout the winter and her strength, as she trailed behind her daughter, had most certainly waned. She could see the mailbox in the distance and hoped the mailman, Mr. Conrad, on his weekly round, didn't pass before they got there.

Clumps of melting snow clung to the scrub grass that bordered the lane. The frost of early morning freshened the air, and maple trees laden with tiny buds awaited the warmth of spring. Catherine gathered her sweater around her middle and gazed ahead at Bertha's long brown curls as they bounced against her back.

It was difficult for Catherine to believe how fast the time had gone. They'd celebrated Bertha's tenth birthday a week ago, and for all her insistence that she was no longer a baby, her delight in walking with her mother to the mailbox had never changed. She squealed with excitement knowing that today she would place their letter inside the box and raise the arm to let Mr. Conrad know there was mail to collect.

They reached the road just in time, and Bertha hurried to place the letter inside. And never one to stand still, she bounced from one foot to the other until the mail wagon came to a stop.

"Good morning, ladies," Mr. Conrad said, stepping down from the wagon.

"I'm not a lady." Bertha giggled. "I'm only ten years old."

"You don't say. Why, I thought you were all grown up," Mr. Conrad said, reaching into the mailbox.

"That day will be here soon enough, Mr. Conrad," Mrs. Willis said. "Though she can already set the table and prepare tea as good as any grown-up I know."

Mr. Conrad looked down at the letter in his hand. "Well now, it's all the way to Prince Edward Island for this one, is it?

"Yes...to Mommy's friend," Bertha said. "Miss Cuthbert."

Mr. Conrad exchanged a knowing look with Bertha's mother then smiled and placed the letter in his canvas bag. Everyone in Stewiacke knew that Bertha had been adopted as an infant and brought from Halifax. He remembered the day they strolled into church, Catherine holding a baby though she'd never been pregnant, and Charles all pumped up and full of pride.

And though the annual letter to Prince Edward Island fuelled rumors of a connection to the mother, not a word was ever spoken. She was the Willises' daughter and that was that.

"I can't wait to have a friend I can write to," Bertha continued. "Wouldn't that be exciting?"

"Sounds like I might need to get myself a bigger wagon," he teased before climbing back up onto his seat. "I best get a move on. Don't want to hold up the mail to the Island, now do we?"

"Thank you, Mr. Conrad," Mrs. Willis said, ever grateful for his kindness.

He tipped his hat and the wagon pulled away.

Bertha held her mother's hand as they headed back down the lane. "Mommy, tell me again about Marilla."

Catherine smiled down at her daughter, who seemed to become more inquisitive about her mother's friend with each passing year. "As I've told you many times before, my dear, she's a friend of the family, that's all. A woman I met many years ago."

"When I was little."

"That's right."

Bertha stooped to gather a clump of snow. She rolled it in her hands and giggled as she ran ahead, then turned and threw it at her mother. Catherine yelped, feigning injury as the snowball landed on her foot, and then took chase. "You come back here, young lady!"

Bertha squealed and headed toward the barn, where her father stood smiling from the doorway.

Charles wiped his hands and watched with delight as his wife, with her skirt gathered in one hand and her sweater flapping around her, ran to catch their daughter.

Bertha didn't see it happen, running as she was with her mother at her back.

And at first Charles thought she'd tripped. Seeing Catherine sprawled across the yard had almost made him laugh, until she didn't move.

Frightened by the sudden change in her father's face, Bertha stopped running and watched as he ran past her toward her mother. "Daddy, what's wrong?" She watched as he fell to his knees and leaned over her mother who was lying on the ground. "Mommy?"

"Bertha, run for Mrs. Levy."

She started to cry. "But Daddy, why is Mommy—"

"Bertha, go." She stood, pinned by the terror in her father's eyes, until he shouted, "*Now!*"

And then suddenly, her legs seemed to move on their own accord. She dodged branches and leaped over rocks. Brambles tore at her skirt and bit into her hands. With tears streaming and heart pounding, she cleared the woods and crossed the field that led to Mrs. Levy's back door.

Bertha banged and screamed, and when the door sprang open she landed in a heap at poor Mrs. Levy's feet, who herself was now shrieking.

"Bertha, my dear child, you frightened the life out of me. What is this all about?"

"It's Mommy," Bertha spluttered between sobs. "She fell and Daddy told me to get you." She struggled to her feet and grabbed Mrs. Levy's arm. "Come quick...please...Daddy's waiting."

"Oh, Bertha dear, calm down. I'm sure it's nothing serious. There's no need for all this fuss, now is there?" She stepped into the kitchen, laid her apron across a chair, then reached behind the door. "Let me just get my coat on now, and we'll walk back together." When she turned around to take Bertha's hand, she was gone. From the back door, Mrs. Levy could see the child running as wild as a colt across the yard and a feeling of dread seized her.

"It was as if her life depended on it, "Mrs. Levy told her husband moments later, when she gathered him, along with the wagon, to take her down the road. "I never saw a child run that fast. The poor thing," she muttered. "Something serious has happened, Frank, I just know it. And her mother's sick, I know that, too. Not that she'd ever say a word, mind you. And now she's fallen?" Frank nodded and steered the horse down the Willises' lane. "Something's wrong. Terribly wrong...I just know it."

When they made it to the house, the back door was swinging unfettered on its hinge. Catherine was sprawled across the floor, head cradled in Charles's lap. Bertha was pressed into a corner behind the woodbox, her eyes pleading and frightened, her face awash with tears.

By the time Mr. Levy had retrieved the doctor, there was nothing more to be done. The seizure had left her paralysed and mute. By noon that day her eyes had closed, shutting out the terror that their words had never eased. And when Catherine's heart, beneath her husband's hand, ceased to beat, he lay across her body and wailed.

∾

Three weeks later, Charles loaded the last of their bags into the wagon and secured the tarp. Bertha was still in the house, rounding up the last of her dolls. "They'll be lonely here all by themselves," she'd announced to him the night before, her eyes brimming with tears. "They need me. I'm their mommy."

The words had cut deep and he struggled to maintain his composure. With no strength to explain that they would be returning and with no desire to be the cause of any more pain, he'd agreed, and now waited while she searched the house.

Charles scanned his yard, his fields, and his pasture. Late May was not a time to leave a farm, but he had no heart to stay. The neighbours had rallied around his loss, and with the cows boarded and the planting done, they promised to see to the rest.

Bertha was not faring well. She was listless through the day and woke screaming through the night. She refused to go to school. In the mornings he'd find her cowered beneath her blankets, or worse, beneath the bed, and now he struggled to get her to eat. This trip to Halifax was for her. She needed a woman's care, and children to run and play with. They would stay with the MacDonald family till the end of July, and he prayed by then she'd rouse.

The ache Charles felt for his wife was unbearable. It crippled him at times, leaving him weak. That morning, leaning in to shave, he stared at the face looking back. And for just a moment questioned who it was. The hair was white where it used to be grey. Eyes deadened by grief stared back. His knees buckled and he grabbed for a chair.

He shook the images from his thoughts as Bertha, hugging an armful of dolls, made her way across the yard.

"Did you find them all, my girl?"

"Yes, Daddy, I did."

They looked toward the lane where Mrs. Levy, carrying a huge picnic basket, was making her way toward them. Charles rushed to meet her and lifted it from her arms.

"I was so worried that I'd miss you," she said, catching her breath. "You can't go all the way to Halifax without a proper lunch, now can you?" She winked at Bertha, hoping for a smile, then noticed all the dolls. "My goodness, I hope they don't eat very much or you'll have to share the biscuits." Bertha finally smiled and Charles felt the tightness around his heart loosen.

"Thank you, Mrs. Levy."

"Oh go on with you, it's nothing. It's the least I can do."

Charles went back to secure the doors while Mrs. Levy settled Bertha and her dolls in the wagon. "Now I want you to have a good time while you're down there in the big city. It won't be easy, my love, but promise me you'll try."

"I promise."

Charles climbed up next to Bertha and gathered the reins. They waved goodbye and Mrs. Levy watched the wagon rattle down the lane toward the road.

"Goodbye, mailbox," Bertha said as they passed the weathered red box, the keeper of secrets, standing seemingly abandoned since that last visit with her beloved mother. Further along she craned her neck trying to catch a glimpse of the pond, hidden behind alder brush and reeds. "Goodbye, pond."

When they approached the church, Charles held his breath. Dirt still covered the mound where she lay, and the cross, fresh with paint, stood out amongst the graves. He said a silent prayer, but would not turn his head. His throat tightened and he swallowed hard. Bertha leaned across him, hugging a ragdoll tight against her, and stared at the grave as they passed. Her words were barely a whisper, but they cut him to his core. "Goodbye, Mommy."

CHAPTER 25

❧∞❧

May 18, 1852

Avonlea, PEI

*T*HE SUN FINALLY CRESTED THE TREETOPS AND MARILLA squinted as she pegged the last of the sheets on the line. "Thank heaven it finally let up," she muttered. The previous month had fulfilled its promise of April showers and on this first decent wash day in weeks, with May flowers perfuming the air, she was grateful to see the sun.

She lifted the empty basket and trudged back to the kitchen. The washtub sat in the middle of the floor with clothes scattered in all directions. Some were pegged on the line strung up behind the stove, and others drooped from the backs of chairs. Two more piles of dirty clothes waited to be washed and a pile of wet overalls waited to be hung. She reached for the kettle steaming on the stove and freshened the water in the tub, the smell of lye filling the air as she poured.

Through the window she could see her mother slowly cross the yard, and it seemed to Marilla that she carried the full weight of her fifty-eight years in each step. She'd been up early and out the door before Marilla finished her tea. The minister's wife was recovering from a terrible fever and with their only daughter now married and living in Charlottetown, the ladies of the auxiliary had taken on the responsibility of her care.

The back door opened and Marilla refilled the kettle and set it on the stove. Her mother stopped just inside the kitchen door and stared. "Good lord, Marilla, what's all this?"

"It had to be done. There's not a clean blouse or apron to be found and I couldn't have slept another night in those sheets." She pointed to the dark pile sitting by the tub. "Matthew's down to his last pair of overalls." Marilla threw up her hands. "And if *you* can convince him to peel off the long johns he's been wearing since last fall, I'll wash them too."

Her mother crossed the room, removed a flannel shirt from the back of a chair, and, bracing her hand on the small of her back, slowly sat down. She reached deep into her skirt pocket, pulled out a letter, and passed it to Marilla. "It's a thick one, that's for sure. From your Aunt Martha no doubt, bragging about how wonderful life is in Halifax." She rolled her eyes. "I was walking past the post office on my way home when Mrs. Webber came out and asked if I could bring it to you. Poor Mr. Webber's not feeling well now either. Hasn't gotten out of bed in three days."

Marilla held the letter and her breath, waiting for the conversation to end, holding back the impulse to rip it open so as not to raise her mother's curiosity.

"Is it the same as what Mrs. Smith has?"

"Oh, I hope not. It's terrible, the coughing never ends."

The kettle whistled and her mother started to rise. "I'll put on a fresh pot. Matthew will be in soon looking for a cup, though where he'll sit in the middle of this...." She scanned the kitchen and shook her head.

"Will you stop fretting, Mother? I'll take care of this." She reached for her mother's arm and helped her to her feet. "Go lie down for a bit, and I'll see to him."

"I never slept a wink all night, my hip was that sore." Her mother leaned heavy against Marilla and winced as she stood.

"And you've been up since when?" Marilla chided. "There are younger than you who can help with poor Mrs. Smith."

"Now who's fretting?"

She watched her mother head down the hall. "I'll go up and finish the beds first, then come back to start the lunch."

"But what about your brother? You said—"

"Surely to God he can make himself a cup of tea."

∽

Marilla closed her bedroom door and sat in the rocker by the window. Her heart raced and her hands shook. Every year for ten years the letters had arrived. At first they came through Mrs. MacDonald to Etta and then on to her aunt. But over time, Catherine Willis had begun mailing them directly to her.

Marilla lived for them, and within their pages. Over the years she'd watched as Rachel and Thomas's family grew, as others married and started lives beyond the shores of Avonlea. And if not for the words that brought her daughter's world to life, filling the void of her own, it would have seemed as if she'd never lived at all. As if she'd never loved. Or been loved.

She opened the letter, gently unfolded the pages, and began to read.

April 28, 1852
Dear Marilla,

Another year has passed and it's hard to imagine our little Bertha turning ten, but she has, and is as much a joy to us today as she's always been. Our trips to the mailbox have become one of her favourite things and she looks forward to what she refers to as her Birthday Letter since our stroll to the mailbox always takes place a few days following the celebration.

To her you have simply been a friend of the family whom I've known for many years. But with every letter I send and with every letter you return, her curiosity has grown.

I know we've always walked a very fragile line between your love for Bertha and ours. We've accepted your place within her life and though you may find this rather unusual, I'd like for her to know you. You, a woman of faith, whom I've grown to admire over the years for your courage in the face of so much tragedy. To know that there are others who care for her. She has so few relatives, you see, and at times I sense she's lonely. How could knowing you ever do her harm?

This past winter, I've not been well. My heart, from as far back as I can remember, has never been strong. At the end of June, at the advice of my doctor here in Stewiacke, we will be taking a trip to Halifax to visit with a doctor who specializes in my condition. We will be staying with Mr. and Mrs. MacDonald, who, as you know, have become good friends of ours over the years. Their children, all close in age to Bertha, look forward to our visits.

If you could arrange to be in Halifax during that time, I would like so very much for you to spend an afternoon visiting with us. Perhaps Bertha, who loves nothing better than playing the part of hostess, could prepare and serve us tea.

Marilla read and reread the words, searching for something between the lines, something that was not being said. Concern for Catherine and hope for this chance that she'd only ever dreamed of battled for prominence inside her head. Thinking she had surely misunderstood, Marilla turned the pages over and over in her hands, looking for something she couldn't see.

"*With kindest regards,*" she finally read aloud, "*Catherine Willis.*"

She pulled back the curtain and watched as the sheets flapped on the line. She felt for a moment as if she'd floated away, and it was only the feeling of the lace in her hand and the sight of Matthew walking toward the house from the barn that pulled her back.

"*Could prepare and serve us tea.*" The words, so incredible when spoken aloud, made Marilla laugh. "Well, of course she could. What's odd about that? My daughter serving tea." The laughter caught in her throat as the word *daughter*, seldom uttered aloud, filled the corners of her room.

Marilla rose quickly and held the letter close. "I'm going to see my daughter!"

Hope finally won, and she ran, her face awash with tears, to find Matthew, the only other person on all of Prince Edward Island who could share in her joy.

CHAPTER 26

June 28, 1852

Halifax, NS

THE END OF JUNE FINALLY ARRIVED AND MARILLA STOOD on the street outside the home of Mr. and Mrs. MacDonald, staring at the front door. It had been ten years since she'd last seen it. Ten years since she'd left part of her soul on the other side. Ten years of daring to dream that one day this might happen, then having it come true, made her hand shake as she raised it and knocked. The weeks of preparation and the days of waiting had passed so slowly she'd almost lost her mind. The impromptu decision to visit her aunt in Halifax raised more questions from her mother than Marilla could handle, and if not for Matthew assuring her they'd survive, she'd have burst from holding back the truth.

The voices of children playing in the backyard drifted to where she stood, and she found herself being pulled toward the sound. She walked the path lined with day lilies and begonia that ran along the side of the house and headed toward the back. The laughter turned to squeals and she peered over the fence as a game of hide and seek looked to be under way. "Five, four, three, two...."

The children scattered in all directions and hid from a young girl leaning her head against the gatepost where Marilla stood. Her hair, a spill of golden-brown ringlets, was held in place by a green ribbon that perfectly matched her dress. Marilla felt the excitement as keen as the children and remained quiet as she continued counting. When she finished, she stepped back, lifted her head, and announced, "Ready or not, here I come."

And then she opened her eyes. Marilla gasped, as startled to see the young girl as the girl was to see her. A beautiful pair of brown eyes, so like her father's, smiled back. Marilla's breath caught, while the words *my baby, my baby* screamed inside her head.

"Who are you?" Bertha said, grabbing the pickets and standing on her toes.

"I'm your…" Marilla struggled against words she couldn't say. "I'm a friend of Mrs. MacDonald's."

The children began to crawl out from where they were hiding and footsteps behind Marilla made her turn.

"Marilla, is that you?"

"I'm terribly sorry, Mrs. MacDonald. I knocked, and then when I heard the children I came back here." Marilla stared into the face of a child she would have known anywhere.

"You're Marilla?" The young girl asked, leaning closer to look.

"Oh Marilla, I'm the one who's sorry. I should have written," Mrs. MacDonald said, her voice shaking.

"You're Miss Cuthbert? You're my Mommy's friend?" Her face clouded over, tears filled her eyes, and she struggled to open the gate.

"Oh dear, she's getting herself all upset again." Mrs. MacDonald moved quickly to intervene, but before Marilla could understand what was happening, the little girl ducked beneath Mrs. MacDonald's outstretched arms and dove straight into Marilla's. She flung her little arms around Marilla's waist and burrowed against her. Marilla felt the space beneath her heart, left empty all these years, begin to fill with joy at the reuniting with her own flesh and blood. She wrapped her arms around her daughter's tiny shoulders and bent to breathe her in.

So lost in her own pleasure at this unexpected moment, Marilla didn't realize the little girl was crying. Marilla spoke softly and kissed the top of her head. "Oh sweetheart, why the tears?"

When she looked to Mrs. MacDonald for reassurance, a man

was now standing next to her, and if not for the outline of his once familiar frame she would never have recognized his face. Brimming with tears and ravaged by sorrow, his eyes filled with something akin to gratitude.

"Daddy." The little girl sobbed, flinging herself toward him. He knelt, shushing and quieting, then gathered her in his arms.

"I'm so sorry, Mr. Willis, please forgive me." She looked at Mrs. MacDonald and pleaded. "I didn't mean to upset her like this. I feel terrible."

"It's not your fault, Marilla. Please come inside." Mrs. MacDonald turned toward the children. "Go on back to your game now, everything will be fine." She gently touched Mr. Willis on the arm as he cradled his weeping daughter. "We'll see you back inside whenever you feel you're ready."

Marilla followed behind Mrs. MacDonald as they made their way back along the path. She waited till they were out of earshot before trying to explain. "I don't understand. I knew this would be difficult, but it's what Mrs. Willis wanted. I came because she wrote to me...you know, the annual letter. This time she said she wished for her daughter to meet me. And so...." Marilla stopped walking.

Her words were the only ones being uttered, and an uneasy feeling swept over her. Why hadn't the little girl cried out for her mother? Why did Mr. Willis look wretched yet somehow grateful to see his little girl gathered in Marilla's arms?

"Where is Mrs. Willis?"

Mrs. MacDonald finally turned around, and with tears of her own now wetting her face, reached for Marilla's hand and whispered, "She's gone, Marilla. Catherine is gone."

Marilla swayed, then lost her balance. Mrs. MacDonald caught her arm just as she started to fall, and held her close. Gently, she led Marilla to the front porch of the house and sat her on the wooden bench just inside the door. She struggled to catch her breath. Moments later, Mrs. MacDonald returned from the kitchen with a glass of water.

Marilla's hands shook as she downed its contents. "How can she be...gone? What happened?"

Mrs. MacDonald pulled out a handkerchief tucked inside her sleeve and dabbed at her eyes. "This was back in April, Marilla. Poor Charles. He was right there. The doctor said her heart just gave out. She collapsed in the yard chasing after—"

Marilla gasped. "No! You don't mean to tell me she saw her own mother…?"

"Yes. Was right there when she died. They were walking back from the mailbox when she collapsed. The poor little thing, that's why he brought her here. She's taking it so very hard."

They clasped each other's hands, comforting and murmuring their disbelief until the sound of children, clamouring through the back door and into the kitchen, could be heard from the back of the house.

"Let me take you into the parlour, Marilla. It'll be quieter there. I'll settle the children with something to eat, then make us a fresh pot of tea." She led the way, and Marilla, too shocked to be of any use, trailed quietly behind.

She opened the door to the parlour, ushered Marilla inside, then headed for the kitchen. Marilla stood in the middle of the room listening as her footsteps faded down the hall, while her memories, freed from their place inside her heart, rushed and swirled around the room. The last time she'd seen her baby girl was in this room. In Catherine's arms. When she'd told Marilla what her name would be.

Marilla spoke it aloud: "Bertha."

"Bertha Willis."

Marilla spun around at the sound of Charles Willis's voice and when she saw him, her own battered heart reached out for his. This man, who'd loved her daughter, who'd treasured and comforted her since the day she became his, stepped into the room and, seeking solace only she could give, walked straight into Marilla's arms.

"I'm so very, very sorry," she murmured while he wept. He clung to her as if to life itself. The bond they felt, forged by the love for her daughter, filled them with a comfort no one else could ever understand.

He suddenly straightened and pulled himself away from their embrace. "I'm so sorry, Marilla. Please forgive my behaviour. I've not been myself for weeks now." He reached for her hands and met her eyes. "But I am so very grateful that you're here. Especially for my Bertha."

They didn't realize she was there until her head peeked out from behind him. "There you are." Charles reached around and pulled his daughter close. "Are you feeling better, my love?"

She squirmed within her father's embrace and glanced up at Marilla with eyes that were bashful yet curious.

"You must be the Bertha Willis from Stewiacke I've heard so much about. I'm Marilla Cuthbert, how do you do?" Marilla presented her hand and waited.

Bertha smiled up at her father and, with his nod of approval, placed her tiny hand inside Marilla's. "How do you do?" She giggled and shook Marilla's hand.

Marilla and Charles stood smiling at each other. Bertha's presence brought a warmth to the room and a lightness to their hearts. Marilla knelt and took Bertha's hands and held them gently in hers. "Bertha, I'm very sorry for the loss of your mother." Marilla struggled to control her voice. "She was a dear friend of mine and I will miss her so very much."

Bertha leaned against her father and whispered, "Thank you, Miss Cuthbert."

"Did you know that every year"—Marilla smiled up at Charles—"sometime around your birthday, I think, she would write me a letter?"

A grin spread across Bertha's face and her hands waved with excitement. "I did! I used to help her. I'm a real good speller. And then we would walk to the mailbox and wait for Mr. Conrad, and then...."

Her eyes clouded with memory and Marilla rushed in. "And she told me all about you."

"About me?"

"She sure did. But I didn't believe a word she said...not for one minute."

Bertha giggled.

"Imagine! Telling me that you could serve tea as good as any grown-up."

"I can!" Bertha said, looking up at her father for confirmation. "Can't I, Daddy?"

"She certainly can," Charles said, and then turned as Mrs. MacDonald entered the parlour and placed a tray piled high with tea and sweets on the table in the centre of the room. "Did I hear someone say tea?"

Marilla watched with pleasure as, moments later, Bertha handed her a steaming cup of tea. It rattled slightly and she quickly steadied the saucer in her hand. Marilla couldn't take her eyes off her daughter and marvelled at how much she looked like William. She was beautiful, well-mannered, and very capable, and Marilla could sense her enjoyment at being the centre of Marilla's attention and affection as she lavished her with both.

When Mr. MacDonald arrived home from work, the excitement of his arrival raised the noise level in the kitchen and Marilla suddenly realized the time had come for her to leave. She placed her cup and saucer on the tray and gathered her shawl from the back of the chair. "Well, it certainly sounds as if you'll soon be needed in the kitchen, Mrs. MacDonald. I really should be going. Thank you so much for a lovely afternoon."

"My dear, you are more than welcome to stay."

"Yes, please, Miss Cuthbert, can't you stay?" Bertha said, taking hold of her hand.

The invitation from Mrs. Willis had been for an afternoon tea, nothing more had been said, and with her gone, so too were any future intentions she might have had. Not knowing if she would ever see her daughter again, Marilla struggled against the pressure building in her chest, the same feeling that had nearly smothered her when she'd first been taken away, and against the longing that engulfed her now for the little girl holding her hand. She knew if she didn't leave now, she may never find the strength.

She blinked away her tears and swallowed the lump in her throat. "Oh, I'd love to, Bertha, but my aunt is expecting me for supper and I really don't want to disappoint her."

The noise from the kitchen grew louder, and Mrs. MacDonald cocked her head toward it. "Will you please excuse me for a moment? The children are likely out there climbing all over him. The poor man can hardly get in the door and get his boots off. I'll just check on them and be right back."

"That's all right, Mrs. MacDonald. Bertha and I can show Miss Cuthbert out." Charles looked at his daughter who was clinging to Marilla's hand. "Can't we, my sweet girl?"

Bertha leaned against Marilla's side and nodded, but her usual excitement at being called upon to usher guests to the door was missing. She seemed reluctant to see her leave.

"Thank you, Charles. That would be lovely," Mrs. MacDonald said. She then leaned close to Marilla and whispered, "Thank you for coming today. You have done wonders for them both."

The walk to the door was quiet and Marilla could feel the same panic seize her as it had ten years before. "Thank you so much for letting me…." Marilla struggled to find the right words. "For inviting me to join you for tea." She knelt in front of Bertha and looked into eyes so like her father's. And like William's, they pleaded for something she couldn't give.

"It was lovely to meet you, Bertha. Your mommy was right about one thing. She said you would always be loved." Marilla pulled her shawl around her shoulders and took a deep breath. She kissed Bertha's cheek. "And you are. So very much."

Somehow the door had opened, the goodbyes had been said, and Marilla found herself once again staring at the desolate side of the same closed door. But this time, unlike the last, she headed to the cemetery to find comfort at William's grave, to the father of the little girl who carried his smile. She gathered her strength and walked away, her imprint the only thing remaining from where she'd laid her hand.

Charles stood on the other side with his hand firmly pressed against it, the only way he knew to stop himself from flinging the door, and all his long-held beliefs, wide open.

CHAPTER 27

July 4, 1852

Public Gardens, Halifax, NS

*C*HARLES DECIDED HE WOULD WAIT. HE WOULD WAIT UNTIL his thoughts returned to reason. Until he felt confident his emotions were firmly under control and his intentions were not self-serving. Before making a plan to see her. That is until today.

Bertha had been asking every morning for the past week when Miss Cuthbert was coming back to visit. And neither he nor Mrs. MacDonald really knew the answer. They'd only known that Catherine wanted an afternoon visit for tea. A chance for Bertha to know her mother's friend. To meet the person behind the letters they'd been mailing since she was a baby. But beyond that, no one knew what was best. After breakfast, Charles decided that a walk through the Gardens might provide a much needed distraction for them both.

"Daddy?"

Charles watched Bertha pick a flower from a patch of daisies nestled beneath a row of maples, shading the narrow path that wound its way through the gardens. "Yes, Bertha?"

"I don't think Miss Cuthbert likes me anymore."

Charles kneeled down beside her. "Bertha, that's just not true. She likes you very much."

Bertha kept her head down, sulking. "Then why hasn't she come back to see me?"

Charles had exhausted all the plausible answers and struggled to explain. "I suppose because she thinks you're busy playing with your friends."

One by one, Bertha starting pulling at the white petals: "She loves me...she loves me not...."

Charles stood, determined to change the subject. "Besides, we'll be leaving soon on our trip back home just like Miss Cuthbert is. She's probably busy packing her bags and getting ready."

The petals dropped and scattered in the breeze. "She loves me...she loves me not...."

"I know how much you enjoyed her visit...but...."

"She loves me—" Bertha's face suddenly crumpled and she burst into tears. "She loves me not!" She threw the stem to the ground and started running, dodging people who were out enjoying their Sunday stroll through the Gardens.

"Bertha!" he shouted, taking chase. "Come back here."

The paths leading in and around the Public Gardens had become crowded since church let out an hour ago, and he jostled his way through. He momentarily lost sight of his daughter among the couples strolling arm in arm while their children, freed from stiff wooden pews, ran circles around them.

The gates leading to the entrance loomed ahead and Charles prayed Bertha would go no further. Sidestepping a group of mothers pushing prams, he turned the corner and nearly knocked them over. Marilla was stopped in the middle of the path, embracing his daughter. His feet skidded to a stop, and if not for wrapping his arms around them both to gain his balance, he'd have knocked them to the ground.

Marilla shrieked and Bertha, still holding tight, stared up into her father's face. "I found her. I found Miss Cuthbert."

The close proximity to Marilla's face, to the warmth of her breath and the scent of her hair, made Charles falter, and he struggled to find his voice. They disentangled themselves and stood, brushing and straightening their clothes.

"And thank heaven she did," he finally said, then knelt to speak to Bertha. "You mustn't ever run off like that again. Do you understand? What if I had lost you?"

Bertha hung her head and whispered, "I'm sorry, Daddy."

Winded from his race through the Gardens and relieved that his daughter was safe, Charles rose slowly to his feet, took a deep breath and looked at Marilla.

"I had just arrived and could see a little girl running along the path," Marilla said, not meeting his eyes, her cheeks beginning to flush at the scene she knew passersby were witnessing. "But I didn't know it was her until she called my name." She looked at Bertha, and as her embarrassment faded her concern for her daughter rose. "Why did you run away from your father? He's right, Bertha, you must never do that."

"Because," Bertha began, "because I plucked all my petals and…." Her lashes fluttered and she lowered her head. "It said you didn't love me."

"You mean petals from a daisy? You were playing the *She loves me, she loves me not* game?"

Bertha nodded silently, her hazel brown eyes finding Marilla's.

When Marilla looked to Charles for guidance on what to say, he knew this was the day. When Marilla's love for her daughter could at last be spoken. And he prayed to God as he laid his own love at her feet, that she needed them as much as they needed her.

"Miss Cuthbert, would you please tell Bertha that the daisy was wrong?"

Marilla's face shone with understanding and she swallowed the lump forming in her throat. "Bertha, sweetheart, that silly old daisy just didn't have enough petals." She knelt before her daughter, looked into her eyes, and spoke aloud the words she'd always held silent within her. "Because…I do love you. I love you very much."

Bertha wrapped her arms around Marilla's neck and Charles let out a breath he hadn't realized he was holding. He looked forward to the days ahead, now that his plan had finally formed. To the time they'd share with their daughter before they each headed back home. Back to their separate lives. He looked at his daughter and prayed. Whatever sins he was about to commit, whatever heartaches he was about to unleash, he was doing so for her.

∾

If sunshine can heal, Charles thought, then so can laughter. The following days passed in a blur of activity and by the end of their week together, the grief Charles and his daughter had carried, and the sadness haunting their eyes, had diminished, leaving father and daughter with a semblance of their former selves. Bertha's cheeks and nose were once again covered with freckles, and the once-familiar darkened skin that Charles had known as a farmer had returned, leaving him, at forty-one, looking as robust as he felt.

The weather had been perfect as they strolled the streets of Halifax, peering into shop windows displaying everything imaginable, from feather-plumed hats to wooden toys and pink-cheeked dolls. He could still see Marilla being dragged through one door after another and Bertha happily walking out cuddling another doll to add to her collection.

They'd strolled the shaded, tree-lined streets of the South End and gazed in wonder at the stone facade of Admiralty House. "It's the biggest house I've ever seen," Bertha said, counting all the windows. She particularly marvelled at the gabled dormers, behind which she imagined endless hours of play, but when she clambered the low stone wall, clung to the wrought iron fence, and pointed to guests enjoying tea in the garden, he'd gathered her quickly and together they'd snickered and all but run down the path. Then back to the Gardens, where daisy picking and questions of who loved whom produced results that had them laughing so loudly that passersby stopped and frowned at their lack of propriety while in public, which made them laugh all the more.

During their days together that entire week, Bertha never left Marilla's side. Charles often found himself staring at the two, as he could see so much of his daughter in every expression on Marilla's face. And even though Marilla's hair was piled high atop her head, the few tendrils that fell across her face and neck bore the same golden hue as his daughter's when warmed by the sun.

The day they picnicked on the slopes of Citadel Hill, letting the sun warm their backs while it sparkled and danced on the water surrounding the harbour, was a memory he would hold forever.

"Miss Cuthbert, could I have another piece of cake? Mine was only small and Daddy said...."

Charles, sitting comfortably on the wool blanket next to Marilla, shook his head. "Daddy did not say you could have another piece of cake, young lady. What he said was you must finish your lunch first and then he would consider your request."

"Oh, Daddy."

Marilla snickered as Bertha held her arms rigid at her side and pouted. At ten, she could be fierce one minute and in tears the next. Hoping to forestall the latter, Charles passed Bertha a handful of crumbs from the bottom of the basket and directed her to the seagulls at the foot of the hill. They watched together as she skipped down the slope, her long brown ringlets bouncing behind her.

Charles marvelled at Marilla's ease with Bertha, and the look of love that radiated whenever she watched her daughter speak. And yes, he'd finally had to admit, he found her very attractive. She was taller than most women he knew, with a graciousness that spoke of strength not vanity, and blue eyes that smiled as though holding a secret. He was not surprised when he felt stirrings of desire for her, but when he had moments believing she could be more than a friendly companion to a grieving widower and his child, he struggled to rein them in.

"I don't know what I would have done without you, Marilla."

She blushed then and he rushed to explain. "What I mean is, I don't know what Bertha would have done without you. She hasn't been this happy in weeks." He lowered his voice, struggled to control his emotions, and finally confessed, "Nor have I."

Marilla's smile had faded then, and he immediately regretted his behaviour. She looked troubled by his words and struggled to speak. Charles hurried to explain.

"I'm sorry, Marilla. Please, forgive me for being so forward."

"No, Charles, I understand. I do. This week has been…more than I ever dreamed possible. And I am so grateful to Catherine, and to you, for this chance to get to know my daughter." Her eyes had welled with tears as she watched Bertha chase the gulls. "I love to hear her laugh, to see who she's become." She wiped her eyes and tried to smile. "You've both suffered a terrible loss and if I can make her smile, let her know how much she's loved." She faced him then and held his gaze. "And if I've brought some measure… of comfort to you, Charles, then I feel I've done what Catherine would have wanted."

That was two days ago. Tonight, he and Bertha were invited for dinner at the home of Marilla's aunt. He examined his reflection in the hallway mirror and adjusted his tie. Marilla's words had landed heavy in his heart. She'd made clear her intentions and left him struggling with his own. Had he really believed she could replace Catherine as his wife, or was it only grief that imagined it so? And what of Bertha?

He could hear the tap of Bertha's shoes along the upstairs hallway and the rustle of her petticoat as she ran. "We're coming, Daddy."

"Finally," he muttered, and then watched as his daughter bounced with excitement down the stairs. He had no practice with ribbons, and the one Mrs. MacDonald secured to her hair matched her pinafore perfectly. She was transformed from when they first arrived. Seeing her face aglow with happiness, Charles reined in his emotions so as not to make her sad.

"Doesn't she look lovely, Charles?"

Bertha gathered her skirt, twirled in front of her father, then giggled. "Do you like it, Daddy?"

"I do. And you do look very pretty."

"As pretty as Mommy?"

The question took his breath, for he had been thinking it himself. In that moment, images of Catherine's beautiful face clouded his vision. He could see the love for Bertha in her smile, her eyes filled with delight at how much their baby girl had grown. His heart, having struggled all week to understand his own feelings for Marilla, now understood his daughter's. Marilla would only ever be a friend. A friend of their family. Catherine, his beloved wife, would always be her mother. Not even Marilla could change that now. At last, the answer was clear and he knew what he had to do.

He swallowed before speaking. "Yes, my dear sweet girl, just as pretty as Mommy."

Bertha wrapped her arms around Charles and whispered, "Thank you, Daddy."

CHAPTER 28

*"A*UNT MARTHA, WOULD YOU PLEASE COME AWAY FROM that window? Neither pulling at the curtains nor staring at the street will get them here any sooner."

Martha didn't budge from her spot, but turned to speak to her niece. "I'm sorry, Marilla, I simply can't help it. The thought that I am going to embrace the granddaughter that my brother never lived to see…it makes me feel as if something of him is still with us."

"I know. And he would have loved her. But you do understand that she knows nothing of our connection to her and never will."

"Of course I do. How could I forget?" Martha pulled a handkerchief from her sleeve and dabbed at her eyes. "And she'll never know that it was I who took her from your arms…that terrible night."

Marilla rushed over to her aunt. "Aunt Martha, please don't keep reliving all that. Of course she'll never know. And you did what you had to do." She placed a comforting arm around Martha's shoulders. "Once you see her, all those old memories will begin to fade. They have for me." Marilla gazed out the window and smiled. "It's the new ones I've gathered this week that occupy my mind now." Her throat tightened as she continued. "I'm so grateful to Catherine. She once thanked me for the gift of Bertha in her life and here I am with the gift of her, even for a short time, in mine."

The knock on the door startled them and they jumped. So caught up in their musings, they'd missed seeing Charles and Bertha stroll down the walkway toward the door.

Etta, who'd been making her way downstairs, reached the front door first and opened it just as Marilla and Martha turned the corner.

Charles looked at the three women who stared in absolute wonder at his daughter. He knew the story surrounding her birth and the struggles each had borne to deliver her safely to him and Catherine. He removed his hat, but before he had a chance to speak, Bertha stepped into the circle of women and basked in their delight. They gathered around her in the hall and began speaking all at once, leaving Charles alone in the porch.

"Hello, Bertha, I'm Miss Cuthbert, Marilla's aunt. It is so lovely to meet you."

"Should I call you Aunt Martha like Marilla does?"

Martha's voice quavered as she held back emotion that had risen at the mere sound of her niece's voice. "I would be delighted."

Etta stepped forward. "Hello, Bertha, I'm Miss Byers, a friend of Miss Cuthbert's. I've heard so much about you. Marilla has been telling us all about your visit to Halifax. Are you enjoying your stay with the MacDonalds?"

"Yes, Miss Byers. Daddy and I—" At the mention of his name, Martha, so enchanted by her niece finally remembered he was there.

"Oh my goodness, Mr. Willis, where are my manners? Please do come in."

Charles stepped into the hallway and extended his hand. "It's a pleasure to meet you, Miss Cuthbert."

He then looked at Etta and, keeping his knowledge of who she was hidden from his daughter's view, nodded in her direction. "How do you do, Miss Byers?"

Sensing the need for a moment of privacy, Etta took charge.

"Marilla dear, why don't you take Bertha into the kitchen. There's a pitcher of blueberry cordial setting in the pantry. Perhaps you could pour us all a nice cool drink."

Bertha couldn't hide her excitement. "I love cordial!"

Martha laughed. "So do I! What kindred spirits we are."

Etta smiled. "Aunt Martha and I will take your father to the parlour and you can join us there."

Once they entered the parlour and closed the door, Etta spoke. "Charles, please accept our sincere condolences on the loss of your wife. Marilla told us what happened."

"A terrible tragedy," Martha murmured as she took a seat. "Just terrible."

Charles took the wingback by the window. "It was a shock to both of us and especially Bertha. She took it very hard. Our time in Halifax has been so good for her. Especially seeing Marilla."

"What did Bertha know of her before now?" Martha queried.

Charles leaned forward. "She's always known her as Catherine's friend who lived in Prince Edward Island and who they wrote to every year. It's only been in recent years that her curiosity, and desire to meet her have grown. So Catherine wrote and arranged for it to happen." He paused, glancing out the window. "Only no one could have imagined the circumstances under which it did."

"When do you plan to return to Stewiacke?" Etta asked.

"We leave Wednesday morning."

"So soon?" Martha said. "Marilla didn't mention anything to me about you leaving this week. Did she say anything to you, Etta?"

Charles rushed to explain. "She didn't, because she doesn't know. I haven't told her, or Bertha, yet."

They quieted as the sound of footsteps and giggles could be heard in the hall. Martha quickly opened the door to allow Marilla to enter. Charles rose and reached for the heavy tray and set it on the table. Bertha followed behind carrying a plate of molasses cookies and set it beside the drinks.

"Daddy, guess what? There's a picnic next Sunday."

"A church picnic," Marilla added, passing around the drinks.

"And Marilla would like to take me."

Marilla smiled. "And your father, of course."

Bertha grew excited. "Daddy, you could do the tug-of-war."

Bertha held the plate of cookies in front of Martha. "Aunt Martha, will you come to the picnic with us?"

Both Martha and Etta looked to Charles for the answer. He shifted uncomfortably and cleared his throat. "Bertha, I'm sorry, but we won't be able to attend. I received a letter from Mrs. Levy and I'm afraid the time has come for you and I to return home. We leave on Wednesday."

Before Marilla could respond, Bertha cried out, "No! I don't want to go home, Daddy. I want to stay here." She threw herself at Marilla and burst into tears.

"Sh now, Bertha, don't get upset. You'll be back before you know it. Won't she, Charles?" Marilla's eyes pleaded for what she herself needed to hear.

"Of course she will. Maybe next summer we can—"

"Next summer? I won't see Marilla till next summer? No!" Bertha wailed and before any of them could react, she'd fled the room and was heading up the stairs.

Charles started after her but Marilla caught his arm. "I'll go, Charles. I'll speak to her."

He hated himself more in that moment than he ever had before. This was the heartache he'd unleashed. Not just his own, but his daughter's. The letter was a ruse, an excuse he'd created to leave Halifax. To leave behind feelings he had no right to feel. For a woman he had no right to love. Grief had consumed him and he could no longer allow himself to believe its easing was caused by anything other than compassion. He knew Marilla cared for him. Respected him. But only as Bertha's father. Nothing more. Charles hung his head and sighed.

Bertha had run the length of the upstairs hall and headed into the only bedroom with an open door. The sight of Bertha curled into a ball on Marilla's bed took her breath away. Her little girl was lying in the very spot where she'd been born. The years fell away and Marilla's longing to hold her, to keep her, felt as strong as it did back then. As did the reasons to let her go. Marilla sat on the side of the bed and gently stroked her hair.

"Did you know that this was my room?"

Bertha shook her head.

"I've been coming to visit my Aunt Martha ever since I was a little girl. And this was always my room."

"I know I'm not supposed to go into people's rooms," Bertha said, sitting up and wiping her face. "But I like this one. And...I knew right where it was. Just like in my dreams. Isn't that silly?"

Marilla froze. "You saw this room in a dream?"

Bertha hesitated for a moment, then nodded. "I did. But I never saw you. I saw my mommy."

Marilla's heart clenched and tears filled her eyes. *Your mommy is right here* she wanted to scream. She calmed her breath and forced herself to say, "You must miss her very much."

"I do. And I wish that she were here. But she's not, she's in Stewiacke where Daddy and I planted the flowers." She remained quiet, lost for a moment in thought, then suddenly swung her legs over the side of the bed and stood. "Marilla?"

"Yes, Bertha."

"Can we be friends...just like you and Mommy were?"

"Of course."

"And can I write you letters, just like Mommy did?"

"I'd like that very much."

Her eyes, still moist with tears, started to brighten. "Daddy will have to help me, of course, and then we'll walk to the mailbox like Mommy and I used to do." Her voice grew excited. "And Mr. Conrad will pick it up just the same as always...."

She hugged Marilla. "I feel much better. And Mommy would be so happy that you're my friend now too."

With tears streaming down her face, Marilla held her daughter and prayed for the strength to let her go. She smiled through her tears and held her tighter. "I'm sure she would."

Bertha wriggled free of Marilla's arms and started to leave. "I'm going to tell Daddy that I *am* ready to go home. We need to check the flowers and the horses and...." She was out the door and down the stairs before Marilla could move. The sudden quiet, the emptiness, felt the same as it had on the night she was born, when the air itself had been pulled from the room along with her daughter. She closed her eyes and tried to breathe.

If Bertha's letters are all I ever have, she thought, *it has to be enough. To know she's loved. To know she's happy.* That's all Marilla had hoped for when she'd given her daughter up. What would she gain if she fought to keep her now? Bertha would grow to hate her. For shattering the only world she'd ever known. Could she tear away Bertha's memories of Catherine's love? Never. No more than she could tear her away from a father who adored her.

Marilla could hear them downstairs gathering in the dining room. She smoothed the quilt on the bed and straightened the pillow. Her hand lingered on the spot her daughter had come back to, letting its warmth seal the memory of her return to the place where her life began.

CHAPTER 29

July 14, 1852

Halifax, NS

*O*N WEDNESDAY MORNING THEY STOOD AND WATCHED AS the wagon drove away. Marilla fought the urge to run after it by wrapping her shawl tightly around her middle and holding herself tight. Etta held Martha as she cried. Bertha turned around in her seat and waved one last time and their faces brightened just for her.

With promises to write and future visits to plan, Bertha had been excited to leave. It was Charles who seemed reluctant. And it was clear to Aunt Martha the reason why. She'd watched as he stood holding Marilla's hands, thanking her for all she'd done, wearing the same expression she'd glimpsed the evening of their visit.

"Come along now Marilla," Martha said, stepping forward to interrupt. "Let's not keep Charles from his journey."

They'd stood, waiting till the wagon rounded the corner and the clattering of the horse's hoofs grew distant before gathering themselves and heading back inside.

"Marilla dear, why don't you make us a fresh pot of tea."

"I'll make the tea, Martha," Etta said. "You two make your way around back. It's a lovely morning. I'll bring it out to the garden."

Aunt Martha leaned heavily on Marilla's arm as they walked along the path leading to the backyard. It was not the first time Marilla noticed frailness in her aunt's step, and she worried that perhaps seeing Bertha had been too much. They settled in chairs out of the sun and Martha pulled her shawl around her shoulders.

"She's such a beautiful little girl, Marilla. Such a dear, sweet child. I never imagined I'd feel so much for her. And you were right. I only see her smiling face as it is now, not the memories of that poor little infant." Martha dabbed at her eyes. "And when she called me Aunt Martha that first night, well…it was that sound that chased them all away."

Tears slid down Marilla's face as her aunt spoke and she quickly brushed them away. "I'm so happy that you and Etta had a chance to meet her." Marilla hesitated then leaned forward. "And her father." She paused before continuing. "Aunt Martha, you must believe me when I say I admire Charles very much…but not for one minute did I imagine…."

"Oh now, Marilla…don't fret. You did nothing wrong. Grief is hard for a man. They don't do well."

"But I could never have replaced Catherine." Marilla said, the thought as incredible as thinking he could ever have replaced her William.

"He knows that now. And aside from the fact that you did nothing to encourage him, he realizes you could never replace the mother that lives in his daughter's heart."

Etta arrived with the tea and they sat quietly, each in their own thoughts, watching as robins fluttered around the bird bath.

Marilla looked across at the woman who'd been a constant in her aunt's life for the past ten years, and a plan began to form. When Etta sold her house and moved in, their relationship, though confusing to Marilla at first, had become such a comfort. Both because she knew that her aunt was not alone and because with Etta, who felt like family now, Marilla could always be herself.

"Aunt Martha? I have an idea. When I leave on Friday to go back to the Island, why don't you and Etta come with me? You haven't been back to visit since father's funeral." Marilla then looked at Etta. "And you've never been to Green Gables, to *my* home. I had hoped that maybe Bertha would have come with me, but…." Marilla waved her hand to dismiss the thought and took a deep breath. "I just know it would be so much easier if…."

Martha and Etta glanced at each other and Marilla could see a hint of a smile.

"If you came with me, especially this time, with leaving my baby, I mean Bertha, behind again…." Her voice trembled. "I wouldn't feel quite as alone as I did last time. And I'd have someone to talk to, aside from Matthew, whose ear I constantly bend." She looked back and forth between them. "What do you say?"

The two women reached for each other's hands, smiled at Marilla, and spoke together. "We'd love to."

$$\sim$$

Matthew held the reins loose in his hands. The horses knew their way. They'd made the trip to Charlottetown many times before. It was early still, the sun only just up, and he breathed in the freshness clinging to the pines.

Not much piqued his interest these days, he had to admit. He kept to himself and spoke only when needed. And with a farm to run, he didn't waste time on what he considered foolishness. Especially his own. But these trips to Charlottetown, though few and far between, always got him thinking of what he once had, and whom he once loved. His Violet.

His quiet musings suddenly flared and he cursed aloud: "Foolishness!" He tightened the reins and urged the horses on. She'd married, of course, though not for some time. When her visits to Avonlea stopped, and when whispers between Marilla and Rachel were interrupted whenever he neared, that's when he knew. He'd overheard once that she lived in Charlottetown, but otherwise he tried not to think of her at all. And thinking it was all foolishness was better than thinking himself a fool.

But the thought of Marilla in Halifax, coming face to face with his niece…well now, that thought had occupied his mind ever since she left and filled him with a feeling he could never have described to anyone, even if they asked. It could be excitement, though he'd had little experience with that. Could be he was just curious. Was Bertha smart and bright and not like him at all? Did she look like the Marilla he remembered as a little girl?

And this was when it always happened. When his breath caught in his chest. When his chin, normally tucked and downcast, lifted. When his lips, buried beneath whiskers and rimmed with beard, spread wide and formed a smile. When he thought of her as family, something like happiness filled the emptiness of his soul and gave meaning to his life.

He'd know soon enough all about her. The ferry would be docking in Charlottetown at noon and he'd be there to listen to all her news. It wasn't just Marilla who lived for the letters from Stewiacke. He did too. Just knowing that his niece was happy and loved was often enough. But knowing he was her uncle, even if she never would, was a feeling he carried with him always.

∾

Nora sat rocking, sipping tea that had gone cold, waiting for the wagon to return. She'd heard the whispers between Matthew and Marilla before she left. And when the reason for the sudden trip to Halifax was given, neither had looked her in the eye. To keep her from the truth, she supposed. That's what they thought.

But in her heart, she knew. She knew she had a granddaughter somewhere out there, and she hated living in a world that would never have allowed it to be. But not as much as she hated herself for being part of that world. Nora reached under her shawl and felt the lump inside her breast. A lifetime of bitterness had finally lodged itself within her. She blinked away tears and swallowed the regret swelling her throat. The only comfort in realizing too late what a waste her life had been was knowing that she wasn't long for it.

The rumble of wagon wheels approaching from down the lane shook Nora from her reverie. She rose slowly and placed the kettle to boil. The table was set and the blueberry pie was warming in the oven. The sound of voices brought her to the window and she was surprised to see that Marilla and Matthew were not alone.

"Now, who in the name of heavens would that be?" she muttered on her way to the back door. She stepped onto the porch and watched as they made their way across the yard. When finally they reached her and the one leading the pack raised her head, Nora gasped at the sight of Martha. So like her brother now, with silver-grey hair. Her smile held his grin and her gait matched his. Nora's defenses faltered and forgetting all that was held between them for a lifetime, rushed forward and gathered Martha in her arms.

The rest, too stunned to speak, stood and watched. Martha's arms, laden with baggage, were pinned by her sides, and only when she felt Nora begin to tremble did she drop the bags, pull her arms free, and gather them around her.

"Nora dear, what is the matter? You look as if you've seen a ghost. And why the tears?"

In that moment Nora's legs gave out and Marilla and Matthew rushed forward and caught her just as she started to fall. "Mother, what is it, what's wrong?"

She lay, her head resting in Martha's lap and looked up into their faces. She gently caressed Matthew's cheek then grasped Marilla's hand and whispered, "I'm so sorry."

ॐ

Nora had fallen asleep as soon as Matthew laid her down, before Marilla had even removed her shoes. They tucked a quilt around her and only then did the outline of her frame appear, small and frail. *Like a child*, Marilla thought, her instinct to nurture rising even as the image of her mother, once so powerful, flashed through her mind. She brushed wisps of white hair from her brow and pressed a hand to her forehead. Her mother's mouth slackened, deepening the hollows beneath her cheeks. They closed the door to their mother's room and joined the others in the kitchen.

"Did you have any idea about this?" Martha said, looking from one to the other. "That she was so sick?"

"She'd slowed down some," Marilla admitted. "I noticed it before I left. But sick?" She looked at Matthew accusingly. "Did you know about this?"

He stared back. "As if she'd tell me."

Etta, sitting quietly at the table, finally spoke. "Perhaps you should get the doctor."

They'd forgotten her amidst the commotion, and they all spoke at once.

"Etta, dear heavens, I almost forgot you were here," Martha said, taking a seat in the chair beside her.

"But I'm so grateful that you are," Marilla said, pulling out another chair to join them. She reached for their hands across the table and held them tight. "So very grateful that you *both* are."

Flustered by all the emotions, Matthew hurried out the door. "I'll ride over to get the doctor."

CHAPTER 30

❧❧❧

October 1852

Avonlea, PEI

ICKNESS HAS A WAY OF SOFTENING THE EDGES, **MARILLA**
thought, staring at her mother's withered body. *Of blurring
our memories and healing our hurts. The fury leaves us, and the need for
forgiveness grows stronger as death gets closer.*

She rinsed the washcloth in the basin of warm water beside
the bed and wiped her mother's face. Water was her only suste-
nance, the only comfort left to give. Water for the body. Water for the
soul. Food did nothing but torture her, and the doctor had advised
them to stop.

"Just be with her," he'd said. "It won't be long now."

Three months had passed since Matthew first brought him
to see their mother. The day Marilla had returned from Halifax
back in July, along with Martha and Etta. The doctor, of course,
had already known. And was angry with her for not admitting it.
For wanting to spare them what she'd known for months. They
who needed to care for her and see to her needs.

Marilla brushed her mother's hair, tucked the quilt back
in place, and gathered the basin. She placed her mother's soiled
nightgown inside a towel, tucked it under her arm, and headed to
the kitchen. The washtub was sitting in its place by the stove and

Marilla tossed the towel onto the pile. She lowered herself into the rocker, leaned back, and closed her eyes.

She thought back to that summer day she'd returned to the farm and marvelled that so much had changed in so short a time. She thought of the evening they'd gathered around her mother's bed. The night before Etta and Martha returned to Halifax. It was a night she would never forget. Her mother had called them all together as she lay propped in bed, and they'd stood awkwardly, not knowing what to do.

"Come in, Martha, Etta, please. Come sit. Matthew, bring a chair. Marilla, would you open the curtains? I want to watch the sun as it sets over the garden." They murmured and shuffled and settled themselves around her. Her strength was waning, and though her voice quavered, it held a sense of urgency. She looked each one of them directly in the eye, held their gaze then finally spoke.

"It's time now and I want to know. I want to know all about her." Her eyes found Marilla's and pleaded. "Please, tell me about my granddaughter."

Marilla gasped, while the others held themselves still.

"You all know. Of that I'm sure. And some of you have seen her. I can see it in your eyes." Her own eyes misted and she started to cough. Marilla reached for the glass sitting by the bed and held it to her mother's lips. She began to cry and her voice rose in frustration. "I'm the reason she's not here, and God knows I don't deserve it...but I want to know her. Before I die, I want to know all about her."

And so they talked and laughed and cried and shared their stories. From the night she was born and taken away to the day in Halifax when, heading back to Stewiacke with her father, she'd smiled and waved goodbye. They'd gathered closer around her bed, some sitting by her side, others with chairs pulled close. Her mother had delighted in hearing it all, laughing and crying till she lay completely spent.

The lengthening shadows of sunset crept across the walls as they talked, lighting her mother's face until the orange glow of sunset deepened and slowly slipped below the horizon. When her mother's eyes finally closed, they crept from the room and closed the door, leaving with her the secrets they no longer held.

∽

"Marilla? Are you awake?" She'd fallen asleep and hadn't heard Rachel's knock. She stood now in the doorway and anxiously peered at Marilla.

"Yes, Rachel, I'm awake. Just resting a bit is all."

"Dear lord, Marilla, but you do look tired. You poor thing." She stepped closer and held out her arms which were piled high with food. "Here, I've brought some fish and potatoes for your supper. It's not much, mind you, but I know it's your mother's favourite. And bread of course."

With no desire to hurt Rachel's feelings by explaining her mother could no longer eat, Marilla simply carried it all to the pantry.

"As if you don't have enough mouths to feed!" She said as Rachel claimed her usual place at the table. "But I do thank you. It's such a help to me."

Marilla looked at the woman who had once been her childhood friend and searched for some semblance of who she'd been. Not yet thirty, she'd already birthed seven children. And with her apron straining against her middle, there'd soon be one more. "How is that brood of yours these days?"

"Well, thank heaven for the school is all I can say, and for my own mother. The new teacher from over in Carmody is wonderful with the children and mother helps when she can. And except for the two little ones nearly coughing their heads off with croup, the rest toddle after Thomas most days." She leaned across the table and patted Marilla's hand. "Marilla, dear, enough about me and my brood, how is your mother?"

Something in the tone of her voice, or maybe the concern on her face, took Marilla back to when they were young, when they'd known nothing and talked about everything. She started to cry, and then found herself leaning into arms that were suddenly holding her. "She's dying, Rachel. My mother is dying.

"Oh Marilla, you poor dear, it's never easy is it? It's only been, what, a few months since you and Matthew knew? Though Mother and I certainly had our suspicions while you were away."

"When I think back to all the times I hated her, when I ran from her…I wish now we had more time."

Rachel quieted her voice. "Really, Marilla? After everything she's done? Please don't think me heartless, but what has changed?"

Marilla moved from Rachel's embrace, wiped her face, and blew her nose.

Rachel stood and placed the kettle on the stove to boil. "I can remember the night when John Blythe sat right there." She pointed to the table. "You told me once how her bitterness had poisoned everything. I know she's dying and I would never wish her any suffering, mind you, but can you really forgive her?"

"Yes, Rachel, I can. She's changed so much from what she was. She's so sorry for it all. You should have been here the morning Aunt Martha left. I never heard anyone wail like that. So much regret. She's making her peace and I need to make mine."

"You're a good daughter, Marilla. Always have been. And I'm only too glad that she finally sees it." She sat heavily back in her chair and sighed. "But you lost so much. Your dear William. Having the chance to marry. To someday have a daughter of your own. You would have made a wonderful mother."

Marilla pressed a hand to her chest and held back a truth she would never tell Rachel, even now.

"So, if you can find peace with your mother and with all that's happened, then you are a stronger woman than I'll ever be. One I've grown to admire more and more."

At that moment, Matthew stepped into the kitchen, and between the kettle's shrieking whistle and Rachel and Marilla's sniffling and crying, his plan for a quiet moment in his favourite corner was upended, sending him back to his mother's rose garden, to the flowers he'd coaxed back to life. To where he'd at last found peace.

౧

Marilla stood at the front door, watching the last of the neighbours walk the path toward home. They were polite and respectful as always, even though in truth they didn't know her mother well at all. It was the graveyard that was full of those who had really known her. Back when she was young and full of life. Before her hopes and dreams, like those of so many others, had been diminished by the need to survive.

She closed the door and walked back to the kitchen, where Matthew sat sipping the last of his tea. His eyes grieved the memory of his mother, for all that never was and never would be. "She died happy...didn't she, Marilla? She was happier just before she died than she ever was when she lived." His voice shook with emotion. "But what kind of life was that?"

Marilla pulled a chair close and sat quietly. The house felt empty without her mother's presence, imposing though it had often been, and the future loomed large. She reached into her skirt pocket and pulled out the envelope she'd been holding, waiting for this moment. It had arrived three days ago, on the morning of her mother's passing, and she'd tucked it away as a nugget of hope amidst the sorrow.

Matthew straightened, his weariness suddenly replaced with recognition, as she tore it open and unfolded the letter tucked inside.

"Is it from her?"

Marilla swallowed, and tried to contain the emotion welling inside.

"Yes."

She took a deep breath and started to read.

October 1, 1852
Dear Marilla,

Though it is not yet time for the annual birthday letter, Bertha could not wait. I sit with her now as she prepares to tell you her exciting news. As for me, taking care of the farm and Bertha is all I can manage. The neighbours help as much as they can and Bertha is a very capable young girl who for the most part takes care of herself.

Our time in Halifax revived our spirits and I will be forever grateful for all that you did in helping us cope with our loss. I'm going to pass this over to Bertha to finish. She's anxious that we get to the mailbox in time.

> *Yours truly,*
> *Charles*

"Do you think I'll ever meet him?" Matthew said, surprising Marilla.

"I never imagined you'd want to."

"I didn't either, until now."

Marilla understood and smiled as she continued reading.

Dear Miss Cuthbert,

There is a boarding school just for girls in Truro and Daddy has arranged for me to attend. As much as I love Daddy and living on our farm, I am excited to go. There is so much to learn about being a young lady and the headmistress is very nice. I met her when Daddy took me for a visit. I will be home on the weekends and for the summer of course, so Daddy shouldn't miss me too much. I want to be like Mommy when I grow up and make Daddy proud. I hope I make you proud too.

> *Your friend,*
> *Bertha*

Matthew wiped the tears he didn't realize had formed and swallowed hard.

Marilla folded the letter and tucked it away. "She's all we have now, you and I. Time has left us too far behind to hope for more."

At thirty-six, Matthew knew his sister was right, and hated the bitterness that had settled in his heart. "Will it be enough, do you think?" His frustration flared. "What kind of life will it be with only her to live for, Marilla?"

"I don't know, Matthew. But just imagine what kind of life it would be without her."

CHAPTER 31

*A*ND SO IT BEGAN. A LIFE LIVED THROUGH LETTERS. A LIFE lived through Bertha Willis.

Matthew and Marilla watched as their fields and pastures surrendered to the seasons while the seasons themselves melded into years. They lived and worked and shared a life that most in the town of Avonlea—though none would ever say—felt pity for, because as time passed they kept more and more to themselves. Hardworking, faithful members of the church and community, they were highly respected. Though at times, in a small community like Avonlea, even they became fodder for the gossip mill run by those with little else to do.

No one saw them huddle together around the table on a day when a letter arrived. Or witnessed their eyes brighten in anticipation of Bertha's news. Charles had added a small greeting to each of the first few letters, but once Bertha had settled into the boarding school that had stopped. And news of Charles, other than word passed on through Mrs. MacDonald or Etta, was only what Bertha shared.

She enjoyed school life and adored her teachers, and so it was no surprise when Bertha announced she wanted to become a teacher herself. Normal School, the teacher's college in Truro, would take her when she turned sixteen and so with only a few months till her next birthday, she was working very hard.

Marilla smiled as she read.

And just think, in only a year I'll be teaching somewhere in Nova Scotia. Though I don't know where, for it's the board of trustees that makes the decision as to where that might be. But just imagine. I'll be teaching children how to read and write and learn and open their minds and their worlds. Is that not the most exciting occupation that anyone could have?

"Aunt Martha would have been so proud," Marilla said, and for a moment a rush of longing blurred her vision. Another grave filled the cemetery, next to her mother and father's, as the row of crosses bearing the name Cuthbert continued to grow.

"Should we tell her?" Matthew asked

"No, Matthew. Not now. If she asks, maybe. It's been nearly six years since she last saw her, and only that one time, so really, what would she remember of her?"

Marilla looked down at the letter and continued reading.

"Please give my best to your brother, Matthew. I do hope that one day we'll meet."

Marilla looked up at Matthew and without meaning to, raised her brow.

"I know, I know. But we've discussed this, Marilla. And I can't. You know I can't."

The thought of leaving Green Gables, let alone the Island, still paralyzed him with fear.

His anxieties, especially after losing Violet all those years ago, had only increased, not waned, as he'd hoped. Matthew stood and started pacing; the pain of all he'd lost and the regret he felt for his part in it, raised his hackles, and he fought the sorrow that pressed against his chest.

He had no way to explain. No words to describe how his world grew smaller every year. How going further than the post office could often squeeze the very breath from his lungs. He was a grown man, for Christ's sake, scared to leave his home. Even if he found the words, who would understand?

Marilla, guilty now for opening an old wound, continued reading.

As you know, Father had to give up our farm shortly after I left for boarding school, and I do miss hearing about the calves in the spring and the harvesting in the fall. The Levys, our neighbours next door, were only too happy to have him stay with them, but with his health being what it is, he tends the gardens now, not the fields. I'm happy he's not alone, but I do get the sense from his letters sometimes that he's lonely. I don't think he ever got over losing my mother. As for me, when I feel lonely and miss her, that's when I write to you.

Marilla sniffled and swallowed the lump that had formed in her throat.

I'm so grateful to have you, Marilla. You've been such a good friend to me. I certainly don't mean to boast, but when your letters and gifts arrive in the mail, the other girls do get a bit jealous. And I know this must sound strange, but knowing that you knew my mother makes me feel closer to her when I write to you. Like I'm writing to her. Like I still do have a mother. I warned you it would sound silly!

I must go now, Marilla, our lamps need to be out by nine and it's already ten past. I'll walk this to the mailbox in the morning, an outing, started by my mother, that I have never stopped enjoying.

Yours Truly,
Bertha Willis

Marilla folded the letter and rested her hands in her lap. She pulled a handkerchief from her cuff and dabbed at her eyes. Matthew stopped pacing and took a deep breath. He looked out the window and could see the cows heading in from the pasture, back to the barn for milking. He could hear the sound of bells clanking and hoofs scuffing as they waddled down the lane.

"Well, it's that time," he said, reaching for his coat.

"It is." Marilla rose slowly, reluctant to get back to work. "I'll put supper on first, then feed the chickens." She stared at the jars of pickles lined up in the pantry. "I need to put those down in the cellar and, good heavens," she said looking out into the yard. "There's still wash on the line and it looks like rain."

They stood looking at each other, and Marilla spoke aloud what they were both thinking. Life had become a drudgery, a time to pass, till they too took their place alongside the rest. "Just imagine though, Matthew, what it would be like without her."

∽

The time passed and in 1860, Bertha finally completed her studies. Her letter, received just after her eighteenth birthday, brimmed with excitement not only because she was graduating but because she'd met a young man with whom she'd fallen madly in love. Their graduation was to take place in Truro in June and she told Marilla how much she wished she could be there. To see her, of course, but also to meet her beau, Walter.

"You'll go then?" Matthew said, tossing a pitchfork full of hay into the horse stall.

"Not likely, Matthew. You do remember what the doctor said?"

"Ahh," Matthew grunted. "He's younger than me, for pity's sake. What does he know?"

Marilla folded her arms and stood her ground. "Matthew, you're forty-four years old. Most everyone you know is younger than you."

"My heart is fine, Marilla. He told me to rest. So I'll rest."

Marilla raised her brows.

"I give you my word."

"And you'll let the farmhand do what you hired him for?"

"I will, if you write her back and tell her you'll go."

Marilla headed back to the house to make the arrangements. It was only two months away, but she needed to make sure Matthew would be looked after. Their father had died young and Matthew was, if nothing else, his father's son.

"You're no spring chicken yourself," Matthew shouted from the barn and Marilla, whose own body ached more and more every day, hadn't the strength to argue.

~

The school grounds were crowded with young people while their parents milled about, anxious to be part of the celebration. Marilla had arrived by train from Halifax the day before. She had secured lodging at the Railway Inn, and on this beautiful sun-filled morning, enjoyed the walk past Victoria Park to where the ceremony would take place.

She stood at the edge of the crowd now, scanning for the little girl she hadn't seen in almost eight years. A prickle of anxiety crept through her as she considered for the first time that she might not even recognize Bertha. Her own daughter. She was, after all, a woman now. The thought made her suddenly weak, and she stood not knowing what to do.

"Marilla, is that you?"

She turned at the sound of her name and did not at first recognize the man leaning against a cane behind her. Until he smiled. And the Charles she remembered, his eyes clouded with something more than memories, his body diminished by illness, stepped forward and embraced her.

Marilla was spared from trying to hide her shock by the sound of footsteps running along the path. A rush of arms, legs, and billowing gowns gathered around them as a small entourage of graduates, trying their best to appear mature and serious, laughed and jostled with excitement.

A young woman beaming with joy, dark hair piled high, stepped out of the crowd and threw her arms around Charles. "Father, what a lovely surprise. I wasn't certain you'd make it in time, but I'm so very glad you did."

Marilla, breathless and overwhelmed by the sight of her daughter, stood watching. When Bertha finally became aware of her, she released her father and stared. Her eyes, at first, did not completely register who she was, but when they did, they opened wide.

"It's you."

Before Marilla could respond, Bertha was in her arms and she melted into the warmth of her daughter while an image of William reached out from the past and enfolded them. And for that one moment, she rejoiced in feeling like family...a family that never was and never could be.

Bertha stepped back to take Marilla in, her brown eyes sparkling. "I'm so happy you made it."

Marilla's hands reached up and held her daughter's face while she spoke the tenderness that engulfed her. "I wouldn't have missed this for anything, my dear."

The group suddenly grew quiet, and a tall man with flaming red hair stepped forward and held out his hand to Charles.

But before he could introduce himself, Bertha rushed to his side. "This is my Walter!"

Charles smiled and shook his hand and without saying a word, the two men exchanged an understanding of the spirited woman who was his daughter.

"And you must be *the* Marilla Cuthbert," Walter said. "I have heard so much about you. Thank you both for being here." Bertha looked up with adoring eyes while he continued. "You've made Bertha and I so very happy."

Marilla was grateful to Charles when he cleared his throat and spoke, for she was trembling with emotion and beyond words. "And you, young man," he said, placing a hand on Walter's shoulder, "have put the sparkle back in my daughter's eyes, which is the one thing that has always made me the most happy. So it is *I* who thanks you."

∽

The journey back to the Island seemed to take forever, and when at last she stepped down from the ferry, Marilla wondered if she'd ever have the strength to go back. Not the physical kind of strength that you can muster when needed, but the kind that fortifies your soul against heartache. Watching Bertha accept her certificate and knowing she was off to her first teaching position had been too much for Marilla to bear.

She'd nearly burst with pride, but only because she couldn't stand up in front of everyone, like she'd wanted to, and shout, *This is my daughter! I carried her and delivered her. And loved her. She's the best part of me. And the worst thing I ever did was give her up!*

And it was then that she'd felt it. Like a hand on her shoulder. A breath in her ear. The image of Catherine, standing near, calmed her. *You didn't give her up,* she whispered, *you gave her life. And now she's a young woman starting her own. You're not alone, Marilla. Not in this. Together now, we give her up. Together, we open our arms and let her go.*

CHAPTER 32

April 1864
Avonlea, PEI

*I*T WAS A DIFFERENT KIND OF EMPTINESS. THE KIND A mother bird must feel when her chicks have left the nest and she pecks and pokes at the empty twigs and discarded fluff, remembering, wondering. There was less guilt, Marilla thought, but no less worry.

And though she was busy with teaching and spending time with Walter, Bertha always found time to write. Long letters filled with all that was happening, or short notes dashed off before bedtime. She could be terribly funny at times, and the sound of Matthew's laughter as he listened to Marilla read breathed life into their quiet existence.

Bertha and Walter taught together at the same school for two years, and when the letter arrived announcing their engagement, Marilla was thrilled. Though as a married woman, Bertha would need to give up her teaching position, a rule she thoroughly disagreed with, the thought of a June wedding and her love for Walter had made the decision easy.

It will be a very small ceremony, Bertha wrote. *Neither Walter nor I have any family and except for you (please say you'll come) and Father, there will only be a few teachers from school, who have become our friends, in attendance.*

"June," Matthew said. "Well now, that's not far off."

Marilla raised her head and glanced hopefully at her brother. He held up his hand to stop her before she could even start. "You know I'll be busy with planting. That's all I'll say on that."

Matthew headed to the pasture while Marilla went upstairs. She tucked the letter inside the box containing all the others and slid it back under the bed. She sat in the chair by the window and gazed across the field. Her daughter was getting married. Of course, she would go. No matter how long the journey, she would be there.

Marilla stood and looked at herself in the long mirror behind her door. She would turn forty this year, and she often found herself wondering *Who is that?* as she passed the mirror in the hallway downstairs. Her hair had more grey than brown, and felt thinner than it used to when she pinned it up. Her face, weathered by sun and wind, held the weight of time passed. The one thing that hadn't changed were the eyes that looked back. They contained all she'd seen, all she'd longed for, and all she'd lost. And now they would be witness to all that her future held.

Her eyes creased at the corners and her lips softened into a smile. "Well, old girl," she said, turning from side to side. "You will, most certainly, need a new dress."

∽

Out of the corner of her eye, through the open window, Marilla could see a skirt flapping across the field and peered closer. Rachel? Running? It couldn't be. Though her oldest daughter was the spit of her mother, Rachel's heft left no doubt as to who it was. "Now what in the name of heavens would she be running for, or from?" Marilla muttered as she made her way downstairs.

The back door opened just as Marilla reached the kitchen. Rachel stumbled in and made her way to the table where she sat huffing and holding her chest.

"Good heavens, Rachel. What is this all about? Has something happened to Thomas? The children?"

Rachel shook her head and held up a hand. When she'd sufficiently got hold of herself she started: "You will not believe this, Marilla. You will not believe what I just heard."

Always one for gossip, Rachel didn't miss much of the goings-on in Avonlea.

Marilla rolled her eyes and headed to the pantry for water. She passed Rachel a glass and took the seat beside her. "No, I probably won't, but you might as well tell me anyway. I can't believe you'd get yourself all upset over something you heard. And running, no less." Marilla smoothed out her apron and drew on what little patience she had left for idle gossip. "Go on then, what did you hear?"

Rachel's eyes went wide. "John Blythe is coming home."

Marilla, shocked at hearing his name, sat motionless for so long that Rachel was not the only one who had to catch her breath.

"Coming home? After all these years. Surely not. Where did you hear this?"

"Lloyd down at the general store told Clarence and Clarence told Thomas." Rachel leaned toward Marilla and lowered her voice. "Apparently, he's coming back to open up the old homestead. Imagine, coming back to Avonlea. A place he said he would never, *ever* set foot in again. Do you remember that, Marilla?"

"Of course I remember." Marilla rose quickly, reached for the kettle, and set it to boil. She stood at the stove, lost in thought. The year Bertha was born, twenty-two years ago. The year her mother had humiliated him with her plan. "Has he been up in Toronto all this time?"

"Apparently," Rachel said. "And he's done well for himself, so they say."

"Now, I'm only asking because I'm curious." Marilla shook a finger at Rachel as she continued. "Don't make something out of nothing." She reached for the teapot and cups on the sideboard and placed them on the table. "But did they happen to say if he ever married?"

The Rachel who jumped up from the table was not the mother of eleven children. The look on her face took Marilla back to when they were girls, and when she grabbed her hand and started twirling her in a circle, Marilla struggled not to laugh.

"Oh for goodness' sake, Rachel. I knew it. I knew you'd go on."

"Oh, but it's so romantic," Rachel said, clasping her hands together. "After all this time. He's come back. And the two of you—"

"What foolishness," Marilla said, stopping Rachel mid-sentence. "And the two of us, what? Pick up from the last time I saw him? You always were a bit fickle, Rachel, I don't mind saying… but this?"

Matthew stepped into the kitchen just then and stared at Marilla, who looked a bit flushed. "Afternoon, Rachel. Saw someone running toward the house. Was that you?"

"Yes it was me. Why?" she said in response to Matthew's smirk. "You never saw a woman run across a field before?"

"Well now, it's been a while. What's happened?"

Marilla removed the whistling kettle from the stove and walked to the table. "Nothing has happened," she said, pouring the water into the pot. She stared at Rachel. "And nothing will."

Rachel, undeterred, started to make plans. "He arrives next Friday. Thomas is picking him up at the ferry. And he'll be in church on Sunday, no doubt, so you can see him then."

"*I'm* pickin' him up," Matthew said, surprising them both. "Thomas already asked me."

Marilla's words were sharp as she faced Matthew. "You knew about this? About John? And never said a word?"

"Thought it best not to, I suppose."

"Right," Marilla said, catching herself. "Well, it makes no difference one way or the other," Marilla said. "Now sit, the two of you. Tea's steeped."

They sat around the table, pouring and stirring. Adding sugar and milk. Rachel trying her best to tamp down her excitement while Matthew sat building up the nerve to speak.

Holding his teacup in his weathered hands, Matthew found his sister's eyes across the table. "Some folks thinking he might be coming back for you, Marilla."

Marilla, so stunned to hear Matthew utter what Rachel had just been saying, coughed and spluttered, sending a spray of tea across the table. Rachel snorted, and Matthew let out a hoot of laughter. Marilla, unable to speak at first, finally joined them, and the sound of their laughter rolled back the years until they were young again. Back before they knew what life had in store. The sound released a memory held within Marilla's heart. Of a time long ago, a time before William, when John had been the first boy she'd ever kissed.

"What foolishness," she scoffed, though a feeling of something like hope flickered. She reached up and straightened her hair while the thought of dresses, for the second time that day, occupied her thoughts.

∾

As expected, the church that Sunday was crowded. The news had spread of John's return, and the curious along with the faithful filled the pews. The rain had not let up in two days, and Marilla stood just inside the entrance, fussing with the hem of her dress. They were late, and Marilla had run ahead while Matthew tied up the wagon. A gentleman entered and stopped right in front of her, blocking not only the light from the doorway but her view into the church as well. Thinking it was Matthew, she raised her head and scowled.

"Marilla?" The man's eyes opened wide as he stared, then dropped from her face to the bottom of her skirt. She flushed under the gaze of her first beau and let the hem of her dress drop, covering her petticoat splattered with mud. It was him.

"Welcome back, John," was all she managed to say before a woman carrying a little boy rushed in behind him.

"John, there you are." She glanced quickly at Marilla then continued, "Darling, could you please run back to the wagon and get the basket?" The little boy wriggled free and ran into the church. She panicked and took chase. "Gilbert Blythe, you come back here."

Marilla stared at John and waited, hoping he couldn't see her heart pounding inside her chest or the disappointment and shame that clouded her eyes.

He smiled. "My wife and son," he said, nodding in the direction she'd run. He fidgeted with his hat, turning it over in his hands, then cleared his throat. "I want him to grow up in Avonlea."

"Yes, of course. That's lovely." Marilla forced a smile. "Congratulations, John."

"So much has changed since I left." He stared at his boots and shuffled nervously. "Perhaps we'll have time later to talk." He looked into her eyes and Marilla, for just a moment, glimpsed the hurt and longing he still carried with him. "I want you to know—"

"No, John, please don't." Marilla held up her hand. "It was a long time ago. Like you said, so much has changed. For both of us." Tears misted her view and she pulled her shawl tight around her, straightened her back, and walked away so he wouldn't see.

Matthew, walking up the stairs, met Marilla on the way out. "Where are you going?" he asked, watching her cross the church-yard and head toward the road. "Marilla?"

She could hear his voice behind her but didn't turn. She kept her head down and walked as fast as her dampened skirt and petticoat would allow. That it hurt so much surprised her. What had she expected? A romantic reunion in the middle of the church? An erasing of all the deceit that had torn their lives apart? She cursed and muttered and walked till she could go no further.

She was struggling to catch her breath when a crack of thunder split the heavens wide open. She stood, unwilling to run, while the rain splattered all around her. She could no more outrun this than she could her past, so she raised her face and let it wash over her. Shame and bitterness heated her face and fuelled her anger.

"I told them it was foolishness." She cursed aloud, then slowly started walking. A chill gripped her and she began to shake. "But I never thought I would be the fool."

CHAPTER 33

⁂

July 1864
Avonlea, PEI

MARILLA LAY IN BED STARING AT THE DRESS HANGING ON the hook behind the door. She'd never made it to the wedding, and the despair she felt kept her in bed long after the croup had run its course. Nearly a month had gone by since she'd arrived home, drenched to the bone, and crawled into bed. It was the fever that finally brought the doctor, and between Rachel and Matthew they'd spent days and nights watching over her until it broke.

When she gained awareness and realized it was too late to go, and that she would have been too weak to travel even if it wasn't, she'd piled that sorrow on top of her shame and burrowed beneath the quilts. Matthew was the one who'd written the letter to Bertha explaining what had happened. But she'd not likely gotten it until after the wedding, and the thought of Bertha standing there thinking she hadn't cared enough to show up nearly broke Marilla's heart. That her own foolishness had been the cause of missing it, the most important day of her daughter's life, made her furious just to think of it. A rage would well up, nearly choking her, and she would cry herself to sleep.

Matthew slowly closed the bedroom door and crept quietly downstairs. Seeing Marilla buried beneath her quilts, fighting all attempts at rousing her, was more than he could bear. That he'd played a part in causing it, going along with Rachel like he'd done, made it worse. She was on her way over now and Matthew prayed she'd break through the weariness that had gripped his sister.

He would be lost without Marilla. He'd always known this, but he felt it more now than ever. Especially since the pain, which sometimes squeezed his chest till he couldn't breathe, seemed to be getting worse.

∾

Rachel sat on the side of the bed and waited. She'd cajoled and fussed and fluffed and finally propped a reluctant Marilla up against her pillows and girded herself for the speech she'd practiced all through her walk over.

"Marilla, I need to apologize."

Marilla raised her hand to stop what she didn't want rehashed. "You managed to get the mud out of the dress. That's enough."

"Please, let me say what I've come to say, then I'll leave you in peace." Rachel cleared her throat. "Let me start by saying I feel terrible. Getting your hopes up like that. It was cruel of me. But Marilla, you have to believe me, if I'd known he was married, I would never have suggested that John was coming back for you."

"Apology accepted. But I will only forgive you if you promise to end any further discussion about it."

"But you almost died," Rachel said, pleading her case.

"Oh for goodness' sake, you and Matthew, making the biggest fuss over the croup. Look at me, I'm perfectly fine."

"Then why have you not gotten yourself up and out of that bed?"

Rachel watched Marilla's eyes fill with tears as she struggled to speak. "Because I can't seem to find a reason to." A single tear slid down her face and it nearly broke Rachel's heart. She'd never seen Marilla like this, and it frightened her into action.

"Well I'll give you one." She pulled back the quilts, then reached for Marilla's robe lying on the floor.

"What are you doing?" Marilla said, startled.

"I'm doing what any friend would." Rachel tossed her the robe and started for the door. "Put that on and get yourself downstairs. I'll start the water and prepare the tub."

"The tub?"

"Yes, the tub. You need a bath. And after that we're going for a walk."

"A walk?"

"Yes, Marilla, a walk." She rushed to the window, pulled back the curtain, and pointed. "Out there!"

Sunlight, which Marilla hadn't seen in weeks, flooded the room and she squinted against it.

"Because if you're looking for a reason to live, you'll never find it in here. Life's out there, Marilla. And I'm taking you, dragging and screaming if I have to, out to find it."

Marilla slowly stood, her legs weak after a month in bed, and struggled to push her arms through the sleeves of her robe. Rachel's retreating back reminded her of poor Etta, stalking out of the room back in Halifax all those years ago, and the steaming, soothing bath that had restored her then.

And as much as Marilla wanted to defy her, Rachel had succeeded in planting a seed. The thought of walking to the shore and filling her lungs with cool salt air pulled Marilla forward, making her reach outside herself, if only just a little bit, to the life that lay beyond.

∾

It was almost the end of September before the next letter arrived. And the only thing that kept Marilla from thinking the worst was the knowledge that Bertha was a newlywed after all, and not likely to be spending much time writing letters to anyone.

Rachel had been successful in pulling her out of the lethargy she'd fallen into and Marilla was grateful, as was Matthew, that she'd finally joined the land of the living. On Monday morning, a week after her recovery, the site of Matthew walking, with a pace he rarely had energy for, down the lane toward her lifted her heart with joyous anticipation. He'd walked to the general store to buy nails, or so he'd said, but with the post office two doors down, she knew he'd pay a visit.

She dropped the sheet she was pinning on the line and rushed to meet him. As she got closer, he pulled an envelope out of his jacket pocket and waved it in her direction. Marilla grabbed it and held it to her chest.

"Thank heavens," she whispered, then looked up into the face of her brother and was once again filled with gratitude.

"Well now come on, let's not stand out here." His attempt at gruffness to hide his own excitement would never be successful, Marilla thought. Not when he himself was grinning from ear to ear.

They made their way to the kitchen and took their places at the table. Marilla tore at the envelope and pulled out the letter.

Dearest Marilla,

I do hope this letter finds you in good health. It was so very kind of your brother to write and let me know you were ill. I was very worried, as you can imagine, especially since you didn't arrive for the wedding. But please, I don't want you feeling guilty. These things happen and can't be helped. Father was there, though his health is poor, and the day was glorious.

Married life has been so wonderful and Walter is the best husband I could have ever asked for. We found a little yellow house to rent and had a wonderful summer together settling in.

"Oh Matthew, they have a little yellow house."
Matthew waved his hand impatiently, urging her to continue.

I felt so sad when he had to return to work. Sad, because I used to love teaching and we always worked together, and because I now have to spend my days without him. But I didn't stay sad for long, because Marilla, I have the most exciting news. I'm having a baby!

Marilla's shriek startled Matthew until she jumped up, walked in a circle, and started laughing. "Oh my, what wonderful news, Matthew! She's having a baby. Our Bertha is having a baby."

The talk of married life and babies made Matthew squirm in his seat and he was about to leave and let Marilla read the rest in private when a thought struck him. "You're going to be a grandmother, Marilla. Imagine that, a grandmother."

The warmth and loveliness contained in that one word brought Marilla back to her chair. Her hands shook as she continued to read.

I can hardly believe it. Not having a mother from a very young age left me unprepared for all aspects of married life, as you can imagine, and so it took my neighbour to finally set me straight and ease my mind. I'd been sick you see and tired and I was worried that maybe I had what my mother had.

"Oh the poor thing," Marilla muttered as she thought back to the day when she herself learned the truth of her own pregnancy. Thank goodness it had been Aunt Martha and not a neighbour, Marilla thought.

Walter, of course, is thrilled with the news and we look forward to spring when the baby is due. Walter's birthday is in March. Wouldn't it be wonderful if she could be born on his? Did I just say she? Oh dear, I better not let Walter hear that. Speaking of Walter, I must finish this letter now and start his supper. Please pass along my gratitude to your brother and please, do continue to write, Marilla. I look forward to receiving your letters, and even though I'm married now, they continue to be a great source of comfort.

With kindest regards,
Bertha

CHAPTER 34

❧⟨♦⟩❧

October 22, 1864

Avonlea, PEI

*T*HE WEEKS PASSED, AND AT THE END OF OCTOBER ON A
beautiful fall day, Rachel's oldest daughter was married.
Marilla finally had the chance to wear her dress and even managed to greet John Blythe, his wife, and his little boy, who were there
attending the event. No one except Rachel and Matthew knew what
had happened on that day back in June when Marilla had run home
through the rain. But now, with Bertha's joyful news tucked inside
her heart, the humiliation was beginning to fade. And she found
herself with enough happiness in her own life that it took nothing
away when she offered it to others.

Christmas came and went like it always did, with little fuss.
Except for the Christmas Eve service. Where Matthew found himself sitting behind Violet and her two youngest daughters. She'd
lost her husband during the summer and they'd come to spend
Christmas with her sister and family in Avonlea. It was the first
time Matthew had seen her in over twenty years. He'd shown not
a trace of emotion during the service, but Marilla had had to help
him into the wagon, so weakened was he by his regret.

The winter of 1865 was soon upon them. And it was the worst
Matthew could remember. The bitter cold kept him and Marilla

inside close to the stove, and with the roads not passable the horses and cows were confined to the barn. And though he hadn't remembered the date himself, Marilla baked Matthew a cake to celebrate his forty-ninth birthday at the end of February. Rachel and Thomas had gladly joined them. Marilla knew Rachel loved sweets, but it was more likely the relief from being housebound with all their children that motivated them to brave the weather. They'd hiked across the pasture, and when Marilla opened the door to greet them, they were so covered in snow they stood like snowmen on the porch.

By the time March rolled around, not a day passed where they didn't wonder about Bertha. And Matthew haunted the post office so often a rumour had started that Violet, who'd started visiting Avonlea more often, was pursuing him once again.

It was well into April before the letter they'd been waiting for arrived. Matthew stumbled into the kitchen to tell Marilla, only to find her sitting at the table with Rachel and her daughter. Marilla knew by the look on his face what he held in his hand, and putting all manners and decorum aside, she shuffled the ladies out the door with apologies that Matthew wasn't feeling well. They expressed their concern and promised to check back with her later.

Marilla quickly poured Matthew a cup of tea while he placed the envelope in the middle of the table. They sat staring, each lost in their own thoughts, thinking of the night Rachel had lost her firstborn and all that could go wrong, until Marilla finally reached for the envelope and with hands shaking, tore it open. It was dated April 20.

Dear Marilla,
My apologies for not writing sooner, but it's been a difficult time.

Marilla started to shake and her vision blurred.

I have the saddest news to tell you along with the happiest. Father died back in February. And knowing he would never get the chance to see or hold his grandchild nearly broke my heart and made the final days of my confinement very difficult.

"Oh, poor Bertha," Marilla said. "What a heartache to have to bear."

The happy news is that I have a beautiful baby girl.

"A granddaughter," Marilla shouted. "I have a granddaughter!"

Our baby was born on March 5 and I always loved my middle name so as soon as I saw her I knew it would be hers.

When Marilla saw the baby's name, her heart filled with love. Catherine had made a promise all those years ago, and within this child was the proof of just how much that promise had endured. She pulled a handkerchief from her skirt pocket and wiped her eyes before reading on.

She's the tiniest little thing, with the most darling face you've ever seen! Walter is so very proud and we're happier than we ever imagined we could be.

She pressed the letter to her chest. "Can't you just picture her, Matthew? Doesn't she sound perfect?"
She picked up the letter and continued.

But I've not been myself since she was born. With the loss of my father and my lack of appetite, I'm finding it difficult to get back on my feet. I'm sure in time this will pass and by summer I'll be carrying her all over town. The feeling I'm having that I can't explain to anyone is that I feel as if I've been orphaned. Which sounds so silly, I know. But with both of my parents gone, I feel as if the connection to my past is lost.

Marilla held the letter to her chest. "My poor, sweet Bertha." She sniffed, wiped her nose, and took a deep breath.

I only wish that my daughter could have grown up with grandparents. I never had any myself and I always thought it would have been so nice. You are the closest person I have now, Marilla, and I would love for you to visit and get to know her. Maybe when the weather improves. It certainly has been a very damp spring. I'll write again soon when I'm feeling better.

With kindest regards,
Bertha

Matthew held his breath, waiting for what would come next. Though he wanted to leap out of his chair and say it, he knew it was not his place. It would be up to her. He wanted it more than he'd ever wanted anything. Bertha and her daughter were the only kin they had left, and they mightn't be long for this world, he and Marilla, but living it as an uncle and grandmother would be the best reward for a life lived in the shadows.

The silence stretched between them as Marilla sat wiping her eyes and swallowing tears. When she finally spoke, Matthew breathed a sigh of relief.

"She does have a grandmother. *I'm* her grandmother. Why can't she know me?" Marilla stood and started pacing. "For that matter, why can't Bertha? I'm *her* mother. She's not orphaned. I'm right here." Marilla thumped her chest. "I'm going, Matthew. I don't care how irrational you think I am. This is not like the last time. There are no other lives to upset. They're all gone." Marilla's head was spinning with the realization that there was no longer any reason for Bertha not to know. The face she turned to Matthew was determined and resolute. "I'm going to see Bertha, and I'm going to tell her the truth."

Matthew, filled with hope, listened as Marilla started making her plan.

"Don't fret, I won't go till the crops are in," she said, pacing and wringing her hands.

"Who's fretting?" Matthew said but knew she hadn't heard.

"And then I'll write Etta. That's what I'll do." Marilla continued, unaware that he'd risen to leave.

"I'll stay with her, I know she'd love that. She gets so lonely now that Aunt Martha is gone. I'll ask her to knit a sweater set for the baby and I'll buy the layette." Marilla's face brightened. "Then I'll take the train to Truro—does it make a run every Sunday, I wonder?"

"I think it sounds like a fine plan," Matthew said, winking at her as he passed. Her prattling stopped for just a moment and she smiled, remembering he was there. Matthew closed the door, leaving the sound of Marilla's excited planning behind him, and headed for the horses. "Uncle Matthew," he said aloud into the hollow of the barn. "I must say, I like the sound of that."

༄

Etta was indeed thrilled to have Marilla visit. At sixty-five she had few friends left, let alone family. She missed Martha terribly, and having Marilla in the house briefly filled the void, bringing the memories of Martha and their time together back to life. And the enjoyment she found in knitting a sweater for Bertha's baby was immeasurable, though thinking of Marilla as a grandmother did nothing to dispel the reality of how old she herself had become. She'd stopped all committee work when Martha died, having lost too much heart to continue, but still did what she could when asked.

The work she'd done for so many years in helping find homes for babies had been improved by the opening of an Orphan Home in Halifax. Mrs. MacDonald, who'd taken in so many babies over the years, had worked hard to fundraise and see that it was built. An older woman by the name of Miss Carlyle had been awarded the contract to operate the facility, and though she spoke of a strong desire to continue Mrs. MacDonald's work, Etta felt it was the financial gain that motivated her more. She often asked Etta's advice, but more often than not it was donations she was seeking.

They wrapped the gifts, packed a lunch along with Marilla's bags, and at the end of June, on one of the first mornings the warmth of the sun shining over Halifax made summer seem possible, they headed to the train station.

"So, your plan is to stay for the week and return on Sunday?"

"That's my plan. But until I arrive, and with all that we have to talk about, and if I'm any help at all with the baby, I may stay longer."

"Oh don't be silly, you'll do just fine. I wish Martha was here. I know she would agree, that this is the right thing to do. And she'd be so proud...." Etta swallowed the lump in her throat. "As am I."

Marilla squeezed Etta's hand and whispered, "Thank you, Etta, for everything."

The train whistle blew and the steam billowed as Marilla climbed aboard.

"I'll be here on Sunday, regardless," Etta said, stepping back.

"And if I'm not on it," Marilla shouted, "I'll be on the next."

"Good luck, Marilla." Etta shouted as the train pulled away. "All the best to Bertha, and your dear little grandchild."

CHAPTER 35

$\mathcal{T}$HE TRAIN RUMBLED INTO THE STATION JUST PAST THREE, waking Marilla, who'd dozed off after eating the lunch Etta had packed. The instructions she'd received from Bertha were that Walter would meet her and bring her to their home. The school was not far from the station and with the train arriving after the end of his workday, he'd be there upon its arrival.

She stepped down along with the other passengers and made her way inside. Her stomach fluttered with nerves and she wished now she'd availed herself of the modern facilities found on the train.

Aside from looking for the tall, well-dressed man she remembered from the graduation, Marilla was quite confident Walter's red hair would make him stand out in any gathering. She scanned the small station, and when she didn't see anyone fitting his description, she found a bench and sat waiting. A woman with two little ones sat perched on the other end and smiled in greeting. "Never fails," she muttered. "He's always late."

Marilla nodded in sympathy just as a man, out of breath and panting, rushed through the door. "Sorry, my darling, but it couldn't be helped. The school is still in chaos, and with only a few days left, the superintendent decided to let the children out early."

He looked at Marilla, furrowed his brow, and spoke.

"You look familiar. Are you from around here?"

"No. I've come up from Halifax to visit with my...family." Saying it out loud, even to a stranger, made Marilla all the more anxious to get to Bertha and let her know she still had one.

"Well, I'm not sure that was a wise decision."

The man's wife stood quickly. Marilla could tell she was embarrassed by her husband's interference.

"Joseph, you're being rude. You mustn't say that."

He continued as if she hadn't spoken. "There's been an outbreak of scarlet fever in the past few weeks. Word's not made it to Halifax yet, I suppose. We've lost several of our students to it and—" His wife huffed, gathered the children, pushed past the people milling about, and headed outside. He hesitated before continuing. "And two of our closest friends." He shook his head as if he still couldn't believe it. "She's frightened, is all. Won't let the children hear a word said about it, and here I am blathering on. But you do look so familiar."

Marilla looked at the large clock hanging on the wall behind the ticket booth and realized it was now past four. A prickle of concern prompted her to ask. "Excuse me sir, but I'm wondering if you know of a Walter—"

The man's mouth opened and his eyes filled with recognition. "You're Marilla Cuthbert."

"Yes, how did you know?"

And though he answered, his voice remained wary. "I remember you from the graduation five years ago when you came to see Bertha. I'm Joseph Smith. I was a good friend of Walter's."

Marilla was so pleased to find a friend that knew Bertha she began to relax. "Oh my goodness, what a coincidence. Yes, I was there, but with so many of you gathered that day, I can't say I remember you."

Marilla's thoughts began to race. *Why did he say that he was a friend of Walter's?* "And were you at their wedding?"

With that, the man's face turned ashen and somehow she knew, but rushed on, racing against a sense of panic that threatened. "She told me there were friends attending"—Marilla tried to keep her voice light, even as the words *scarlet fever* circled—"and some teachers from the school...."

But then she stopped and stared in horror as tears glistened in this man's, this stranger's eyes. Marilla's breath caught in her throat and she jumped up from where she'd been sitting and rushed outside looking for Walter. To end this silliness. This misunderstanding. She rushed back inside. "Joseph, where is Walter?"

"Miss Cuthbert, when last did you hear from Bertha?"

She rambled on as panic seized her "Well, not since sometime in May. The poor thing. She wasn't feeling well and said she was looking forward to my visit..."

The words *We lost two of our dearest friends* echoed in her head.

"...And that Walter would come to the station to meet me. Why, Joseph? Why do you ask?"

Joseph's wife came in search of her husband, was calling out his name, till she saw the look on his face, then stopped.

"Didn't you know?" he said, reaching for her hand. "She's dead, Marilla. So is Walter. They both died. The fever took them two weeks ago."

Marilla faltered as the words tilted her world, as the image of their bodies lying cold in the ground pierced her. Then like an explosion, she lunged at him, clutched at the front of his jacket, and screamed. "Where's the baby? Where is she?"

It was then he spoke the words that crumpled Marilla to the floor and frightened them both with the ferociousness of her scream.

"I don't know. She was taken away. Given to a family." He watched as her legs gave out and tried to explain. "They had no choice. There was no one else."

ᔿ

Marilla fought to breathe and flailed against those who reached to help her. She raged and wailed and prayed she'd wake from a nightmare she couldn't understand. The rest remained a blur. Of voices raised and feet scurrying.

She was carried. Felt air on her face. The bump and rattle of a wagon. Doors opening and closing. The sound of hushed whispers till at last, the nothingness of sleep released her.

The room was dim when she finally woke, and someone placed a cool cloth on her brow.

"How are you feeling?"

Marilla struggled to speak. "Where am I?"

"You're in our home, Miss Cuthbert. I'm Lenore, Joseph's wife, the man you met at the train station. Here, drink some of this."

She lowered a mug to Marilla's lips and tilted it forward. The whiskey seared Marilla's throat as she swallowed, making her splutter and gag.

"It's horrible, I know, but I can assure you, it will help."

Marilla grasped at the woman's hand and started pleading. "Please, tell me this is not true. Tell me this is all a dreadful mistake."

She tried to sit up but Lenore gently lowered her back against the pillow. "I'm so sorry, Miss Cuthbert. We'll talk more of this later, but right now you need to rest. You've had a terrible shock." Mrs. Smith tucked the blankets around Marilla and quietly slipped from the room.

Marilla lay as if weighted. Her limbs felt detached, severed. And all that was left was her heart, with its secret tucked inside, beating alone in the middle of the bed, while Walter and Bertha lay in their graves. And her granddaughter, whom she'd never know, taken. She hadn't any strength left to cry, but could feel tears, blistering with anger and regret, slide down her face and wet the pillow.

∽

Etta had been summoned and arrived three days later to take Marilla back to Halifax. When she stepped into Mr. and Mrs. Smith's parlour, the woman that stood as she entered was almost unrecognizable. Marilla's hair, dirty and dishevelled, had been gathered into an untidy coil at her nape. The dress she wore was wrinkled as if slept in, and her eyes were hollow and lifeless.

When she finally recognized Etta, for she'd been staring as if from a distance, Marilla's eyes brimmed with tears and a strangled cry escaped her. Etta gathered her into her arms and cradled her while she wept.

Etta whispered and shushed, unable to hold back tears of her own. "I've come to take you home, Marilla. And though there are no words for the depth of your loss, I want you to know that I am so very, very sorry."

෴

Etta had written to Matthew as soon as she'd received word and she prayed it would be delivered before Marilla arrived home. And though Etta had struggled to get answers as to the baby's whereabouts, no one had any to give. The outbreak had left people frightened and the town in mourning. They'd laid flowers at Bertha and Walter's graves and Etta had had to coax a reluctant Marilla to board the train for the trip back to Halifax.

For the week remaining before she left for the Island, Etta focused on restoring Marilla's strength, for this journey back to Green Gables would be on her own. Though thoughts of Bertha and Walter prompted tears on their walks, the fresh air did prove to be a source of comfort for Marilla. Especially by the waterfront, where the sight and sound of gulls circling the fishing boats and the smell of salt air seemed to relax her and on occasion produced a lifting of her face, if not a smile.

With the purchase of a fresh cod wrapped and tucked in their basket, they made their way along North Park Street. Marilla stopped and stared at the grey stone building set back from the road. Behind the gate, children could be seen playing in the yard as their laughter filled the air.

"I don't remember this building, Etta. What is it?"

"It's the orphanage I wrote to you about a few years back."

"The Orphan Home?" Marilla said. "Yes, I do remember." She looked at Etta. "And these children, the ones playing there, are who all those socks go to?"

"Hats and mittens too," Etta said proudly. "It comforts me to know that I'm still able to help."

Etta could see sadness gathering on Marilla's face and hurried her along.

"At least my granddaughter did not end up there," Marilla said and trailed behind. "My Anne."

~

Marilla packed her bag in preparation for the trip back home and placed it in the front hall. On their last night together, Etta had prepared roast chicken, normally one of Marilla's favourites, but her appetite had yet to improve and she felt guilty for leaving most of it on her plate.

"Not to worry, Marilla," Etta said as she watched her struggle. "I'll pack the rest for your journey across the water."

Tears welled at the kindness of Etta's words and the reminder that she was going back to Matthew with nothing but sorrow to offer. She slept fitfully, and in the morning gathered herself for the moment when she had to leave.

Marilla looked one last time at the bedroom where Bertha was born, the room she'd once told Marilla she dreamed of, and headed down the stairs. Etta was outside talking to her neighbour, Mr. Roberts. He was driving Marilla to the ferry and had arrived early, eager to help. Her bag was already stored inside the wagon and Etta was patting the horse as it snorted and huffed.

When Etta heard the front door open, the smile she'd worn for her neighbour fell away and she walked quickly toward Marilla.

"Come inside, dear. I have something to give you."

Marilla stood in the hallway and watched Etta scurry to the kitchen. She returned with a basket, whose bright red napkin did little to ease the ache that clutched at her heart.

Etta's eyes were bright with tears, but her voice remained firm. "There's biscuits, a little jar of jam, and of course there will be tea on the boat. There's chicken and...."

Marilla removed the basket from Etta's hands and placed it at their feet. She gathered Etta and held her close as she wept.

"You were right. There are no words for my sorrow and there never will be," Marilla whispered. "But there are also no words for how much you mean to me except to say, I love you. Goodbye, Etta."

Marilla picked up the basket, headed out the door, and never looked back.

PART IV

COMING
HOME

CHAPTER 36

April 25, 1876
Orphan Home, Halifax, NS

*T*HE MATRON HAD SUMMONED ANNE TO HER OFFICE. Terrified they'd found yet another fault in her behaviour, one deemed worthy of punishment, or to right the wrongs of being an "ungrateful, heathen child," as matron often called her, Anne sat on the opposite side of Miss Carlyle's desk, squirming in her seat and fiddling with the buttons on the collar of a dress that was too small.

"Anne Shirley! Sit up and stop fidgeting. You are eleven years old, not a child. And you must begin to demonstrate behaviour more becoming of a young lady rather than that of a street urchin."

I've only been here a year, Anne thought, *and already I'm grown up?*

"Yes, ma'am," Anne said, keeping her head down, thus avoiding any criticism for the insincerity matron would undoubtedly see in her eyes.

"There's a visitor here to see you, Anne. A Mrs. Hepworth of Truro. She and her husband owned the property on which your parents lived and where you were born."

Anne sat up and leaned forward. Hearing the words *home* and *parents* caused a fluttering in her chest. "She knew my parents?"

Matron continued as if Anne hadn't spoken. "After your parents passed away, the house, which they rented from the Hepworths, was boarded up. Well, according to Mrs. Hepworth, they sold the house recently to a young family and when they were cleaning it out, they found a box that belonged to your mother. And after considerable effort in tracking your whereabouts, Mrs. Hepworth brought it here. She felt it was important that you have it."

Anne paled at the significance of the words. Miss Carlyle, not wanting a scene in view of Mrs. Hepworth and hoping a small financial gain might be forthcoming, spoke softly. "Now Anne, listen to me. I'm going to bring Mrs. Hepworth in to meet you, and you must behave. Do you understand?"

Anne already knew that children not behaving well reflected poorly on matron. And though it was often used, along with the strap, to put the fear of God in all of them, knowing that it was in fact matron's own worst fear gave Anne a small measure of her own worth.

"Yes, ma'am."

Miss Carlyle opened the office door and ushered Mrs. Hepworth inside. In her hands was a small metal box, which she placed on the desk in front of Anne before taking a seat beside her.

Anne stared. She had never owned anything that belonged to her mother. And the very thought that the same hands that held her as a baby had held this box sent shivers along her arms. And meeting someone who had known her mother, who had been in her presence, made her seem real and not just something her imagination had dreamed up.

"Hello, Anne. I'm sure Miss Carlyle has explained everything to you. And she, of course, could have simply given you the box herself. But I was so anxious to meet you and to see for myself that you are well cared for."

Anne reached out and touched Mrs. Hepworth's hand, hoping some warmth of her mother still remained. Mrs. Hepworth's sharp intake of breath caused matron to scowl. But when she placed her hand atop Anne's and blinked away tears, matron relaxed.

"You were just a baby. And it all happened so fast. The next thing I knew, your parents, and you, were simply gone." She patted Anne's hand and smiled as she remembered. "She was such a lovely person, your mother. And she adored you. It was all so tragic." She reached for her handkerchief and dapped at her eyes.

"So when we found this box belonging to her, I knew I had to find you. I feel I owe it to her...and to you. This is not the life she hoped you'd have, Anne, but perhaps you'll find some comfort in having something of hers to cherish."

Anne reached across the desk, heedless of matron's reproach for not having asked permission, and picked it up. She placed it in her lap, felt the weight of all that was left of her mother's life, and forced back tears she dared not show.

"Thank you, Mrs. Hepworth," Anne said "I am very grateful to you for finding me, and for bringing me something of my mother's."

Mrs. Hepworth then slid an envelope across the desk. "This is a contribution to the fine work of your orphanage, and of course to Anne's care."

Miss Carlyle snatched at the envelope, then, realizing she may have looked much too anxious, demurred and slid it slowly across the desk.

"And perhaps this goes without saying, but I would like Anne, as rightful heir to her mother's belongings, to be assured that, regardless of the value of the contents, this box now belongs to her and her alone."

"Why yes, Mrs. Hepworth, of course. You have my word."

Mrs. Hepworth reached into her handbag and removed a key tied to a tiny yellow ribbon and handed it to Anne. Suddenly overcome with emotion, Mrs. Hepworth stood, indicating the meeting was over. Matron came out from behind the desk and walked her to the door. When she turned around to say goodbye, Anne rushed forward, clutching the box under one arm and throwing the other around Mrs. Hepworth.

Mrs. Hepworth held her, kissed the top of her head, and whispered, "Goodbye, Anne."

❧

Anne carried the box to the ward she shared with ten other girls. The large east-facing room was empty at this time of morning and the silence felt peaceful, something the room rarely was. Anne sat with the box in the middle of her bed, and though she knew she would be late getting back to the laundry, she just had to see what was inside.

Anne placed the key inside the lock. The latch clicked and the top loosened. She opened it and looked inside. A beautiful handkerchief rested on top of the contents. The initials *B.A.S.* were stitched along the edge. Anne picked it up and brought it to her face. A hint of rosewater lingered and Anne closed her eyes and tried to imagine the woman who'd once held it.

At the bottom of the box lay a bundle of envelopes tied with ribbon, and she reached in and pulled them out. They were addressed to *Miss Bertha Willis of Truro Nova Scotia*. Her mother. She lay the stack on her bed and untied the ribbon, picking up the first one that fell free. It was dated July 14, 1862.

> *Dear Bertha,*
>
> *I enjoyed our picnic on Sunday past so very much, and hope that, with your permission, I can accompany you to the annual church supper on Saturday. All of the teachers will be there, of course, so we will be well chaperoned, but it would mean so much to me if we could share a table together. Please don't think me forward. It's no secret to anyone that you mean a great deal to me.*
>
> *Yours truly,*
> *Walter Shirley*

My father, Anne thought. *This is from my father.* Tears stung her eyes and she held the letter close to her heart.

Anne reached out and pulled another envelope from the pile. This one was addressed to *Miss Marilla Cuthbert in Prince Edward*

Island and had never been opened. "Who might that be?" Anne whispered as she opened the letter. It was dated June 1, 1865.

Dear Marilla, I have not recovered as hoped and Walter has now fallen ill. We desperately need your help and ask that you make arrangements to visit as soon as possible. You are a dear friend and I feel as close to you as I did my own mother and father. We are struggling to care for Anne and there is no one we'd rather have to care for her than you.

Yours truly,
Bertha

Anne could hear footsteps in the hall and quickly placed the letters back in the box, locked it, and placed it in the nightstand beside her bed. She straightened her quilt and headed to the laundry to finish her chores before lunch. Her steps were light and her heart was filled with hope. There was someone out there, beyond these stone walls. Someone who knew her. Someone like family. As soon as lunch was over, she would write her own letter. To Miss Marilla Cuthbert in Prince Edward Island.

∽

The front parlour of Mrs. Stevens's house was packed. The mail wagon, driven by her husband, had been late, and while she sorted and stamped, the grumbling from those gathered in the front parlour and down the hall had begun. She'd taken over the position of postmistress after Mrs. Webber, God rest her soul, passed away. And after ten years of providing the residents of Avonlea with their mail, Mrs. Stevens felt strongly that Mrs. Webber's name be added to the list of saints displayed at St. Luke's for having endured the previous thirty-five.

"Already May, and here we are still waiting for word from that bunch over in Charlottetown."

"Last year it was grass they wanted us to plant. In a field meant for potatoes! Did you ever hear the likes?"

"What about the year before? When they wanted us using manure for fertilizer instead of seaweed? Made no sense at all."

"Imagine thinking some fancy Agricultural Society knows better what to plant than the ones farming the land for years."

"And feed prices!"

Mrs. Stevens stared at the envelope in her hand and cleared her throat. "Excuse me, gentlemen. Has anyone seen Matthew Cuthbert this morning?"

"Saw him over at the blacksmith's earlier."

"Keeps to himself that one." .

"There was a time I could set the clock by him," Mrs. Stevens said. "He'd be here every Friday morning, right at nine."

"Would've done him no good this morning, seeing how the mail was late."

Mrs. Stevens glared at the men as they nudged elbows and enjoyed a laugh. She then hollered for her husband who was sipping his tea in the kitchen: "Vernon, take over here while I run down the road."

The envelope was addressed to Miss Marilla Cuthbert, but since she'd stopped coming to the post office herself over ten years ago, after that trip to Halifax, Mrs. Stevens needed to find Matthew and give it to him to pass along.

The poor woman. Mrs. Stevens would never forget that day at the train station in Charlottetown, or the sight of Marilla when she'd arrived.

"Now when was that?" she mumbled aloud as she made her way down the road.

Had to be eleven years or more. It was just before she and Vernon had taken over the post office, she knew that. They had gone to the station to pick up his cousin, and who had been standing there? None other than Matthew Cuthbert himself. That was surprise enough, because everyone knew he didn't venture far from his fields. But when this woman had stepped down onto the platform and almost collapsed into Matthew's arms, well now. All she remembered thinking was *Who in the name of heavens is that?*

And when she finally stepped back and they'd seen who it was! Dear lord in heaven, it was Marilla. The poor woman had aged a hundred years. She and Vernon had stepped away, not wanting them to know they'd been seen. And of course they'd never said a word.

But it wasn't long after that Marilla stopped coming to the post office. And she hated to say it, even though others relished the opportunity, but it was after that Marilla became more like her own mother with each passing year. Keeping to herself. Bitter. Snappish if you looked at her the wrong way.

And Mrs. Stevens could have waited and spoken to her in church on Sunday—though it was beyond her how Marilla had continued to teach Sunday school—but a feeling of urgency, and yes, she supposed curiosity, propelled her to do otherwise.

She looked down at the letter in her hand. It wasn't odd that Marilla received mail from Halifax, she had for years and Matthew always picked it up. It did, however, seem odd that she'd be receiving a letter clearly written by a child.

CHAPTER 37

ᓚᓄᓄᓄᓚ

MATTHEW THANKED MR. SLOANE FOR HIS FINE JOB IN replacing the broken shoe, held the horse by the reins, and led it down the road toward home. The horse's best years were behind him but the thought, or even the suggestion, of putting him to pasture made Matthew bristle.

"Might as well put me right out there beside him," Matthew would argue whenever Marilla tried. But when she'd suggested he get help with the farm work, he knew he needed to listen. It was when he turned sixty a few months back that he'd realized it wasn't just the horses getting old, it was him as well.

He could see Mrs. Stevens walking toward him and he lowered his head, hoping she'd pass by silently like most women did, leaving him in peace. But when she called out his name, his chest tightened. He talked as little as needed, and to most women—other than Rachel and the minister's wife—not at all. His world had always been small, but in the past ten years it had closed in around him, leaving little room for anything beyond his own loneliness and sorrow.

"Good morning, Matthew."

"Morning ma'am," Matthew said, tipping his hat.

Mrs. Stevens held out her hand and showed Matthew an envelope. "A letter has arrived for Marilla and I felt it important she receive it. Would you please see that she gets it?"

Matthew hesitated before taking the envelope, wary now on hearing the word *important*. "Yes ma'am, I'll see to it." He then raised his head. "What makes you say it's important?"

"Well now, I don't really know. It may be nothing at all, but I couldn't help but notice the handwriting."

Matthew turned the envelope over as she spoke, and stared at the letters scrawled across the front. Memories pierced Matthew's world and he struggled to breathe. Memories of those first few letters that Bertha had sent all those years ago collided with the image of a grave and he staggered to recover. Though her voice seemed distant, Mrs. Stevens's hand reached out and steadied him as he waited to gain his footing.

"Are you all right, Matthew?"

Unable to speak, he walked away, leaving a shocked Mrs. Stevens behind holding the reins of his horse.

∾

The rocking chair had been moved years ago from its place beside the stove, where it had sat for as far back as anyone could remember, to the kitchen window overlooking the fields and barn. Marilla sat in her nightdress sipping the last of her tea while she waited for Matthew to return. She looked down and tried to summon the shame she should have felt at not yet being dressed at this hour of the morning. But she couldn't. There's no shame where there's no pride. And she felt neither.

Rachel had tried, she'd give her that, but it was no use. Over the years, Marilla had watched herself do exactly what she'd once sworn she never would: let the kind of bitterness that consumed her mother find its way into her heart and into her life. But it had. At first it was anger that made it nearly impossible to speak and she'd had many a fight with Rachel, who tried her best to help, but without knowing what happened and with Marilla refusing to say, the friendship had been strained. And then, when year after year went by, and Marilla heard of yet another grandchild being welcomed into the Lynde family fold, and when she could no longer bear to greet Rachel's smiling face at the door, the friendship they'd once shared became distant and awkward. They were neighbours nonetheless and she was grateful for that. Thomas, without fail, still checked in on Matthew each morning and evening and Marilla often left a basket of rolls or biscuits for him to carry home.

The rocker had been moved for just that reason. From here, Marilla could watch out for him as well. Ever since that day when Matthew had lain an entire morning in the field before Thomas found him, she would panic when her brother was out of sight for long. And farmhands were hard to find. The shipyard took most and the rest had gone to Upper Canada.

The decision had been made, though Matthew had fought it, to get a boy from the orphanage in Halifax to help with the farm work. Etta had written with the suggestion, no doubt thinking it would alleviate their loneliness as well as that of an orphaned boy. So when they found out the Spencers from over in Carmody were heading to Halifax at the end of June to adopt a little girl, and even though she knew Rachel would question the sanity of it, once she heard, they asked if they could bring back a boy for them. And so it had been arranged. She would write and let Etta know of their decision. Poor Etta, confined to the house more and more these days, but at seventy-six, as sharp as ever.

Marilla wasn't keen on the idea herself, though she would never say. When she thought about her own daughter who'd never set foot on the Island and then her own granddaughter who'd been flung to the far reaches of God knows where, and here they were taking in someone's else's child, her insides would churn at the injustice of it all.

Tears began to form and Marilla fought the urge to once again give in. To wallow and rage. But the minister's wife had spoken to her just that week, and if her approach to the children did not improve she would not be welcome back to teach Sunday school in the fall. Imagine! But no one understood what it was like to be surrounded by the children's laughter, their joy, their love of life when she had none. Or seeing the innocence in their eyes, their hope for the future, when all she could see was the misery that lay ahead for them.

And not one of them was hers.

They were someone else's children and grandchildren and they all looked at her with pity, knowing she'd never had her own and never would. Her pursed lips and stern voice made people shy away, Marilla knew that. They saw her as an old woman incapable of kindness, without ever knowing that, at one time, her heart had beat as strong as theirs.

Marilla placed her hands on either side of the rocker and pulled herself upright. Time to get on with it. She picked up the steaming kettle and headed to her room to wash. Just as she stepped inside, the door to the back porch flew open and banged against the wall. Startled, she set the kettle down and headed back to the kitchen. Matthew stood in the doorway, breathless and shaking.

Marilla panicked at the site of him. "What's happened?"

Matthew reached into his pocket, fought to catch his breath, and waved an envelope at Marilla.

"Matthew, look at you! All this fuss over a letter from Etta. Will you please come and sit down?" Marilla said, heading to the table. "Remember what the doctor said about your heart. It's not good to get overexcited." She turned suddenly, realizing what it could be. "It's about Etta, isn't it, Matthew? She's ill. Did someone send word that she—"

He dropped the letter on the table and collapsed in his chair. Marilla stared at the envelope and then back at Matthew. The letters that spelled out her name were boxy and crooked, and looked nothing like they should. A prickle of recognition crept up her arms and weakened her knees. She dropped into her seat at the table and reached for the envelope. Her hands shook as she tore it open and unfolded the letter.

"*Dear Miss Cuthbert,*" she read aloud, "*my name is Anne Shirley.*"

Marilla dropped the letter and screamed. Her hands clamped over her mouth to squelch the sound, and when she looked over at Matthew his eyes were filled with tears. All the hows and whys scrambled to connect and Marilla stood, snatched the letter off the table, and started pacing. "Where is she? Where is she, Matthew?"

She held the letter in shaky hands and scanned the words. "She lives in the…orphanage. In Halifax." The image of the iron gates and stone walls made her falter and Matthew rushed to her side just as she crumbled to her knees. The letter fell to the floor and Matthew picked it up and continued reading.

"She says she found your name in amongst her mother's things, and wants to know if you'll be her friend." The innocence of the words pierced Matthew and he lowered himself to the floor and cradled Marilla as her keening filled the room. "She found us," Matthew said, his voice choked with tears. "Oh thank God, she found us." He rocked Marilla and spoke gently. "We'll bring her home, Marilla. We're her family, and we'll bring her home."

Marilla looked up, and though her face was awash with tears, the light, doused when Bertha died, sparkled in her eyes. This child, her own flesh and blood was the gift, the hope, after all she'd lost. Her granddaughter, Anne Shirley, was coming home.

CHAPTER 38

～～✦～～

June 20, 1876

Orphan Home, Halifax, NS

*E*TTA STOOD OUTSIDE THE IRON GATES AND PEERED AT THE orphanage. It was dusk, and the children were inside for the night. The windows glowed with light and she wondered which room was Anne's. That she was here was a miracle. The joy Etta felt when she received Marilla's letter had not waned. She had little time left on this earth and making this one last request, for Marilla and for Anne, assured her that she'd rest in peace.

"Thank you, Mr. Roberts. I can make my way from here. I won't be long." Etta watched as her long-time neighbour, one of the few left, made his way back to the wagon to wait.

Etta, with a small satchel hanging from her arm, leaned heavily on her cane and made her way to the large front door. She knew Miss Carlyle but not well. She fingered the envelope in her coat pocket and hoped that what she had to offer would alleviate any worries the matron may have for what she was about to ask.

Miss Carlyle recognized her but seemed wary to open the door. She ushered Etta in and led the way to her office. The absence of children's voices, or any sound of laughter, made the walls feel cold and the echo of her cane on the stone floor gave Etta the chills. When they were both seated, Miss Carlyle spoke.

"It has been quite some time since you've visited the orphanage, Miss Byers. I must say I'm surprised to see you. What is it that you would like to discuss?"

Etta took a deep breath and leaned forward. "Some time in the next few days, a Mrs. Spencer from Prince Edward Island will be arriving to adopt a little girl from your orphanage. Is that correct?"

Miss Carlyle's eyes widened and she placed her hands on the desk. "Why yes, that's correct, but how—"

"I received a letter from Miss Cuthbert, who is a dear friend of mine."

"The same Miss Cuthbert who has requested a boy from this very orphanage?"

"Yes," Etta said, reaching into her pocket. She placed an envelope on the desk and watched Miss Carlyle's interest pique. Its bulk left no secret as to its contents.

"There is a young girl housed within your institution and Miss Cuthbert has requested, through me, to have her released into her care. When Mrs. Spencer arrives, please assure her, though she'll think it a mistake, that you are quite clear on Miss Cuthbert's instructions. And what she requested was most definitely a girl."

"I would not even consider a request of this kind, Miss Byers, as you well know. However, given that it is you. And given that Miss Cuthbert is a friend of yours and you trust her intentions for this request, I will do as you ask." She slid the envelope toward herself and tucked it into a drawer. "What is the child's name?"

"Her name is Anne Shirley. And I would like to see her."

༄

Anne was summoned quickly and brought to the office. When she stepped inside, her dear little face, framed by long red braids and dotted with freckles, was pale with fear, and Etta felt terrible for being the cause of her stress.

"I'd like a moment alone, Miss Carlyle, if you don't mind."

She hesitated for a moment then stepped out and closed the door.

"Hello, Anne. Please don't be frightened. My name is Miss Etta Byers and I'm a dear friend of Miss Marilla Cuthbert."

Anne's face softened with relief and she stepped toward Etta. "You know Miss Cuthbert?"

"I do," Etta said, smiling at the sound of Anne's voice. Bertha was not much younger than Anne was now when Etta had met her. And the memory of her voice filling their home tugged at her heart.

Anne's brow creased as she spoke. "I wrote her a letter. But she never wrote back. She knew my mother." Anne's face brightened with hope. "Did you?"

Etta closed her eyes. The rush of time swirled, taking her back to the night Bertha was born. To the tiny, wailing infant. To the stormy night she was thrust into.

Anne's soft fingers touched her arm and pulled her back.

"Yes, I knew your mother."

A memory flashed of Bertha's smiling face, so like Anne's, as she waved goodbye and drove off with her father, the day they left Halifax. Etta placed her hand over Anne's and fought back tears, then reached for the satchel on her arm. "Anne, I have something to give you."

Etta reached in and pulled out a bright yellow shawl. It was knit with the same yarn as the sweater set she'd knit and sent with Marilla to Truro all those years ago. The sweater set that Anne had never received. That Marilla never got the chance to give.

Etta stood slowly and when she held it out to Anne, she could see her hesitate. "Anne, listen to me carefully. Miss Cuthbert—Marilla—didn't write back to you, and certainly not because she didn't want to," Etta reassured her. "She wrote to me instead and asked that I come and speak to you directly. She didn't wish to have what she wants to say written in a letter. Do you understand?"

Anne held her breath and nodded.

"Marilla and her brother, Matthew—"

"She has a brother?"

Etta smiled. "Yes. And he's a kind, gentle man whom you will like very much."

Anne's eyes widened and Etta realized what she'd mistakenly done and rushed to explain. "They cared for your mother very much and want nothing more than to provide for you. So, they have decided to adopt you and make Prince Edward Island your home."

Anne's breath caught and she stood completely still. Etta waited a moment, unsure by the expression on Anne's face that she understood. Then, before she had time to organize her thoughts, Anne rushed into her arms and burst into tears. "Prince Edward Island? I'm going to Prince Edward Island? They want to adopt me?" She stepped back and stared at Etta. "Please tell me you mean it. Sometimes people say things that they don't mean."

Etta reached for the chair behind her, and Anne helped her sit, wiping tears and sniffing as she did. "Please say you mean it. Please, don't make me so happy I could burst and then—"

"Anne, you poor dear, please listen." Etta could feel her strength ebb and though she hated to quell the excitement in a life that had had so little, she needed Anne to listen.

"Sometime in the next few days, a Mrs. Spencer will be coming to the orphanage to take you and another little girl that she and her husband are adopting, back to the Island. She thinks she's coming to get a boy for the Cuthberts. And she will think this is all a mistake. I want you to know that it's not. But because this is a private family matter and no one else's concern, you understand, they didn't tell her otherwise. Best to let her think it is."

Anne's eyes filled with tears and Etta beckoned her to come closer. When Anne stepped toward her, Etta reached for her hands.

"This may all seem very confusing to you, Anne. I'm sorry. But I want you to trust that everything will work out as it should."

Etta handed Anne the shawl. "Keep this close. Let it comfort and keep you until the situation settles. And when it does, trust me when I say, you will be very happy."

Anne looked into Etta's eyes. Eyes that held the memory of

her own mother. She then placed the shawl around her shoulders, held tight to Etta's words, and felt the warmth of something like love wrap itself around her.

∾

Green Gables had been cleaned from top to bottom. Marilla's old bedroom had been dusted and dressed for Anne's arrival, with lace curtains at the window and a rose-patterned quilt for her bed. Cookies had been baked. And beans and brown bread were warming on the stove for when she arrived.

Marilla tried her best to settle in the rocker and await their return. Matthew had left earlier that morning for the train station where Anne would have been dropped off by Mrs. Spencer, who would then journey on to the station in White Sands.

Where there once had been no words to describe Marilla's sorrow, there were now no words to describe her joy. The flutter and anticipation she felt brought back memories of her escape into the night so long ago to meet the man she loved. She'd been searching then for the kind of joy that made life worth living. And now, thirty-four years later, it had found her.

She and Matthew had argued fiercely over not telling Anne the truth. They were friends of her parents and that's all. Matthew desperately wanted to be called Uncle. A word he'd waited a lifetime to hear.

"I don't understand, Marilla. What difference does it make now?"

"They would never look at me the same, Matthew."

She'd raised her hand to quiet him until she'd finished explaining. "And I don't care about any of that. For myself. But they'd never look at her the same, either. The illegitimacy that taints me taints her, too. She'd be shunned everywhere she went. You know that, Matthew."

He'd nodded, thinking of Anne's future, and knew she was right.

"It's not what I want either, but it's the way it has to be."

He'd agreed and now she waited. The clock ticked and the wood sizzled in the stove. The white lace curtains fluttered in the breeze and the clucking of chickens pecking in the yard settled her heart. All was ready.

From a distance, Marilla could hear the rattle of a wagon as it left the main road and headed down the lane. She waited till she was sure it was them. Over the rise, she could see the top of Matthew's hat and she stood to see more. A little girl, whose smile she could see from the window, sat beside Matthew. Her head twisted from side to side and Marilla could tell, even from where she stood, that she was talking Matthew's ear off.

She felt tears gathering in her eyes as she hurried to the door. When she reached to open it, something held her back. A feeling of not being alone in this moment made her turn. And without ever seeing them, she knew they were there.

Her mother and father, united at last, warmed her with their smile.

And dear Aunt Martha, steadfast and loyal, stood by her once again.

Bertha and Walter's contentment spread around the room while Catherine and Charles's pride filled it with light.

Marilla smiled then and touched her face. She felt the warmth of Williams's kiss on her cheek, his love pure and gentle, with her now as it always was.

They'd all gathered to share this moment. To watch the circle of their lives close around Anne Shirley. Marilla stepped out into the yard, and opened her arms.

ACKNOWLEDGEMENTS

A NUMBER OF YEARS AGO, MY FAMILY DOCTOR, during one of my visits, said, "You should write a book." I never forgot that, and so I want to thank Dr. Art Parsons for his support over the years and in reinforcing the idea that we are so much more than what we believe ourselves to be.

I want to thank Penelope Jackson, editor and manuscript reviewer, whose encouraging words at the very beginning of my foray into writing spurred me on.

To the many Atlantic Canadian authors who've answered my e-mails, led workshops and classes, provided encouragement and inspiration, and whose books have made me laugh and cry, I want to say thank you: Sheree Fitch, Donna Morrissey, Lesley Crewe, Jane Doucet, Pamela Callow, Linda Little, Carol Bruneau, and Shandi Mitchell. That I am now counted among you is as much an honour as it is astonishing.

A special thank you to the Sherbrooke Writers Guild for hosting the first Sherbrooke Village Writers Camp in September of 2018 and to the instructors, Clary Croft, Sheree Fitch, Harry Thurston, and Whitney Moran, who nudged this book into reality. I will be forever grateful!

From that inaugural event, I had the pleasure of meeting three wonderful women who have become my Halifax Words 'n' Whimsy

Writers Group. Big hugs to Jean Hillman, Melanie Mosher, and Trish Joudrey.

A big thank you to my Tarpon Springs, Florida, Fiction Writers group, who were there from the very beginning! Especially to David Edmonds, Bill Fredericks, and Gino Bardi for their leadership and support over the past five years. Every writer needs a group, and I am so lucky to have found them!

To my sisters Joyce Baxter and Judy Warner, who provided encouragement at every phase of this writing journey. And especially to my sister Corrine Stevens, the best reader any writer could ask for, who was never too busy when I called and said, "Do you have a minute?" and listened patiently to every chapter I wrote. Thank you!

To my daughter in law, Debbie Scallion, a strong, resourceful, creative, community-minded woman, who holds my son and grandson close to her heart, I simply want to say thank you.

To my son Sean Scallion, a musician to the core, who is the definition of what it means to be a good husband and father, I hope this book reinforces for you that no matter how far away you are or how much time goes by, Nova Scotia will always be your home.

To my son Matt Scallion, a creative, gentle soul, whose journey has taken him through darkness and light, I want this book to remind you that within the very DNA you carry are the hearts and souls of all those who came before you. No matter where you travel, your East Coast roots will hold you firm, and like you, they will endure.

To my Greek family and friends, both here and abroad, who have, for the past fifteen years, embraced me as one of their own, especially my mother-in-law, Zoe Michalos, who values family above all else, I hope this book helps you understand the pride with which I carry the family name.

And finally, to my husband, Trifon Michalos, the one who keeps the real world turning while I'm buried deep in the world of my characters, I want to say thank you. For cooking meals, paying bills, keeping gas in the car and groceries in the fridge. Your quiet, gentle presence is the rock on which I stand. And your love, the soft place where I land.

*B*ORN IN MUSQUODOBOIT HARBOUR AND raised in Halifax, Nova Scotia, Louise Michalos brings an authentic voice to Marilla Cuthbert's story. The second youngest of a family of nine, whose mother was raised in a lighthouse and whose father was raised in a home that housed the post office, Louise's life was infused with the stories of love and loss that are held within small communities throughout Atlantic Canada. Louise currently lives in Bedford, Nova Scotia, with her husband, Trifon. *Marilla Before Anne* is her first novel.